A WEDDING FOR THE SPITFIRE GIRL

The Spitfire Girl Series

The Spitfire Girl
The Spitfire Girl in the Skies

A WEDDING FOR THE SPITFIRE GIRL

Fenella J. Miller

First published in the United Kingdom in 2019 by Aria,
an imprint of Head of Zeus Ltd

Copyright © Fenella J. Miller, 2019

The moral right of Fenella J. Miller to be identified as the author of this work has been asserted in accordance with the Copyright, Designs and Patents Act of 1988.

All rights reserved. No part of this publication may be reproduced, stored in a retrieval system, or transmitted, in any form or by any means, electronic, mechanical, photocopying, recording, or otherwise, without the prior permission of both the copyright owner and the above publisher of this book.

This is a work of fiction. All characters, organizations, and events portrayed in this novel are either products of the author's imagination or are used fictitiously.

A CIP catalogue record for this book is available from the British Library.

ISBN 9781788548410

Aria
c/o Head of Zeus
First Floor East
5–8 Hardwick Street
London ECIR 4RG

WWW.ARIAFICTION.COM

For my beloved husband. Always in my heart.

One

January 1942

Ellen Simpson. Her name was on the list to attend a conversion course at White Waltham in order to become qualified to ferry light twin-engined aircraft. Ellie turned to her friend Amanda who was also included.

'I hope we don't get any more snow. I know it will be helping the war effort to be able to fly a bigger range of planes, but I love flying Spitfires. Do you think we'll still be able to deliver them afterwards or will the other girls take over?'

'Whilst we're based here, I should think the bulk of our work will still be fighter planes as Southampton is where most of them are built. I was told we've got to shift three hundred thousand Spitfires in the next few months as the factory is too vulnerable to attack,' Amanda said.

'That can't be right – whoever told you that must have meant three thousand. The air transport auxiliary service might be efficient but we'd all have to deliver hundreds of Spitfires each in order to clear that many.' Ellie laughed with her friend.

'Of course, how silly of me. It doesn't matter how many it is, we've obviously got a lot of work ahead of us.'

There were two other girls scheduled to go to White Waltham with them but they weren't back from yesterday's delivery so hadn't heard the good news.

Since the Yanks had joined in the fight, the atmosphere at the all-female Hamble ferry pool had been more cheerful – not that any of the girls moped about, however bad the news.

Already the US servicemen were pouring into the country but as yet she'd seen none of them. There were, so she was told, American women joining the ATA along with other female pilots from all over the world.

She had joined last year and was one of the more experienced flyers. Already the original eight were delivering bombers and now she thought about it, she was long overdue to do this conversion course herself. The fact that she was the youngest member, despite having the most hours logged, was probably why she'd not been put forward until now.

'Amanda, you joined almost at the beginning – why haven't you been sent before this?'

'No idea, but after I blotted my copybook last year I think I was deliberately overlooked. Despite Margot and Pauline's assurance that they were on my side I think Margot didn't want to upset her friends. Telling the world about how that bitch tricked your fiancé into marrying her made me rather unpopular.'

'Please, don't remind me. I'll never forget Greg. I loved him so much, but he's gone and what that dreadful woman did to us is in the past. Jack's home now and I'm going out with him.' Even as she said this, she knew Jack would never mean the same to her as Greg had done.

'It's amazing how the lack of his left hand makes so little difference to his flying. He's the redheaded hero of the ATA.'

'I'm not sure that's true. Isn't the commanding officer at White Waltham the man all the girls dream about? When he was seen without his shirt last summer it was the talk of the pool.'

'He is a bit of a heartthrob but your Jack's just as attractive and half the women here are a little bit in love with him.'

'I don't blame them – I am too.'

'Then what's holding you back?'

'He's not the same man he was before the accident. I always loved his sense of fun. We used to sit and talk for hours, but now he's so much quieter I don't think I really know him any more.'

'Give him a chance – he's obviously besotted with you. If I wasn't already having an affair with Nigel, I'd jump into bed with him if he offered.'

A year ago she'd have been shocked by such plain speaking, but since Greg had died without them having slept together she viewed things differently. 'Hands off: he's mine. I've only seen him twice since he got back last December – we're both so busy and White Waltham is miles away from here. Our days off haven't coincided so far but as soon as they do, he'll be staying at the cottage with us.'

'How will you feel about being eventually promoted above him? If we're cleared to fly the light twin-engined operational aircraft then we're bound to go onto the heavy class and then we'll be ranked higher. I doubt that he'll ever get above third officer. With only half an arm he won't be able to fly anything but fighters.'

'It won't bother me and I don't think it will worry him either. He was a squadron leader when he was demobbed – so as far as I'm concerned, he'll always outrank me.'

'What about Wing Commander Hugo Lambourne? Didn't you get a phone call from him the other day?'

'I did, but I told him I was no longer available, that I was now going out with Jack and couldn't see him again.'

'How did he take it?'

'To tell you the truth, I'm not sure. He said if I changed my mind and things didn't work out as I'd hoped to get in touch.'

'Two strings to your bow? Actually, I think if I was in your position I'd do exactly as you're doing and give Jack a test flight. If he fails to live up to expectations then you can always move on.'

Ellie couldn't prevent her cheeks from turning pink. She was trying to be sophisticated, talking blithely about sleeping with Jack at the earliest opportunity, but if she was honest she thought doing this would just complicate matters. Initially she'd regretted that she'd never made love with Greg, but now she was glad she hadn't. Her views might be considered old-fashioned by her friend but she would much rather wait until she was at least engaged to Jack before taking the next step.

'Unlike you, I've no experience in that area to compare him with. In fact, the more I think about it the more certain I am that I'll wait. Hopping in and out of bed with a string of handsome officers might suit you…'

'Hang on a minute – I resent that remark. You make me sound like a floozy...'

'I'm sorry, but you do have different views on the subject. I'm an old-fashioned girl and not quite ready to step into the modern world if it means behaving...'

Amanda's eyes narrowed. This was the first row they'd had and Ellie didn't want to fall out with her. She grabbed her arm before either of them could say something they'd regret.

'Please, I'm sorry. I sound like my mother and I promise you I don't really believe any of that nonsense. I'm just nervous about making a commitment. I do find Jack very attractive though.'

'He's been through a lot. Which brings me back to the fact that you're almost bound to meet up with him as he's based where we're going.'

'I'm glad we've talked about it as it's got things straight in my head. Fortunately, I've not said anything about spending the night with him. We've kissed a few times but he didn't make a move to take things further when we were together over Christmas.'

'Golly! I should hope not – not under your parents' roof.'

'It was quite embarrassing as Mabel and Dad kept leaving us alone together and I think they were expecting us to announce our engagement after spending just two days together.'

'You've known him for two years and were already good friends. He was in love with you whilst you were still with Greg – I expect he's happy to wait until you're ready.'

'We'd better get a move on; the Anson is waiting on the apron. We'll be able to fly the taxi when we come back but only if it's empty. How do you feel about that?'

'As long as I'm flying, I don't care what it is.'

They ran to the locker room and quickly pulled on their flight suits, boots and helmets and then snatched up their parachutes. Lugging this lot at high speed across the tarmac, as well as their overnight bags, was hard work but they'd been doing it for so long they didn't think twice.

They scrambled into the aircraft and took the remaining seats at the rear. Talking was impossible whilst in flight because of the racket, so Ellie settled back to mull over what they'd been discussing. Maybe Jack would be off base whilst they were there and the question wouldn't arise.

Jack, having his own cycle, was usually first to arrive at his base. Pointless really, as often it didn't get light enough to fly until after nine o'clock. He'd joined the ATA a couple of months ago and so far had had no difficulty flying even the most damaged Spitfires and Hurricanes. With only one arm, flying single-engine fighters was a doddle but he doubted he'd ever graduate to twin engines.

He was resigned to his limitations and as long as he was doing his bit for the war effort, most of the time he was just grateful he was alive. He wasn't sure how he felt about the Yanks arriving and acting as if they were God's gift. They didn't have a bloody clue about how things were in England at the moment. Their home country had never been bombed or endured rationing and blackouts.

The ops room guys and gals were always there early as they had to organise the pilots' duties and write the chits that would send them off to deliver and collect whatever kites needed to be ferried about the place. The weather was dire, as soon as one lot of snow thawed and life went back to normal a second cold front rolled in and it all started again.

He'd been fortunate to get an extra day's leave over the Christmas period and had been able to spend it with Ellie at Glebe Farm. Her parents, Fred and Mabel, were his family now and he had their support in his wish to marry their daughter. His mood lightened a little as he thought about the woman he loved. She didn't feel the same way about him, wasn't in love with him, at least not how she had been with Greg.

He sat nursing his mug of tea. The more he dwelt on the situation the more fed up he was. He couldn't have competed with a ghost even with both arms – what bloody chance did he have now?

'Reynolds, for God's sake, man, wake up. You're wanted on the blower.'

Jack slopped his tea and swore. 'Right, coming, I wasn't asleep – was thinking – not something you do much of.' His grin took the sting from his words. Billy Walker had become a good mate of his, although anyone listening to them would think they were deadly enemies.

One of the girls in the operation room handed him the phone. He raised an eyebrow and she shrugged. Whoever it was obviously hadn't identified themselves – he'd hoped it might be Ellie.

'Reynolds here. To whom am I speaking?'

'Jack Reynolds? Former Squadron Leader Reynolds?'

'Yes. Who the hell are you?'

The rich, plummy voice continued as if he'd not interrupted. 'You are required to report to Oriel College, Oxford, immediately.' The line went dead leaving Jack staring in astonishment at the receiver.

What the blazes was that all about? He could hardly abandon his duties here and scuttle off to Oxford. He'd have to speak to the pool commander before he did anything else. The chits were already being spread out on the shelf outside this room and he didn't have to look at them to know that he'd have at least half a dozen ferrying jobs allocated to him.

Frankie Francis, pool commander, met him at the door. 'Good show, was coming to find you. There's a car outside for you. You're off the rota for today.'

'Some toffee-nosed guy, who refused to identify himself, told me to report to Oriel College. What for?'

'Buggered if I know, old chap. Something hush-hush, that's for sure.'

'Bloody hell, that's all I need. Don't fancy being mixed up with the SIS or any of the intelligence brigade. Hopefully, they've got the wrong guy and I'll be back in a couple of hours.'

Sure enough a brown job was standing by a large, black car. The soldier saluted – not necessary as, although he was an officer in the ATA, this was a civilian operation. He didn't return the gesture, just nodded and jumped into the back.

Frankie was the best-looking guy in the ATA – he seemed oblivious to his charms and Jack had rarely seen him in the company of any of the hopeful young ladies who swarmed around him.

It was only twenty miles or so to Oxford and the worst of the snow had been cleared by the soldiers who had very little to do at the moment. As soon as Frankie had mentioned it being hush-hush, he'd guessed what this was about.

Joe Cross, his uncle, had given him Glebe Farm Aero Club just before the war started, and had been involved in dodgy dealing. Joe had died two years ago in jail and Jack was no longer in contact with his aunt. He had never known exactly what his uncle had been incarcerated for – but he was damned sure it was something to do with blackmail and Mosley's lot. All the fascists had been rounded up now as far as he knew.

Ellie's mother had buggered off to live with her own father, Sir Reginald Humphrey, and she and Fred had been divorced. He was now happily married to Mabel and since Ellie's eldest brother Neil's funeral none of the Simpson family had had any contact with the fascist bastard Humphrey.

At one point everyone at Glebe Farm had expected to be arrested, but fortunately this hadn't happened. The more he thought about it the more convinced he was that this unexpected summons to Oxford was something to do with what had happened back then.

He frowned. There was another brother, George, who had sided with his grandfather and mother – he hoped for Ellie's sake her estranged family weren't going to drag her into something unsavoury. He didn't give a damn about his reputation, but if the woman he loved was damaged by something his uncle had set in motion he would be appalled.

Perhaps it would be better for both of them to stop seeing each other until whatever was going on was sorted.

There were very few private cars on the road nowadays – petrol rationing had seen to that. Therefore, apart from military vehicles of various sorts, he didn't see much traffic and the vehicle entered Oxford sooner than he'd expected.

He looked around with interest, never having been to this university town before. Students on bicycles, their black gowns flapping behind them, showed that life went on more or less as usual here. The car pulled up in front of an impressive archway.

The driver jumped out and opened the door for him as if he was someone important. If the guy only knew the real reason for his being here, he wouldn't be so polite. The car roared off leaving Jack standing in front of the college, not sure where he should be.

A young man in mufti rushed up to him. 'Squadron Leader Reynolds? Excellent, please come with me. I apologise for not being here to greet you but you're earlier than we expected.'

Jack followed and was led across the quad and into the hallowed hall itself. Strangely there were students and professors wandering about the place as well. If this was the home of some secret service or other it seemed odd that they were sharing the accommodation with regular guys.

'It's the third door on the left, sir.' His guide vanished, leaving him to make his own way, and he was still none the wiser as to why he was there.

*

The Anson juddered to a halt on the tarmac at White Waltham. Ellie had been here before when she'd delivered and collected aircraft but this was the first time that she'd had the opportunity to look at it properly.

'It's very posh. Was it built especially for the ATA?' She asked Amanda who tended to know the answers to these sorts of questions.

'It was a Flying Training School and built a few years ago but we've booted them out and taken it over.'

'I heard talk that they're going to build us a better home this summer. With so many more women joining we're going to need a bigger place.' Ellie pointed at the building ahead of them. 'Look at the size of their operations room – they must have a dozen people working in there.'

'Alison does amazingly well considering how small her ops room is.' The Anson that had ferried them from Hamble had collected the two pilots waiting for a lift and was now taxiing around the apron preparing to take off again.

Carrying a parachute and the bag with what she would need for the next few days, whilst wearing a padded flight suit, was something she'd become accustomed to and she didn't think twice about it nowadays. In fact, with her thick leather flying jacket, helmet, boots and gloves, as well as the Sidcot suit, even the harshest weather was bearable.

They went to the restroom to find themselves an empty locker each and, once their baggage was safely stowed, they headed for the ops room where they would discover which instructor would be training them and on what aircraft.

'We'll be able to fly the light twin-engined aircraft but not any bombers. We won't even be able to take the Anson with a full load. I wonder how long we've got to fly the Airspeed Oxford, de Havilland Rapide and Anson before we can do the conversion that will make us Class IV and be able to fly the bombers,' Ellie said.

'We'll be promoted to second officers once we do the second conversion.'

'Seems strange we'll be designated Class III but remain only third-class officers. Why is that?'

Amanda didn't answer as they'd now arrived outside the operations room. They were told to wait in the Mess and have a cuppa until their instructor turned up.

Once they were settled and happily drinking tea Ellie returned to her previous question. 'We've both been flying Spits and Hurries for months and have only just been recommended to do this conversion. Do you think we're going to have to wait as long to move up again?'

'Just enjoy the fact that we're going to have a few more shillings in our pockets at the end of the month.'

An hour later someone from the ops room came in. 'Sorry, ladies, the Rapide you were going to be trained on is out of service for the next few days. We're up to our necks and one of our pilots has called in sick and another has been sent somewhere by some bigwigs – God knows where – not good enough when we need every flyer we can lay our hands on. Will you help us out today?'

'That's the ticket! Of course we will – we'd rather be working. Have you okayed it with Hamble? They might want us to come back and deliver for them?'

'Already spoken to Alison – she'd rather you remain here until you've completed your conversion course.'

They followed him back to the shiny wooden shelf that ran alongside the ops room. There were two rows of unclaimed chits.

''Fraid one of you has got a Walrus – hope you've got your little blue book as you're going to need it.'

'I'll take that,' Ellie said. 'I've not flown one before and I'm up for a challenge.' He pointed to the pieces of paper nearest to her and she gathered them up and flicked through. Nothing too alarming or too taxing amongst them apart from the distance involved. 'I've got to take the Walrus to Prestwick.' She wasn't keen on flying through the balloon barrages of Manchester, Liverpool and several other industrial cities, but wouldn't dream of saying so.

'I'm taking a Barracuda to Burtonwood first, then collecting a Spit and taking it to Debden,' Amanda said. 'There's a damaged Hurry needs ferrying for repair. I hope I can catch a lift back here. We don't know where we're staying tonight either.'

'I'm sure there's accommodation near the base somewhere we can use. It's going to take me two and a half hours to get to Prestwick. I'm picking up a Spit and bringing it back here. Let's hope the weather doesn't worsen and we get stuck overnight somewhere else.'

'My chits have got Jack's name on them. He's one of the men absent from duty today. I wonder if he's the one who's ill or the one who's been sent somewhere.'

'No doubt I'll catch up with him at some point.'

After reclaiming their flight suits and other paraphernalia they sat and studied their ferry notes as they both had to fly aircraft they weren't familiar with.

Ellie was satisfied she understood the foibles of this plane and slung her parachute over her shoulder and headed for the tarmac. The Walrus was a bulky kite that could land on water and was known as the waddling duck. It was a biplane with an enclosed cockpit and although made by the same company who made the wonderful Spitfire it had none of its sleekness. After climbing into the cockpit, she spent another fifteen minutes familiarising herself with the controls then went through her preflight checks. She taxied onto the runway and was given the green light to take off.

The flight to Prestwick was uneventful, the weather remained clear and she landed smoothly. After minimal delay she had signed the necessary papers to allow her to collect the Spitfire. She loved this fighter. She would be happy to just ferry these from the factory to the airfield every day of the week.

Two

Jack knocked on the door and was asked to come in. He wasn't sure what he'd been expecting – a row of accusatory faces sitting behind a desk, sinister men in plain clothes waiting to arrest him; but what he saw was nothing like that.

'Ah, Squadron Leader Reynolds, welcome, welcome. I'm Roger Mainwaring. Find a pew, shove the papers onto the floor, more important things to talk about than those tedious items.' The speaker was a bespectacled young man about his own age, untidily dressed, and as far from accusatory or sinister as he could possibly be.

He did as instructed and moved the chair up to the desk, which was as untidy as the man behind it. 'I'm a civilian, no need to address me so formally. Jack will do.'

'Excellent, excellent. I expect you're wondering why you're here. Help yourself to coffee if you want it – it's in the thermos over there.' He gestured vaguely towards the table by the window and then continued. 'Fine, fine, let's get on with it shall we?'

'I'm assuming it's something to do with my deceased uncle, Joseph Cross.'

'Exactly, exactly, you hit the nail on the head, Jack.' Then the young man's expression changed from benign to something very different. His eyes were hard, his friendly demeanour gone as if it had never existed.

Jack couldn't stop himself shifting uncomfortably on his seat. The guy was his age, half his size for God's sake, why should he be nervous of him? But there was something formidable about Mainwaring despite his glasses and slight figure.

'You will be aware that the list Cross had was used for the purposes of blackmail. Our inquiries relating to that matter were concluded last year. However, we discovered that Cross also had connections to the major crime families in London. We've not been able to locate items that we think are pertinent to this investigation and are hoping you can help us with this.'

'Exactly how? I didn't spend more than a couple of weeks at his home in London before moving out. I'd no idea he was crooked until I was shot.'

'We've searched his property from top to bottom and found nothing. We think he must have had a lock-up somewhere, or a second address, and are hoping you can point us in that direction.'

'Sorry, I don't know anything about my uncle's criminal activities. You've wasted my time and yours by bringing me here. I would have been better off doing my duty.' He braced his good arm on the edge of the desk and pushed himself upright. 'Do I get a lift back or have I to make my own way?'

'Please, Mr Reynolds, have some coffee before you leave. I apologise for dragging you away from your vital duties but I didn't do it lightly. There's more to this than you realise.'

Reluctantly Jack resumed his seat and accepted a mug of the surprisingly decent coffee when it was handed to him. 'Okay, shoot – I'm listening.'

'Would you like a sandwich to go with that coffee?'

'That would be great – thanks.'

Mainwaring rushed off to organise the food. Jack was tempted to look at some of the piles of paper but refrained – not that anything secret would be left lying around for someone like him to see.

As he munched an excellent meat sandwich – he'd no idea exactly what was between the slices of bread – Mainwaring explained. 'Extortion, prostitution, the black market – criminal activity is rife in London and all the major cities where the remaining police force are too busy dealing with the bombing to keep this in check.

'When the sirens go off, the streets are empty and the criminals have *carte blanche*. These felonious families are a threat to the war effort.'

'I know that. My uncle was arrested before the war started so I can't see anything he's got hidden away will be of much use to you even if you could find it.'

'It is my considered opinion, Mr Reynolds, that if Cross had obtained a page from the Right Club and was using it to blackmail members, he might well have similar information on the families that rule the East End.'

'I understand and wish I could help you. What I can do, when I get a day off, is go to his house and see if anything in the area jogs my memory. It might not be for a while as transport isn't always available.'

'Thank you, that would be a great help. The sooner the better. I'll see what I can do about getting you some extra leave…'

'No. Delivering aircraft is more important than messing about in the East End. I've said I'll go when I can – that will have to do.'

Mainwaring's expression hardened for a second, then he resumed his friendly approach. 'Absolutely fine, old boy, go when you can.'

The remainder of the visit was more relaxed and he entertained Mainwaring with stories of his exploits in the desert until the car returned to collect him. Being late January, it got dark so early there was little chance of him being able to ferry any kites today.

He was still of the opinion that he'd have been better off doing his job than sodding about in Oxford. He thanked the driver and strode into the building at White Waltham. He almost fell over his feet when the first person he saw was Ellie.

'Honey, what the hell are you doing here?' He opened his arms and she flew into them and a satisfactory five minutes later he raised his head. Her eyes were shining; she'd enjoyed the kiss as much as he had.

'Actually, I'm here for a Class III conversion course but the aircraft's out of service for the next few days. Amanda has taken your chits. She should've been back by now but it's almost dark. I've been to Prestwick and only just made it.'

'Nothing else will land tonight so she'll have put down somewhere. Hang on, I'll check with ops. They'll know where she is.'

*

Ellie had been as surprised to see Jack as he was to see her – but she hadn't expected to be swept into his arms and so thoroughly kissed. If she was honest, he hadn't done any sweeping as she had gone to him. She scarcely noticed the lack of his left hand anymore and was quite certain if she didn't want him then there were a dozen girls who would take her place.

She wasn't sure if Amanda being away was a good thing or not. Did she want to spend so much time alone with him? He was attractive and made her tingle all over when he kissed her but she didn't love him in the same way she had Greg and didn't think she ever would. When he returned, his smile reassured her that her friend was safe.

'Have you got a billet for tonight? I can give the pub a bell and see if they've got a spare room you can use.' His smile was wicked and she knew what was coming next. 'Unless you'd care to share?'

'I certainly wouldn't – I didn't sleep with Greg and I'm certainly not sleeping with you. I'm not that sort of girl.' She hadn't meant to say this, the words had just tumbled out and she immediately regretted them. It was none of his business and she sounded like a prude.

Instantly his expression changed and his eyes were sad. 'God, I didn't know that. I'm so sorry. You know how I feel about you and I'm well aware that you don't feel the same. I've no intention of pressurising you into anything you don't want to do.'

'I am very fond you, but even if things were different it's too soon for me to take that sort of step. In fact, I'm not sure I ever will be able to. I'm still in love with Greg. I'll understand if you don't want to wait until I'm ready.'

'I won't be changing my mind. I love you and hope one day you'll feel the same way. Now, do you want me to ring the pub or do you have somewhere to stay?'

'Amanda and I know of a B&B half a mile from here. I've got the directions already. But I'd like to get a meal with you in the Mess if they still serve at this hour.'

'If we go now we'll get something decent. I'll tell you where I've been all day.'

When he'd finished explaining she touched his arm sympathetically. 'It's horrible having a relative you disapprove of – you know how I feel about my grandfather, Sir Reginald. In some ways I wish he'd been arrested like some of the others were but then my mother would have been miserable.' Talking about her estranged family made her sad. He immediately picked up on this.

'Why don't you go and see your mom and brother? You've not met his new wife and she doesn't know about Fred or that you've joined the ATA.'

'I couldn't just turn up out of the blue – also, I don't think it would be very tactful telling her about Dad and Mabel.'

'I can think of something that you might wish to tell her in person. We could pretend to be engaged. That would be reason enough to visit uninvited.'

'I'm not sure that's a good idea, but I'll give it some thought.'

'We're a couple, aren't we? We enjoy each other's company. I don't think either of us has to put on a show – we just have to behave as we always do.'

'I'm still not convinced. My mother would expect there to be a notice in the paper. George would no doubt talk to his cronies and before you know where we are the whole world will think we're really engaged. What about Fred and Mabel? Do we lie to them too?'

'Do you think your mom will approve?' She shook her head. 'Then I can't see there's a problem. You can say that you've changed your mind after the visit and there's no reason for it to become public knowledge.'

'If you put it like that, I think it might work. I was never very close to her, was relieved when she left so suddenly, but life's too short to hold grudges. I always wanted her to approve of me but she never seemed to. Any of us could be blown up at any minute and I wouldn't want that to happen without mending our relationship.'

He laughed. 'Blown up? That's a bit extreme, but I get your drift. Then the next time we get leave at the same time we'll go and see them. Where do they live? I've never thought to ask.'

'Just outside St Albans. I'll cadge a lift and join you here as I don't think it's more than forty miles from this ferry pool.'

Surprisingly her appetite hadn't deserted her at the thought that she might come face-to-face with her obnoxious grandfather in the near future. She thoroughly enjoyed the spam fritters, chips and peas followed by spotted dick and custard. She looked around the crowded room and several of the people smiled in recognition. This ATA ferry pool only had a couple of women pilots and neither of them were there tonight, but there were several other girls; presumably they were admin staff.

Strangely the dark blue uniform worn by ATA pilots was in the minority that evening – and she was proud that she was one of the few wearing it.

'That was delicious, Jack. You're lucky you get such good food. Do you eat at your digs as well?'

'Breakfast, and sometimes a sandwich to go with a pint if I'm there in the evening. It's a village pub not a hotel.'

'Can we stay and talk here or shall we go to the restroom?'

'They're closing the serving hatch but we can sit here as long as we like. I'll get us both a cuppa – no coffee, I'm afraid.'

She was going to offer to come with him as she didn't think he could carry two mugs at the same time but decided he might be offended. She tried to treat him the same way she had when he'd had both his hands. He collected the drinks and by gripping both handles in his right hand and carried them over without spilling a drop.

He grinned. 'I know, amazing isn't it what a one-armed guy can do.'

'Absolutely spiffing! I should have known if you can fly a fighter one-handed you wouldn't have any difficulty carrying two mugs of tea.'

He moved his chair so he was sitting beside her and not opposite. Probably wise if they didn't want anyone to overhear what they were talking about.

'I don't want my dad and Mabel to know anything about this…'

His eyes widened. 'Good God! Of course we don't want to involve them.'

'I remember at Neil's funeral that I wasn't allowed to speak to Mum and she looked really cowed and miserable. I should have tried to keep in touch.'

He squeezed her hand and his smile made him seem almost like the old Jack. 'Our pretend engagement will give you the perfect reason to go and see them. Humphrey won't approve of me – I wonder if I'll be banished to the servants' rooms.'

She laughed at his nonsense. 'Over my dead body.'

'Do you know when you're going to get any leave?'

'I'm stuck here until the Oxford's in service. Alison doesn't want any of us to come back until we're converted to twin-engined aircraft. If you could get a couple of days off, we could do it now. We'll go home first, and then go to Sir Reginald's house.' He raised an eyebrow and she laughed. 'You're right. We can't do both, so it had better be Herford House. I just hope that obnoxious man isn't there.'

'We're going to have to take that chance. Are you sure you want to do this now? With two days off we could go to London and see a show and I could do what Mainwaring wants.'

'I've made up my mind I want to see Mum and if I don't do it right away I might never go.'

'In which case I'll speak to Frankie – he's the guy over there just finishing his pudding.'

She watched him weave his way through the other diners and everyone he passed spoke to him. He was obviously popular here. Would she have agreed that they should get engaged, even though it wasn't a genuine arrangement, if she hadn't, deep down, decided she wanted to marry him eventually?

It was all such a muddle. If she'd been married to Greg, Jack would have found someone else by now and none of this would be happening. Life was so complicated – it was much easier flying a Spitfire.

He turned and smiled. He'd obviously got his time off. Heaven knows what he'd said to his CO and she hoped he hadn't mentioned the so-called engagement.

Jack couldn't believe his luck. Frankie had been great about his request, saying that there wouldn't be much ferrying done for the next few days as the weather was closing in.

'Congratulations on your engagement, old chap, you deserve to be happy after what you've been through.'

'Thanks, it's worked out rather well for both of us.' As soon as he said this, he felt a stab of guilt – Ellie would much rather be married to Greg than him and she was only his by default. He smiled ruefully. Who was he kidding? They weren't really engaged and he'd better remember that.

He smiled at her and nodded and she looked equally pleased. 'Do you think there's any chance I can borrow a vehicle? God knows how long it will take to visit her mother using the train.'

'Don't see why not. Can you still drive?'

'The only disadvantage to losing my left hand and not my right is that I can no longer change gears. Ellie will drive.'

He rejoined her and she seemed a bit taken aback that everything had been arranged so easily. Maybe this was all moving too fast for her. As far as he was concerned the more time he spent in her company, the happier he was.

She frowned. 'Poor Amanda will be stuck wherever she is. I hope it's somewhere comfortable as not all RAF bases have accommodation for women.'

'She's not at an RAF base but a ferry pool. Hopefully someone has offered her a bed. I've got my overnight things, as always, in a locker. I'm glad you agreed to come back to the pub later. My digs are only a mile from here so we can set off really early tomorrow for St Albans.'

'I wish I'd bought my greatcoat. I don't think my flying jacket on its own will be warm enough.'

'We're travelling in a car and that will have a heater so we'll be fine.' Something else occurred to him. 'We've got two nights free – one of them will be spent here but why don't we try and see Fred and Mabel after visiting your mom?'

'We won't have enough petrol for that. I think one side of the family is more than enough at the moment. What about going into London and doing what you have to do for that Mainwaring chap?'

'That's too far as well. I'm hoping we'll get time off again together in the not too distant future and we can both get a flip to Hatfield. It's easy enough to get to Town from there.'

'And with any luck we could nip down to Romford and see my parents at the same time. I don't want to keep tomorrow's visit a secret from them for ever.'

'Okay, we'll do that. I doubt that we'll have time to visit them before we're both back on duty.'

'We were only there a month ago so they won't be expecting us to turn up so soon.'

'It's more comfortable in the restroom – shall we move there? There might be a few blokes we could play a rubber or two of bridge with.'

She looked at him in surprise. 'Golly, I didn't know you played bridge. When did that start?'

'When I was in Africa – had to do something at night. There were never enough books to read. Do you play?'

'I do, but I much prefer to be the dummy, put my hand down and let my partner try and make the tricks. I do enjoy the bidding though and trying to stop the other couple making their game.'

There were half a dozen people lounging about in the room where the pilots waited for the weather to clear when they were flying. No one was interested in playing bridge but someone suggested they played Monopoly.

He was bankrupted first as his mind wasn't on the game and he wandered off to the can. Ellie was engrossed and didn't notice his departure. He paused at the door to watch her. She was completely at ease with the guys and they treated her as an equal. He wouldn't have left her alone if he'd suspected for one minute one of them might make a pass at her.

There was no heating in the passageway and no lighting either. There were too many windows to put blackouts up so everywhere was dark and you had to use your torch to move about. He paused to look out of the window.

Bloody hell! There was a blizzard blowing outside. He didn't fancy cycling back to the pub in this and he didn't want Ellie walking to her B&B either. With the blackouts down in the restroom, nobody there would be aware the weather had deteriorated.

'It's snowing heavily. I don't know about you blokes, but I'm going to kip here.' Jack's announcement had the desired effect. There was a chorus of swearing, the game was abandoned and Ellie rushed over to him.

'We should have gone ages ago. If we put on our flying gear, I think we'll be warm enough. I've slept on the floor a few times over the past couple of years and it won't hurt to do it again.'

Two of the men opted to risk the weather as they lived no more than five minutes from the gate of the base, but the rest of them decided to bed down where they were. Fortunately, all those who were staying were flyers so had overnight bags and the same gear that he and Ellie had.

'The radiators are already cold; it's going to be freezing in here by morning,' she said.

'Then it's sensible for all of us to sleep in here together. Shall we get our stuff from the lockers?'

'If you get yours, I'll bag us the best place. The padded seats on those sofas will come off and we can use them as a mattress. Our overnight bags will do as pillows.'

He left her making them somewhere snug to sleep. By the time he returned she'd set up a bed for them both in the far corner of the room where they wouldn't be trodden on if anyone got up in the night.

'Give me your key and I'll fetch your stuff for you next. No point in both of us getting cold. I think it's unlikely we'll be going anywhere tomorrow as there might well be a foot or two in the morning.'

Both of them had suffered the lack of privacy and communal living of boarding school, so sharing their sleeping space with four others wouldn't bother either of them. When he returned with her belongings she was busy moving furniture with the help of a couple of the guys.

'The others have gone in search of more makeshift mattresses. I feel a bit mean about bagging the only two full-length ones for us.' This had been said in a whisper.

'As the rest of us are men I hardly think anyone's going to object to the one female having the most comfortable billet.'

'I don't expect to be treated any differently because of my gender. However, on this occasion I'm grateful not to be sleeping directly on the floor.'

They stepped into their Sidcot suits, pulling them on over the top of their fur-lined flying jackets, then shoved their feet into their boots and buckled on their helmets. 'We might look ridiculous, but I don't think any of us will be cold despite the temperature dropping.'

They settled down and the nearest bloke turned off the central light. There'd been no smutty remarks about him sharing his bed with her. He'd have flattened anyone if they'd made any.

He lay down first and turned on his left side. 'Turn your back and snuggle into me. It'll be more comfortable and much warmer for both of us.'

He sensed her laughing in the darkness. She reached out and her hand accidently brushed across his face, making him catch his breath. 'At least no one will think we're up to no good dressed the way we are.'

Three

Ellie slept soundly, as did everyone else; they were all permanently fatigued. She stirred when Jack got up but didn't open her eyes – he'd probably gone to the WC. She drifted back to sleep and was woken by the delicious smell of hot toast and tea.

She rolled over and saw him putting a tray down very carefully on the nearest table. He'd balanced it somehow on the remains of his arm. He was now just in his uniform; his hair was brushed and he'd even had a shave.

'Is that a fresh collar? I'm impressed. I'm also absolutely sweltering. I'm going to get this lot off before I have my breakfast.'

At the mention of breakfast two of the remaining pilots sat up. 'Is the Mess open, Jack? It must be later than I thought,' one of them said as he scrambled to his feet whilst rubbing his eyes.'

'Nope, made this myself.'

'Tea first, please, and then I'll have my toast.'

As they were munching happily one of the men pulled back the blackouts. 'Bloody hell! There must be a foot of snow out there. At least it looks as if it's going to be bright and there's not a cloud in the sky. With luck we won't get any more today.'

The restroom smelled stale and she wrinkled her nose. 'I'm going to open the window when I finish this, hope no one minds.'

'No need to apologise. It's reminiscent of the boys changing room at school,' Jack said with a grin.

The nearest chap did the honours and a blast of icy air whistled through the room, clearing the air immediately. The remaining sleeper sat up and protested loudly at the howling gale.

'Sorry, I've got my orders. I'll close it in a minute.'

'Do it now, I'm freezing my balls off here.'

Before Ellie could stop him, Jack stepped across and pushed the speaker over with his foot. 'Watch your language, lady present.'

The poor man sat up, his cheeks scarlet, and mumbled a hasty apology to her.

'No need to apologise, I've heard a lot worse. It's you who should be apologising to him, Jack, I don't need you to fight my battles.'

His smile sent a flicker of heat through her. 'I'm well aware of that, honey, but as your temporary fiancé aren't I entitled to express my disapproval?' He'd spoken softly so no one else would overhear.

'No, you're not.' She drained her mug and collected her overnight bag. As so many women worked at this ferry pool there were adequate facilities. On one never to be forgotten occasion, she had been forced to pee behind a hangar and still wasn't sure that no one had seen her. She was always uncomfortable when she was obliged to deliver an aircraft to that particular base.

When she returned the room had been restored to its usual appearance and only Jack was in there. He was staring gloomily out of the window and she joined him there.

'I don't reckon we'll be going anywhere today. Only half the girls have made it into the office this morning and it looks like a couple of the guys are missing too.'

'I think the nearest army barracks is at Didcot and that's more than fifty miles away so I doubt any of them will come as far as here to clear the roads.' As she spoke, a tractor pushing a snowplough turned into the gates and began the laborious task of removing snow from the runways.

'I think that's a lost cause,' he said gesturing towards the tractor. 'I went outside and it must be several degrees below freezing. Even if they clear the snow the runways will be lethal. There'll be no flying today.'

'I hope that means there'll be no bombers coming here either. I wonder if the RAF will be grounded or will continue to attack German warships in the Atlantic?'

'Let's not talk about that.'

'We won't be going on our trip today as the weather's so bad. I only brought enough things for a couple of nights – I'm going to have to wash my smalls and shirt but I can hardly do it in the ladies.'

'If you don't mind the walk we can go back to my billet – I'm sure my landlady will let you do it there and then hang them in the scullery.'

'Don't you have Greg's bicycle? I've travelled on a crossbar many times and I'm sure between us we can compensate for your lack of a hand.'

She checked her watch – it was just after eight o'clock. 'I'd like something a bit more substantial than toast if that's available.'

'I don't think it'll be safe on my bike so we'll walk. Better than staying here.'

Warmly dressed in their fur-lined flying jackets, their overnight bags slung over their shoulders, they headed for the exit. It took them an hour to reach the pub he was lodging at but he'd enjoyed the walk as Ellie happily clung on to his arm for most of the way.

The front would be locked at this time, but the back door was always open as none of the ATA guys knew exactly when they'd be returning.

'Stamp the worst of the snow from your boots and then I'll brush it off your clothes. You do the same for me. My landlady, Vera, won't appreciate us bringing this lot in.'

They'd just finished when the door flew open. 'Don't hang about out there, Jack, you and your young lady come in and get warm. I was that worried when you didn't get back last night – where did you sleep?' Vera clucked and fussed over Ellie but left him to his own devices. They vanished upstairs and he followed them as soon as he'd hung up his garments and kicked off his boots. It had been madness not to have worn his greatcoat in this weather – he wouldn't make the same mistake again. He dropped his dirty laundry into the hamper and despite his disability was ready before Ellie.

From the racket coming from the bar, at least two of the other lodgers were here and playing a noisy game of darts or possibly shove-halfpenny. He wandered in and was greeted with a cheer.

'Good show, getting boring beating this blighter so often,' one of them said.

'Ellie Simpson's upstairs – she came back with me. We kipped on the floor last night and don't want to do that again.' He aimed a friendly punch at his friend when he leered suggestively. 'No, we won't be sharing a bed.'

He was called into the kitchen for what would be a third breakfast. Ellie was happily munching more toast and drinking tea.

'You look quite different, Ellie, like a new woman.'

'Vera has loaned me some clean things until mine have been washed. She's an absolute treasure…'

'Thank you, ducks, glad to know I'm appreciated. Fat chance of any of these lumps telling me I'm doing a good job taking care of them like a mother hen.'

The two blokes in the bar had joined them – nobody turned down tea and hot toast even if it was only spread with margarine or dripping.

The snow thawed the next day and they were all back on duty. 'Ellie, be careful flying the twin-engined kites, especially in this weather.'

'I'm always careful. Let's hope we can make that visit soon. Do you think your CO will still let you borrow a car when we can go?'

'If there's one going spare then I'm sure he'll stick to his word. I had to tell him we just got engaged and that's why we needed it. I told him to keep it under his hat until we'd spoken to your family.'

'I wish you hadn't done that. If anyone overheard, they'll gossip and before we know it everyone will be congratulating us. I really don't want to be engaged to you even like this – I just want to be your friend.'

Somehow, he kept his dismay from showing. 'Remember, this is a temporary deception. As soon as we've seen your mom and your brother, we can break it off.' He hadn't hidden his distress well enough.

'Don't look so hurt, Jack, I can't bear to see you unhappy. I still want to go out with you and I don't mind the occasional kiss. You're a very handsome man and I'm only human.' Her smile was sad as she continued. 'Are you quite sure you want to keep seeing me when you know I don't feel the same way and might never do so? Wouldn't you be better finding yourself a girl who will love you as much as you love her?'

He swallowed the lump in his throat. 'No, honey, things are okay the way they are. You'll get over Greg one day and I want to be there when you do.

Ellie tried to relax and enjoy the enforced break from her work but knowing how much she was hurting Jack made that difficult. He deserved better than her – a girl who would reciprocate his love in a way she feared she never could.

That evening in the bar she voiced another of her concerns. 'I hope Amanda's not having a rotten time. I should have asked if I could use the telephone. It's all very well being told I'm not needed at Hamble but I should have checked with Alison.'

He waved a sandwich towards the window. 'It's snowing again. There'll be no ferrying until that lot clears.'

'Now the Americans are here do you think we'll be delivering aircraft to them?'

'I expect they'll have their own ferry pilots. Although the instructor seems to think if I have someone with me, I can fly anything.'

'Hang on a minute, I've not passed the conversion course for Class III yet – in fact if the weather doesn't improve, I won't even be able to attempt it.'

'Piece of cake for you as you're the best flyer I know. In case you're wondering, I'm proud of you and don't care that I can't ferry twin-engined kites myself. The Yanks will have coffee, chocolate, nylons, gum – in fact most of the things no longer available because of rationing here. I reckon delivering to an American base would be a popular run. Shame we won't get to do it.'

'Do you think some of the pilots from the aerial circus you were with will come over?'

'There was only one other guy my age, the rest were much older and I doubt they'll be wanted for active service. Most of our guys are early twenties.'

'It's too late to ring Hamble but whatever the weather tomorrow morning I'm going to try and get back. I'm not comfortable hanging about doing nothing.'

'Make the most of it, you'll be flying non-stop to catch up with the backlog once the weather clears.'

'I suppose you're right. Are you quite sure it's still snowing? I'm going to have a look myself.'

Vera was behind the bar polishing glasses. 'No need to, ducks, it stopped a while ago and it's a deal warmer. It should be safe enough for you all to get back to work tomorrow sometime.'

*

The following morning Jack rang the base and was told not to report until after lunch as that would be the earliest it would be safe to fly. When they crunched towards the administration block just after midday there was the roar of an engine above them and an Anson landed on the now cleared runway.

'Things are getting back to normal. I wonder if the Oxford has been repaired so I can do my conversion course.'

They reported immediately to Frankie Francis and he was delighted to see them. 'That's the ticket! If you get into your flight suits pronto you can hop on the Anson and go and collect a couple of Hurries for me.' He handed them the necessary chits. 'Priority job and there's no one else available. Miss Simpson, you'll be pleased to know the Oxford will be in service tomorrow.'

It would be dark in a couple of hours and the skies were now heavy with either snow or rain. Ten minutes after their arrival they were airborne. The fighters might well be delivered in the dark unless they were prepared to wait until tomorrow morning.

It was a fairly short hop to the MUs, where the repaired aircraft were waiting. The handover was swift and she was so familiar with this kite that her preflight checks were all she had to do – there was no need for her to spend time looking in her little blue book.

Jack took off first and she followed him. He had instrument training so if the weather closed in before they landed, he would be able to lead her in safely.

*

Once in flight Jack waggled his wings to indicate to Ellie that she should fly beside him. They were cutting it fine but he was more concerned about icing on the wings than flying in the dark. These were fully operational kites with everything installed and in working order. He hoped he didn't have recourse to use the radio.

It was a short flip to Kenley so they should be able to land before it became too dark for Ellie to see. The barrage balloons were lowered to allow them to approach safely. He circled the strip allowing Ellie to make the first approach.

The flaps and undercarriage were down. Her position was perfect.

Bloody hell! There was another Hurry coming in to land from the opposite direction. Jesus H Christ! She was going to die and there was nothing he could do about.

Ellie must have pulled the stick back hard but instead of climbing, the aircraft went into a spiral dive. She was hurtling nose first towards the hangars. She was seconds away from certain death. But then she regained control and the brave little Hurry levelled off and she was able to land.

The silly bastard who'd caused a near fatal collision had landed safely. If he got his hands on him he'd knock his bloody head off. Jack landed perfectly in the fading light and taxied to a standstill beside the kite Ellie had been flying.

She was already on the ground and had her parachute slung over her shoulder and her overnight bag in her other hand. It was slightly more complicated for him to remove himself from the cockpit one-handed but he was getting expert at the job.

'God, sweetheart, that was close.'

'Too close. It all happened so fast I scarcely had time to take it all in. I hope whoever came in the wrong way gets the book thrown at him.'

He squeezed her shoulder. 'He'll get more than that if I find him.'

'Don't you dare, Jack Reynolds, I told you before that I can fight my own battles. Do you think he was an RAF pilot or another ATA?'

They were now walking briskly across the tarmac and a group of three RAF guys were heading their way.

'Bloody poor show, you almost went for a Burton. Not one of ours, a foreign bod who's not got the hang of things yet. Can't apologise enough. You're doing a grand job.'

The officer reached out to take Ellie's parachute but she shook her head. 'I can manage, thank you. We'll have to stay the night so I hope you've got somewhere for us.'

'Sorry, no empty beds – you'll have to kip in the Mess. If you go to the NAAFI, you'll get something to eat.'

'Right, thank you. We'll just let them know we've arrived safely and then head that way.'

It was strange being back at Kenley and not knowing anyone. Quite possibly all the guys who'd been here in his day were now dead. The life expectancy of a pilot wasn't great.

'Ellie, we need to check in. Frankie knows you've got your conversion course tomorrow so I'm hoping he'll send the Anson at first light.'

'I'm surprised we didn't have some time in the lecture theatre – there's bound to be technical stuff I should know.'

'I expect they'll do that at the same time. We weren't there long enough to see if Amanda was back – but I expect she is.'

The Mess wasn't vacated until the small hours so neither of them got much sleep. The room smelled of stale smoke and beer.

He was forced to guard the gents whilst she used it. The WAAFs had their own accommodation elsewhere but she didn't want to leave him just to use the bog and have a wash. When their taxi turned up in the morning they were waiting on the apron eager to leave.

The sky was strangely quiet – had been all night. He wasn't sure how he'd have felt if the squadron had been scrambled whilst he'd been there.

They got in the Anson; it got clearance and took off immediately. They were the only passengers. As soon as they landed Ellie hurried off to find her friend, leaving him to report for duty. He collected his chits and saw he was taking a repaired Hurricane to Dumfries and then collecting a damaged one and flying it to be repaired.

His final ferry of the day would be a new Spitfire from Hamble to Debden. He doubted he'd get a lift back so he resigned himself to another uncomfortable night. The fact that he had no clean collar did nothing to improve his mood.

There was no time for social chitchat, he had to get on with his job and hope that Ellie was successful with her course.

The first flight of the day was to Prestwick, which was over 350 miles. He should do it in a couple of hours if he pushed it a bit – ATA weren't supposed to fly above 2,000 feet as they didn't have instrument training. Today he was going to ignore that rule and fly the way he always had when he was still a fighter pilot.

Four

'There you are, Ellie Simpson. Did you have an enjoyable night with Jack?' Amanda winked knowingly and Ellie couldn't prevent her cheeks turning pink.

'I've no wish to discuss my private life with you.' Her remark was accompanied by a smile. 'Are the other two here now?'

'They are. We've to report to the instructor, haven't the foggiest who he is, in full flight gear. Presumably the technical details will be demonstrated rather than explained in a classroom.'

'Because we're so experienced, have so many hours in our logbooks, the powers that be must think we already know about hydraulics, undercarriages and flaps.' Ellie hefted her parachute onto her shoulder but shoved her overnight bag into an empty locker.

The air was slightly warmer and the snow at the edge of the runway was soft underfoot. As she and Amanda trudged across to the designated hangar the other girls joined them.

'I say, Ellie, is it true you've just got engaged to that delicious redheaded chap?' Maggie asked as soon as she arrived at their side.

Ellie was about to deny it but decided it might be safer to go along with the pretence just in case word got back to Sir Reginald. She knew it had been a bad idea for Jack to have mentioned it to Frankie.

'Yes, Jack and I are engaged. I'm not sure how you know about it as we've not told anybody yet.'

'You certainly haven't told me and I'm your best friend. Who told you, Maggie?'

The girl looked slightly uncomfortable but then shrugged. 'The news is second-hand – someone overheard your chap talking about it to Frankie Francis.'

'Before you ask, we're not making any plans to get married at the moment. There's a war on, in case you've forgotten, and that has to come first.'

'Fair enough – but I envy you. He's an absolute dish and a hero as well.' Maggie sighed theatrically. 'I'd love to be engaged to a handsome fighter pilot – even one with only one hand.'

'Thank you for your congratulations. Good heavens – look over there – that must be the man who is going to train us.' She pointed to the muffled shape hopping from foot to foot and gesticulating madly at them. 'He looks ancient. I hope he knows what he's doing.'

She needn't have worried; their instructor was certainly past his prime but he knew everything he should about twin-engined aircraft. In fact, because they were such eager and intelligent students he also ran through the vagaries of the next class, that of the light bombers.

'The most crucial thing you have to understand is how to fly with one engine. You will spend most of the time learning how to do that.'

She exchanged a glance with Amanda and her friend shrugged.

'Now, Miss Simpson, as the most experienced flyer I want you to go first. I'll do one circuit and bump and then we will change places. You need to complete a minimum of three perfect circuits to be passed.'

'Okay. This might take some time as we'll have to wait each time before we can take off. Why don't you three go back to the Mess and have a cup of tea? You'll be able to see me coming and going.' She turned to her friend. 'If we're going in order of experience then you'll be next, Amanda.'

The instructor nodded and pointed to the elderly Oxford parked on the apron. 'No need to dilly-dally, Miss Simpson. I want to get all of you through this before we lose the light if possible. I've got another batch coming tomorrow.'

This aircraft had been designed to train flight crews so shouldn't have any unpleasant quirks. She had travelled many times in the Anson but this was the first time she would be flying a twin-engined kite. She took her seat on the left of the cockpit and her instructor took the other one.

She watched him go through his preflight checks and by the time they taxied to the end of the runway to wait their turn, she was familiar with all the dials, switches and knobs. The green light shone and moments later they were airborne. At no time did he speak – she had expected a stream of instructions – and was somewhat unnerved by his silence. He obviously intended that she learn by observation.

He climbed to 2,000 feet and flew in a large circle around the area. As she'd flown over this landscape dozens of times she'd no need to peer out of the cockpit. She concentrated instead on watching how the aircraft responded, exactly when the undercarriage was lowered and the flaps opened.

They had to circle twice before they got permission to land and she was pleased as this gave her longer to take note of everything. She'd already memorised the page in her blue book and was pretty sure she'd have no difficulty when it was her turn.

He landed and taxied to the end of the runway then turned the aircraft and switched off the engine. The two huge propellers stopped spinning.

'Right, young lady, your turn. The same as I did with me beside you and then you do it three times solo.'

'Yes, sir. Got that.'

'You will then do the same thing with one engine throttled back. Essential that you know the critical speed below which your kite won't maintain height if an engine fails.'

Her circuits and bumps went perfectly and then began the tricky hour of learning how to fly with one engine. Apart from the aircraft having a tendency to crab sideways it all went as planned. When she taxied to the apron after the last time, she was confident she'd passed. She checked everything was as it should be, collected her parachute, walked towards the rear of the Oxford, opened the door and dropped the ladder.

The instructor nodded and handed her a slip of paper. 'Excellent, I expect to see you back shortly to take the next conversion. You're more than capable of flying the bombers.'

'Thank you. I think I'll have to do at least three months before I'm sent back here.'

'Not if I have anything to do with it you won't.'

Amanda was waiting for her test. 'Well? Easy? Hard?'

'Piece of cake. You just need to watch him like a hawk as he doesn't say much. It took me two hours so I'll wait inside. I'll give Alison a call and let her know. With any luck we'll all be able to hop in an Anson and be back at Hamble tonight.'

She was sorry she wouldn't see Jack again today, as he couldn't possibly make it back before she left. The light was closing in by the time the last girl had successfully completed her circuits and bumps and their taxi was ready to go.

'Come on, girls, if we don't get away now we'll be stranded here for another night.'

Ellie and Amanda had to walk in the dark to the cottage they rented. Not a pleasant experience especially after the last couple of days. Eventually, they reached the gate and trudged wearily up the path.

As Ellie was about to open the door she froze. 'There's somebody inside. I heard movement.'

'Mice?'

'No, a person. Do you think it could be Nigel?' Amanda's gentleman friend was also in the ATA – the only reason he wasn't in the RAF was his age.

'I doubt it, he was on his way to the Isle of Man when I spoke to him yesterday.'

They had kept away from the front door in order to whisper to each other. 'We can't stand around out here freezing to death. I'm going in. I'll use my torch to bash him on the head if necessary.'

She reversed it and dropped her overnight bag on the doorstep. Amanda stooped down and put a heavy stone into her bag, obviously intending to use this as a weapon.

After taking a deep breath Ellie shoved the door open so violently it crashed against the wall. She heard someone swear in the kitchen – definitely a man.

'We know you're in there. Come out with your hands up.'

Amanda had closed the door behind them and they were standing in total darkness. Her heart was hammering so hard she could hear it. She took several steadying breaths the way she did when something untoward happened while she was in the air.

The kitchen door slowly opened, filling the passageway with light, and a scruffy unshaven man emerged. He didn't have his hands up. She stepped forward with the torch raised and his sneer changed to alarm. She had no intention of actually hitting him – unless he forced her to do it.

She glared at him. 'Remove yourself from my house immediately.'

He looked as if he might refuse but then saw Amanda swinging her bag threateningly and changed his mind. He shoved past them and ran out, slamming the door behind him.

'Did he have a bag full of our possessions with him?'

'No, Ellie, but he could have had things stuffed in the pockets of his revolting coat. God – we'll have to fumigate.'

'We better check what's missing and I suppose we'll have to inform the police. But I need a cup of tea after all that excitement.'

They stepped into devastation in the kitchen. The cupboards had been ransacked and everything edible had gone. The stench of unwashed male made her catch her breath.

'No tea then, and there won't be anything else until the van comes tomorrow. What a mess. I think we'd better change out of our uniforms before we tackle this.'

It took them a solid hour before they were satisfied their kitchen was clean. The intruder hadn't ventured anywhere else and by the time they'd finished Ellie was feeling a bit sorry for him.

'The poor man must have been starving to have risked imprisonment. I'm not going to tell the police but we'd better make sure we lock the door in future.'

'He could be a deserter – he was certainly living rough. His life is miserable enough without us adding to it. Although maybe he'd be better off in custody – at least he would be warm and fed.'

'Don't they shoot deserters?'

'No, that was the last war. I'm absolutely bushed, Ellie, I'm turning in. Are you excited about what we might be asked to ferry tomorrow?'

'Actually, I'm not. The only difference is that now we can fly an empty Anson, the Rapide and the Oxford. I hope we'll be moved up to Class IV pretty quickly so we can fly bombers.'

'I'd rather fly a Spitfire or Hurricane than anything else – but being promoted is a good thing. It's strange isn't it that last year we were overjoyed we could fly operational aircraft at all and now we're moaning we can't fly the twin-engined bombers.'

The next morning the thaw had continued and instead of crisp white snow underfoot there was grey slush.

'Whoever borrowed our bikes had better return them soon or I'll kick up a stink. It's just too far to walk after a long day.'

'I've been keeping my eye out but haven't spotted them so far.' Fortunately, this morning they snagged a lift and didn't have to walk to Hamble.

Alison congratulated them. 'Well done, both of you, not that I expected anything else. Your instructor got in touch with me, Ellie, and said he'd be happy for you to move up to Class IV as soon as I'm prepared to send you back. With that in mind, I'm going to give you as much experience with twin-engined aircraft as I can. You'll be far more useful to me when you can deliver Blenheims, Wellingtons and Dakotas.'

'I'll ferry whatever I'm given, Alison, you know that.'

'Excellent. I think half a dozen trips should be enough and then you can move up to Class IV.'

Was her friend going to be cross because she'd not been singled out for preferential treatment? No such thing – Amanda slapped her on the back.

'You deserve it. You must be one of the most experienced flyers in the ATA, male or female. Don't look so glum, I'm not jealous, not really. Two things for you to celebrate now.'

Ellie hated deceiving her friend about the true state of affairs between Jack and herself. The sooner she made that visit to Herford House, her mother's ancestral home, the better. All this nonsense could be put aside and life could go back to normal.

There was still twenty minutes to go before the chits would be put on the table so there was ample time to have a much-needed cuppa whilst they waited. 'Thank goodness there's something in the biscuit tin today. I'm absolutely starving,' Amanda said.

'Going without supper or breakfast in this weather's no fun. I hope we go somewhere we can get something decent to eat.' Ellie was just sipping her tea when Amanda nudged her.

'Oh my God! Look who's just walked in.'

Jack had an uneventful trip and arrived a good deal earlier than he would have done if he'd stuck to the rules. He filled in the paperwork, signed the necessary forms, collected the operationally ready Spitfire, and was back in the air less than forty minutes after his arrival. Sometimes one was obliged to hang about for hours whilst the admin Johnnies got themselves organised.

He was determined to get back to base tonight regardless of the weather and the lack of light. When he'd been operational himself, he frequently flew at night. He'd met a couple of ex-fighter pilots in the ATA and all of them ignored the ATA manual, which said there was to be no flying above 2,000 feet and to stay grounded if the weather was bad.

Most of the blokes and girls were happy to fly in appalling conditions – conditions that kept the RAF from the air. When a kite was needed anywhere in Britain the ATA did their best to deliver. Unlike the RAF, who had to follow orders, Jack was free to make his own decisions about the weather conditions and if it was safe to fly.

He'd loved flying his Hurry but had to admit that the Spitfire was his absolute favourite. It wasn't just its elegant shape, although that was part of it, it was the way it handled.

Somehow the kite seemed almost as if it was eager to be in the air. If he took his hand from the controls in fine weather it would continue to fly in the same direction. Yet at the lightest touch of a finger it responded instantly. The cockpit was as comfortable for him at over six foot as it was for one of the girls at only five foot four.

Again, he flew at 10,000 feet using his instruments to guide him. The light was fading whilst he was still some distance from home. They wouldn't expect him to arrive in the dark and the runway might not be clear. Nothing for it but to risk it and land anyway.

No point in using the radio as he'd only get static – no one at White Waltham would be listening. He supposed he wasn't the first flyer to arrive in the dark so there must be some provision. Obviously, runways couldn't be lit because of the blackout, but all he needed were a couple of blokes with torches and he'd be able to land safely.

He roared around the airfield a couple of times to indicate he was there and sure enough on his third circuit half a dozen torches were shone into the air on either side of the strip. He throttled back, lowered the undercarriage and the flaps and was pleased with his perfect landing.

As soon as he was down the torches were shone in a straight line to show him where to taxi. He switched off, unclipped his harness, pushed back the cockpit cover and was ready to get out.

'I might have known it was you, Reynolds – no one else is damn fool enough to arrive in the middle of the night.'

Frankie was waiting on the ground and made no effort to help him with the difficult task of climbing out of the cockpit whilst carrying his parachute and overnight bag.

Sod him! Jack did what he always did in these circumstances and tossed his bag out, rapidly followed by his chute. He was almost sorry neither object hit his CO.

'Evening, sir, thought I'd be here a bit earlier…'

'You should have stayed at Prestwick – there's only one way you got here so soon.'

Jack had excellent night vision and his eyes had adjusted to the darkness. He scooped up his missing bags and slung them over his shoulder. 'If I'm going to get a bollocking can we do it inside? Too bloody cold out here.'

Frankie Francis strode ahead and this time used only a tiny pinprick of light from his torch and not the full beam. This was enough to follow safely into the admin building.

As soon as the door shut behind him the blackout curtain was pushed back and they both stepped into the corridor.

'I'm not going to reprimand you this time – you're one of the few men I have who are perfectly competent at night. However, rules are rules and in future you damn well stick to them. That clear?'

'Sure thing. Are Ellie and Amanda still here?'

'No, all four girls successfully completed their course and have returned to Hamble.'

Jack knew he'd got off lightly this time and hoped he had the sense not to do the same thing again, but he doubted it. He dumped his flight gear, grabbed his bicycle and set off for his billet. Ellie didn't have a telephone at the cottage so he'd have to wait until tomorrow and see if he could catch her before she started her ferrying duties.

He avoided the noisy public bar and made his way directly to his bedroom. With any luck he'd be able to snatch a quick bath whilst the rest of the guys were downstairs swilling beer and playing darts. He was safely in his pyjamas and dressing gown when someone knocked on the door.

'Jack, I heard you come in and have made you a sandwich and a cuppa.' Vera was a good sort who looked after him better than he deserved because she felt sorry for him.

He opened the door and she walked in and put the tray on top of the chest of drawers. 'There you are, love, get that down you. Some posh bloke has been ringing asking for you. What do you want me to tell him if he rings again tonight?'

'I don't think he will. He won't expect me to have got home in the dark. Thanks for the sandwich. Much appreciated.'

There was only one person he could think of who would be ringing him and that was Mainwaring. Not his problem. He needed his kip. He'd worry about it in the morning.

Five

Wing Commander Lambourne looked handsome in his uniform as he strode towards them. 'Ellie, I need to speak to you.'

'Hugo, what are you doing here? Is bomber command still grounded? We're just waiting for our chits so I haven't got long.'

Her friend had politely drifted away, leaving them to speak privately. 'We've been posted to the Isle of Man and leave tomorrow. I need to speak to you urgently.'

'I explained to you that I'm involved with someone else. In fact, we got engaged a couple of days ago.'

His smile was remarkably cheerful for a man who was supposed to have feelings for her. Was there another reason for his being here?

'Good show, congratulations, you deserve to be happy. I'm not the marrying kind and you're better off with that other chap. You told me that you're related to a George Simpson – I've heard the most disturbing news about him and I thought you ought to know.'

'Go on, I'm listening.'

'I've got a brother at the war office and a cousin in intelligence – we met up for a farewell dinner last night in London. I think they forgot I'm not part of their circle and the conversation drifted to their search for a traitor sending information to the Nazis. When they mentioned the name Simpson I began to pay attention.'

'There must be hundreds of people called Simpson – why did you immediately think of me?'

'I remember you saying you had a grandfather called Sir Reginald Humphrey and his name was mentioned too.'

'I've not seen George or spoken to him since our brother's funeral.' She forced her fingers to unclench. 'Why do they suspect him?'

'It's possible he's leaking material about naval manoeuvres in the Atlantic – at the moment he's just one of the possible traitors. I think it's because Sir Reginald was once associated with Mosley that he's on their list.'

'I don't understand why you've come rushing here to tell me this? There's nothing I can do about it.'

'I know you're no longer in contact with him, but I wanted to give you a chance to warn him. If he's arrested and found guilty, he'll be executed.'

'A traitor should be hanged – if my brother is spying for the Germans he deserves everything he gets.'

He looked shocked by her vehemence. 'Right. I'd better be going. Take care of yourself, Ellie. Goodbye.'

She offered her hand and he shook it vigorously. 'Cheerio, Hugo, fly safe.'

He strode off, leaving her with a sour taste in her mouth. Now it was imperative she and Jack made the abandoned visit. Whatever she'd said to Hugo, she had no intention of allowing her brother to be hanged. Surely he couldn't be a German spy?

'Ellie, he didn't look too upset – I suppose you gave him your good news.'

'He didn't come to say goodbye.' She explained and Amanda was horrified.

'That's bad news. I'm sure your brother's innocent but I expect you want to warn him anyway. I know I would – family first.'

Ellie felt sick. 'I'm beginning to think that I shouldn't interfere. I don't believe it for one minute, but if George is a traitor then he might well have caused the death of British servicemen. Might do so again – I can't let him get away with that.'

'Horrible dilemma for you. Go and see him and decide then what you're going to do.'

'I'm going to forget about it for the moment as there's nothing I can do until I've completed my work rota. Hopefully, Jack and I will get the same time off again.'

'Alison's just bringing the chits, Ellie, we'd better go.'

The head of an admin girl poked out of the hatch that divided the ops room from the Mess. 'Ellie, urgent phone call for you.'

It was Jack on the other end of the line. 'Congratulations on your promotion, honey. Mainwaring's been trying to get hold of me but I'm avoiding him. God knows what sent him into a tailspin.'

She turned her back and moved as far away as the flex would allow before telling him what had just happened.

'Bloody hell! Not good, I agree. Can you get a flip here? I met the guy. He was one of us – I can't see him changing sides.'

'I'll come as soon as I can. I've got to go. Take care.' She replaced the receiver and dashed into the pandemonium in the Mess where everyone was milling about collecting their chits for the day.

Amanda had already gone – like Ellie she put duty first. Hers were the only pieces of paper left on the table. Usually she was one of the first to leave.

She was taking an empty Anson to be repaired, then collecting a Spit and delivering it to Debden in Suffolk. She was then taking an Oxford to White Waltham and would be collected by the taxi Anson and flown home at the end of the day.

When she landed at White Waltham there wasn't time to enquire if Jack was at the pool as the taxi was waiting. The day had flown past. She smiled. It had done so both literally and figuratively. When she was airborne there was no time for thinking about personal matters. Flying had helped with her grief when Greg had died so tragically.

Her thirteen-day roster was busier than usual because of the poor weather, which had delayed a lot of deliveries. Amanda was going off somewhere with Nigel for her two days' leave and Ellie had managed to arrange for a flip to White Waltham. She was looking forward to seeing Jack again, but dreading what they had to do.

What if her mother didn't want to see her? Didn't even let them in? It wasn't just re-establishing contact with Mum that mattered now but protecting her only surviving brother. She and George had never been as close as she and Neil had been but they'd never actually fallen out.

Six

Jack had somehow managed to avoid being in the building each time Mainwaring had telephoned. Frankie wasn't impressed. 'Next time that blighter rings you damn well speak to him. Who the hell is he anyway?'

'It's something to do with national security – I'm sorry I can't tell you anything else.'

'Righto! The car you want has a full tank of petrol but I doubt you'll get any more so make sure you get it back before it runs out.'

'That's great, Frankie, and I give you my word you'll not be pestered anymore.' In fact, he'd been so busy he'd only been able to speak to Ellie once. The weather had improved, the snow gone for the moment, and the backlog of deliveries had finally been cleared. As neither of them had more than the two days free before they were back on duty, he just had his usual overnight bag. He was unlikely to get a car with a tankful of petrol again and travelling by rail was a bloody nightmare.

Like all ATA flyers he dreaded being told there was no taxi to collect him and he had to catch the train home. This had happened to him twice during the past two weeks and on both occasions he'd only just got back in time to start the next day's ferrying.

He was waiting on the edge of the apron when the Anson bringing Ellie landed. She wasn't on duty so she hadn't had to lug her parachute with her and like him just had her small travelling bag. He waved and she increased her pace and trotted over to him.

Her lips were cold but her enthusiastic response to his kiss reassured him that at least she found him desirable. 'Morning, honey, let's get a move on before anyone finds us a priority delivery to do.' He slung his bag over his left side and put his right arm around her shoulders.

He was well aware that he was the luckiest guy in his pool to be engaged, even if it wasn't genuine, to this beautiful girl. They made a striking couple. With his height, red hair and one arm, no one ever forgot him. Ellie was tall, slim and quite beautiful. Several guys had told him he'd got the best-looking gal in the ATA. His lips curved at the thought.

'What are you smiling at, Jack?'

'Just happy to see you. If the spooks haven't been able to prove your brother's a traitor then I don't see that he's in any immediate danger.'

'Do you think George will confess to me?'

'Don't let him say anything incriminating. Just tell him what that Hugo guy told you and leave it at that. Remember, you're going there to see your mom and your brother. With any luck Humphrey will keep out of our way.'

Ellie drove the car with the same skill she flew a kite. As the roads were relatively empty it only took a couple of hours to get there. A few miles from their destination he spotted a massive stately home set way back on a hill. He'd expected her to be nervous at meeting her mom again but if she was she was hiding it well.

'My God, Ellie, is that your grandfather's pile?'

'I think it has to be. Mum never said she'd grown up in a palace.'

When they arrived the imposing iron gates were open and she drove straight in. The drive curved to the right, making the house invisible at first but they both knew what to expect.

'It's a perfect early Georgian manor house and I think the grounds might have been done by Capability Brown.'

'There must be more than fifty windows and none of them with tape on them. Does he think he's immune to…?' His voice trailed away as the possible implication of the untaped windows sunk in.

'I know what you're thinking, Jack: that Humphrey hasn't bothered with the tape because he knows this house won't be bombed. He can't be that stupid.'

'Maybe just arrogant? Do we go around the back?'

'The back – where the carriages used to turn. The front is the park and formal gardens.'

'So the servants' entrance must be at the side somewhere.'

'Yes, but we're certainly not going there. I'm going to pull up in the same place that invited guests would. I wonder if anyone has seen us or whether we're going to have to knock on the door.'

'Will it be opened by a butler in tails?'

'Very likely – but I refuse to be intimidated. It's not us that's under suspicion of spying for the enemy.' Her smile made his pulse skip. 'And you, Squadron Leader Reynolds, are a hero of the RAF.'

They left the bags in the back seat and with some reluctance stepped out onto the raked gravel. She slipped her hand into his without him asking and this gave him the confidence to approach the imposing front door without shaking in his boots.

As she was holding his only hand she reached out and hammered loudly with the shiny brass dolphin knocker. 'Sod it – quickly, I've got a ring here and forgot to give it to you. They'll expect you to be wearing one.'

Hastily she pulled off the leather glove on her left hand and held it out expectantly. The ring wasn't in a box but tucked into his pocket, making it easier for him to recover it and push it over her knuckle.

'Jack, it's quite beautiful. Is it an emerald in the middle and diamonds around the edge?'

'It is.' His smile was somewhat lopsided as he continued. 'Take care of it, love, that's the equivalent of a Tiger Moth.'

She had just replaced her glove when the door slowly opened. He heard her sharp intake of breath.

Mrs Simpson was acting as butler. She was thinner than he'd remembered, but looked well enough and was certainly expensively dressed. He was staggered that she looked pleased to see them. 'Ellen, Mr Reynolds, what a pleasant surprise. Do come in. My father, you'll be relieved to know, is away on business but George is around somewhere.'

Jack was shocked when Ellie let go of his hand and hugged her mother. For a moment the woman's hands hung limply by her sides, then she returned the embrace. 'I'm so pleased to see you, Mother, and it will be good to catch up with George as well. Is his wife here too?'

'No, Fiona is staying with her parents this week. She will be sorry to have missed you both.'

They were now inside the vast entrance hall and Jack looked around with interest. This was the sort of place Ellie would have lived in if she'd married Greg. Not his cup of tea – but it was certainly impressive.

No uniformed maid or footman rushed forward to take their coats, which he found a bit odd considering the size of the house and the wealth of the owner. His breath condensed in front of him. It was as cold in here as it was outside.

This time they'd both worn their uniform greatcoats as well as their peaked caps. As civilians they could have worn mufti, unlike service people, but the general population frowned upon men out of uniform so he always wore his.

He shrugged off his coat and dumped it on a spindly gold chair. Ellie grinned and did the same. Hats and gloves were added to the pile and then they followed their hostess who had walked through the hall and vanished down a wide, freezing passageway.

'God, it's perishing in here. I think we should have kept our coats on,' he whispered to her.

'Shush, behave yourself. Things are going okay so far. Thank goodness that man isn't here.'

Mrs Simpson took them to a small, thankfully warm, room and hastily closed the door behind them. 'This house is horribly cold in the winter. If I'm honest, it's cold all year round. It does have rudimentary central heating but Pa refuses to have it on. I hide away in here most of the time as it's the only warm room in the place apart from the kitchen.'

'Do you have staff, Mother? It's a huge house to run without any.'

This was the second time she'd used 'mother' instead of 'mum'. Ellie was really making an effort. The atmosphere was strained. He was glad there was a substantial fire, with a small sofa and two armchairs grouped in front of it to remove the chill.

'We have a cook and two housemaids inside and three ancient gardeners. The rest of the staff left last year to do war work. We only use this room and the breakfast parlour downstairs and obviously three of the dozen or so bedrooms.'

He gazed out of the window, surprised the park hadn't been ploughed up to grow vegetables. 'No potato fields here, Mrs Simpson?'

'Pa refused. The Ministry of Agriculture weren't at all pleased with him but he agreed to use the paddocks and they seem to be happy with that for the moment.' She gestured that they take a seat.

'You look quite splendid in your uniform, Ellen. How long have you been in the ATA?'

'Eighteen months – I was in the WAAF before that. Jack and I have just got engaged and we wanted to tell you in person.' She held out her hand and the wildly extravagant ring he'd bought for her sparkled satisfactorily. They were talking as if they were strangers, which was hardly a surprise after the way Mrs Simpson had treated Ellie.

Her mother gave it a cursory glance. 'Very nice. Are you planning to get married soon?'

'No, not until after the war ends. We're both far too busy working. I heard that George was forced to leave the RAF. What does he do now?'

'He's got an absolutely splendid job at the Admiralty in London. He is indispensable to them, you know.'

'That's good. Does Fiona do anything useful?'

'Good heavens, no. Their baby is due in April, which is why she's gone to see her parents as it will probably be the last time she can do so before the birth.'

'Congratulations, you will be a grandmother and I'll be an aunt. Dad will be pleased even if he's never going to see the child; he's happy that George's doing well.'

So far Jack had been ignored, which suited him just fine. He stood up in his usual ungainly way. 'We've come a long way to see you, ma'am, and could both do with a hot drink. If you give me directions, I'll find the kitchen and get that organised.'

'Yes, an excellent idea. The bells don't work at this end of the house. Return the way you came, cross the hall and go down the corridor opposite. There is a flight of steps on the left that leads to the kitchens and so on.'

'I'll leave you to catch up with your mom, honey.'

None of the windows he passed had blackout curtains – how the hell did they manage at night? Probably like White Waltham the residents had to make do with torches. He stopped to have a look and saw solid shutters neatly folded at the sides of each window. Holy cow! They would take hours to close every night and open again in the morning.

He found the stairs okay and when he pushed open the swing door a welcome wave of warm air enveloped him. He was smiling when he poked his head around the kitchen door. He knew who he'd rather be in this house – servants had a far more comfortable existence than those living in so-called luxury upstairs.

This wasn't going well. 'Jack was a squadron leader when he lost his hand, Mother. Don't you think it's wonderful he can still fly for the ATA?'

This comment was ignored. 'I was sorry to hear that Greg married someone else. It must have been so difficult for you.'

'It was, but we would have been together if he hadn't died.' Her eyes filled and she swallowed the lump in her throat.

'I didn't know that. Can you bear to tell me what happened?'

When Ellie had finished things were easier between them. Her mother's sympathy was genuine. 'So, you see, it's really very hard for me to let go of my feelings for Greg and…' She'd revealed too much.

'My dear, give it time. Jack's a good man and Greg wouldn't want you to mourn for him for too long. I know the family of that dreadful woman – they were never favourites of mine. To think that Greg's inheritance went to her.'

'Actually, Greg left everything to me. I've invested it in war bonds for the moment.'

'Good heavens! I should think that didn't go down well.' Mum paused and then continued, 'I am sorry for the way I left and for the way I behaved whilst I was there. I don't regret marrying your father but it was a mistake for both of us. If I hadn't, you and your brothers wouldn't be here.'

'I didn't make things easy for you. Can we move on from that and start again?'

'I'd like that. I had an unrealistic memory of my life here and coming back opened my eyes. I did the right thing for Fred and me but wish I had taken his offer and found my own home.'

They chatted about the war and the shortages and then returned to the subject of her brother.

'Now, tell me what George is doing that's so important he was able to leave the RAF.'

'I'm so proud of him. He suffered a perforated eardrum and could no longer fly. He could have managed the estate and been safe but he chose to work in London and risk being killed by German bombs.'

'He must miss being able to fly. I know I certainly did until I joined the ATA.'

'I don't know exactly what it is he does as he isn't allowed to talk about it.'

'Goodness, how exciting. Why is he home today? Is he unwell?'

'His immediate superior insisted that he took a few days' leave – he hasn't had a day off for months and things are quiet there at the moment.'

Ellie rather thought her brother wasn't wanted anywhere near secret information whilst he was being investigated. 'I think things are quiet everywhere, thank God. Now the Americans are fighting alongside us I don't think it will be long before Hitler's defeated. I will probably be flying their kites soon.'

'Surely not? They will want their own people to do that.'

'Not the Yanks' own, but ones they've given us.'

Footsteps approached the small sitting room and they both looked towards the door. It opened and George stepped in. His eyes widened when he saw her.

'Ellie, I didn't know you were here. I saw the car outside and came to investigate. How the hell did you get any petrol?'

'Jack borrowed it from his CO. Congratulations on your forthcoming baby. I hope Fiona's well.'

'Perfectly, thank you. I must say I'm surprised to see you both here.'

She held out her hand so he could see her beautiful engagement ring. 'I wanted to tell Mum in person that I'm engaged to Jack. I've only stayed away because I dislike Sir Reginald but I wanted to share my good news with you both. There's no reason for us to be estranged unless you support his views, of course.'

'Grandpapa severed all connections to Mosley as you well know. We fully support Churchill.'

'I'm delighted to hear you say so. However, don't you think that if Sir Reginald was totally committed to beating the Nazis he wouldn't have refused to plough up the grounds?' She stood up.

Her mother moved across to take her hands. 'Please stay and have your drink.'

'I'm not going anywhere, Mum, just thought I'd see if I could help Jack. Could we meet in London occasionally? I get a couple of days' leave every fortnight.'

'I'd like that, but it will have to wait until after the war. I have no transport and it's too far to walk to the station.'

The rattle of crockery approaching interrupted them. George made no move to open the door and turned away as if he'd lost interest in the conversation but she knew he was listening.

'Jack finds it difficult balancing trays with only one hand. I'd better go and help him, Mum.' She squeezed her mother's fingers and her mother returned the gesture.

When she stepped into the icy passageway it wasn't Jack outside but an elderly woman wearing a maid's uniform. 'Let me help you.'

'No, Miss Simpson, I can manage. Your young man will be along with the sandwiches and cake. Cook is just cutting off the crusts.'

This was frowned on nowadays – one wasn't even allowed to throw the crusts to the birds. The maid saw her face and hastily clarified her remark.

'Good heavens, miss, them crusts don't go to waste. They make a tasty bread pudding for afters.'

Ellie held open the door and was about to go in search of him then thought better of it. The delicious aroma of real coffee drifted across to her – this certainly wasn't the ersatz, barleycorn concoction that was masquerading as coffee at the moment.

Her brother was sitting next to Mum on the sofa and the tray was on a small hexagonal table beside them.

'Do you take cream and sugar, Ellen? I can't remember how you like it.'

'Neither, thank you. Jack likes it the same way as me. Real coffee is a treat – not something I've had for more than a year. Jack says the Americans will have things on their bases that are rationed here.'

'Sit down, my dear – don't hover, it's most disconcerting.'

Ellie was at a loss to know how she could possibly mention what Hugo told her. Maybe Jack would be able to turn the conversation to this difficult topic. 'Jack's taking a long time. I'm going to see what's happened to him. I won't be a minute.' She was out of the door before either of them could protest and met him halfway down the passageway carrying a tray with sandwiches and cake one-handed.

'Let me help you. It would be criminal if you dropped that.'

He grinned and happily handed it over. 'How's it going in there?"

'My brother's there and he's not as unfriendly as I remembered. Do you have any idea how we can introduce the fact that he's being investigated for spying?' She smiled. 'Mum and I have talked and she apologised for being so hard on me. I'm so glad we came. I'll have two mothers now.'

'Leave it to me, you spend time with your mom and I'll persuade him to come and talk shop to me. After all, we were both fighter pilots. We must have something in common.'

'She wants to be part of my life, our lives. It's a shame that will have to wait until the end of the war but at least contact has been re-established.'

There was no room on the coffee table for the sandwiches and cake but Jack picked a second one up and placed it adjacent to the other. She put down the tray. As her mother didn't get up to serve them, Ellie did it herself.

'Coffee, sandwiches made from real bread and not the horrible national loaf that tastes like wet newspaper, and proper cake – I hope you've not used up all your rations on us.'

'We have two farms on the estate so rationing isn't a problem here,' George said. 'I'm sure it's the same at Glebe Farm. I hear that our father married the housekeeper.'

'Yes, he did. Mabel and he are very happy together.' She wasn't going to get into an argument about this so bit into her sandwich.

Jack, true to his word, suggested to her brother that they take their coffee and cake to the other side of the room so she and her mother could continue to catch up. She thought at first George wouldn't move, but then he nodded.

'I flew Hurries. I wish I could be back with my unit and not spending my days paper pushing at the Admiralty.'

Seven

Jack would have to take his coffee but leave the food behind. He was surprised and touched when George piled everything onto the empty tray and carried it across to the window.

'Not as warm here, but we can talk freely. Why has my sister decided to make this unannounced visit? What's changed? I don't buy your story about the engagement.'

For a moment he thought George had seen through their pretence but then realised he was referring to the fact that getting engaged wasn't sufficient reason to make the trek.

'You're partly right. Ellie might not have been close to you or Mrs Simpson but you're still her family. So many good guys are dying as well as civilians and she just wanted to see you both again just in case she went for a Burton.'

'I should think that the death of Neil and then Greg Dunlop really shook her up. I'm not surprised she's going to marry you – I've always thought you were a better fit than Greg. Ellie's a matter-of-fact sort of girl and I think would have hated being stuck in a place like this. I can't say I'm enjoying it myself but I can't leave my mother on her own. It's a good thing Fiona likes it here.'

'Thanks – but she still holds a torch for Dunlop and I'm not sure she's committed to this engagement. Don't be surprised if you never see it announced in *The Times*.'

'I'm sorry to hear that. Whatever the reason, I'm glad you came.'

'Great. How does your mom get to see anyone, stuck out here? Does she have the use of a car?'

'She doesn't have any friends within walking distance. Mother's trapped as she doesn't drive and even if she did there's no petrol to put in the car.'

'What about a pony cart? I noticed your stables are still occupied. Surely she could drive herself to the station occasionally.'

'Mother's not overfond of equines – Grandfather made her hunt when she was a girl and that's put her off for life. But it's a good idea and I'll see what I can do to persuade her to have a go.'

A squadron of Spitfires roared overhead and he watched them go, wishing he was up there with them.

'I feel the same way, Jack, it was bloody bad luck damaging my ear.' George looked longingly at the sky. 'I know I'm doing a vital job but it just doesn't feel the same. To be still fighting the Nazis would be so much better. At least you're still flying.' He scowled at the departing planes. 'I bloody hate the Germans. Can't stand the sight of Sir Reginald either.'

Jack came to a decision and hoped it was the right one. 'Look, George, I said earlier there was another reason we came today. A friend of Ellie's came to see her and told her that you're being investigated for treason. She wanted you to know. If I thought for one minute you were spying for the Germans, I wouldn't have told you.'

George turned the colour of an old sheet and if Jack hadn't reached out and caught it, his cup would have smashed to the floor and attracted unwanted attention. He raised his voice slightly so he would be overheard. 'Yes, I'd like to see the horses. I learned to ride when I was in the States but I've not been on one since I got back.'

He kept talking and kept his bulk between George and the women – if they saw him now there would be awkward explanations to make. Once they were outside, he guided the trembling guy rapidly down the passageway and out into the fresh air before he could throw up on the polished boards.

He all but pushed his companion behind the shrubbery where he wouldn't be seen. Not a moment too soon. He moved away rapidly and left him to it. Was this reaction a sign that the bloke was really a spy or was it just the shock of being investigated? Suddenly he didn't care – this was hopefully his future brother-in-law and whatever sort of mess Simpson had got himself into he would do everything he could to protect him.

'Christ almighty! That was close. You might have given me some warning when you dropped that bombshell.' George was wiping his mouth on a spotless white handkerchief as he spoke. 'I wondered why I'd been given this leave when we're so busy. It's not me – in case you were wondering. I do have access to state secrets but I'm one hundred per cent loyal to this country. Thank you for your faith in me.'

'We'd better go around to the stables as they'll expect us to be smelling of horse when we go back.'

'Do you really ride or was that just quick thinking on your part?'

'Actually, it's true. I've only used a western saddle so not sure if that counts.'

'Don't look so worried, I'm not going to suggest we go for a hack. I didn't even know there was an investigation in my department. There are four of us – and I don't blame them for thinking I'm a prime suspect.'

The horses were stabled in individual loose boxes and all looked in good shape. He rubbed noses and pulled ears and inhaled the smell with delight. 'Do any of these go in harness?'

'Not the hunters, but there's a cob in the end box that the gardeners use. He'd be ideal as he's past his prime and good-natured.'

Jack kept the conversation light, allowing George to recover. On the way back to the house he asked the question that had been hanging between them. 'Right, if it's not you it has to be one of the other three. You work with them, who do you think it is?'

'I know exactly who it is but I'm not going to tell you his name. I don't want you and Ellie involved in this just in case I'm arrested.'

'If you didn't know the spooks were onto it, presumably the real culprit is also in the dark. Do you think you can catch him at it before he twigs?'

'Bloody well hope so.' He gripped Jack's shoulder. 'I'll never forget what you've done for me. Prewarned is forearmed – or something like that.'

'Do you know if the other blokes are going to be given leave?'

'Good thinking. One of them had last week, I'm off until Friday and then the other two go in turn. Their thinking might well be that if the leaks stop whilst one of us is away then they've got their man.'

George's colour had returned and he looked almost cheerful for a man who could be arraigned for treason at any moment. 'It's the chap going on leave last that I suspect is the traitor. I'll be back at work soon and will have a week to keep an eye on him.'

The gust of icy wind made Jack look skywards. 'Bloody hell! It's starting to snow. I thought the weather had changed for the better.'

Ellie watched Jack almost push her brother from the room and could think of only one thing that could have upset George so much. He'd been told about the investigation. A wave of relief swept over her. He wouldn't have reacted so violently if he was actually a spy.

She turned back to her mother who hadn't noticed the men's rapid departure. 'Mum, you don't have to live here. Dad has given you a generous allowance and would buy you somewhere more comfortable. He wants you to be happy.'

'I grew up here and this might seem an unfriendly sort of place but it's the only home I have.'

'You're not answering the question. Wouldn't you prefer to be living somewhere you weren't so cut off?'

Her mother looked away and the delicate porcelain cup rattled against the saucer. Ellie had obviously touched a nerve.

'I know you had to leave. You and Dad should never have got married in the first place but he doesn't regret it either as, if you hadn't, none of us would have been born.'

'I let my father push me into trying to take the farm away from Fred. I couldn't ask him to help me after that.'

'Then don't. I keep forgetting I've got an enormous amount of money in war bonds – but I can access enough of it to buy you somewhere. What about George? Surely he and Fiona would rather have their own place?'

'I shouldn't really tell you this, but I think Fiona only married George because of his connections. She loves being the lady of the manor and is a great favourite with my father.'

'Where would you like to live? There are some lovely Georgian houses near the cathedral in St Albans. Shall I look there for you?'

Her mother wiped her eyes. 'If you're quite sure, then yes, please do. Leaving Glebe Farm was the right thing to do but coming here wasn't. I'd no idea my father was involved with the fascists before the war and would never have come if I'd known. George didn't want to lose contact with me – we've always been closer than I was to you and Neil.'

Ellie had always known this was true but for some reason hearing it confirmed was hurtful. 'You always wanted me to be more like you and I was always a tomboy. I think we could have tried harder to get along. Anyway, that's in the past. I want us to be friends in future.'

'So do I, Ellen. I don't quite know what George will do when I move.'

'I'm sure he'll move out as well and Fiona has no choice but to go with him. She's having a baby in a few months and would be a lot more comfortable somewhere smaller.'

Something caught her eye and she scrambled to her feet in dismay. 'It's snowing again. The Met office didn't forecast any more snow this week. We'd better leave before it gets any worse.'

Her mother joined her at the window. 'It's settling already. It's getting dark even though it's scarcely midday. Why don't you and Jack stay here overnight?'

'Is Sir Reginald likely to be back?'

'No, he's gone to Liverpool on business and won't be back for a few days.'

'In which case, if Jack agrees, then I'd be happy to stay.' She began to put the crockery and cutlery on the trays. 'I'll take this back to the kitchen. Even if we decide not to risk getting snowed in here, maybe we could still have lunch before we leave.'

'I'll come with you and speak to Cook. As George said before, we are lucky as we don't have to rely on the meagre rations we're allowed. I'm sure your father and his wife eat as well as we do here. One of the many advantages of having a farm.'

They took a tray each and as they stepped into the hall the front door opened and Jack and George came in, closely resembling snowmen. They stamped the worst off their feet and brushed themselves down before moving any further.

'It's arctic out there, Ellie. I don't think we'll be going anywhere today. I've moved the car into the coach house and covered it with a blanket. With any luck it'll start when we do want to leave.'

'Mum has suggested that we stay here tonight, Jack, and I'd be happy to do so if that's okay with you.'

'Great – I'm going to ring Frankie and see what the Met office has to say about this cold front. You do realise we're likely to be stranded here until the snow clears.'

George had smiled and vanished somewhere. She was still holding the tray. 'You make the phone call and I'll take this to the kitchen. Our greatcoats are still on that chair where we left them – if you put yours on could you get our overnight bags from the car?'

'Was about to suggest I did so – no point in us both getting cold and wet.' He leaned closer and spoke quietly. 'Your brother's not involved with the leak but he thinks he knows who is. He had no idea he was under suspicion.'

'Exactly what I thought. I'm so glad we came.'

The servants' quarters were far warmer than upstairs. The elderly maid emerged and removed the tray from her hands. 'You run along, Miss Simpson, I'll take this.'

They had a delicious lunch of leek and potato soup and freshly baked rolls, followed by apple pie and custard. When Mum told George that she intended to move and suggested that he and Fiona came with her he couldn't have been happier.

'That's very generous of you, Ellie. I won't be sorry to move from this depressing place. Fiona won't be pleased. However, I'm sure once we're settled in St Albans, and not stuck out here miles from anywhere, she'll see the advantages.'

The weather worsened to blizzard conditions. The shutters weren't closed so one was obliged to move about the house without lights.

'What did Frankie say when you rang him, Jack?'

'It's as bad at White Waltham as it is here and everything's ground to a halt again. Why don't you ring Hamble and see if the weather has deteriorated in Southampton?'

Alison confirmed the snow was widespread and not to worry if she couldn't get back the day after tomorrow as there was unlikely to be any flying for the next few days.

They spent an enjoyable afternoon playing bridge and were then served an excellent supper. When they finally ventured into the icy corridors both she and Jack stopped to put on their greatcoats, caps and gloves before they had to find the bedrooms they'd been allocated.

'Wise move,' George said. 'We collect hot water bottles to take up as there's no heating allowed. Our grandfather thinks it's healthy to be cold.'

'You can't bring a new baby into a freezing house…'

'Ellie, there must be thousands of families who can't afford to heat the bedrooms – what do you think they do with new babies?' Jack, like her, had never had to experience such privations.

'You're right. But it's outrageous that there's no heat when it could be provided.'

Her brother held open the door that led down to the kitchens. 'I agree, but I'm only a guest here so must put up with things if I want to stay. Why don't we all go into St Albans tomorrow, weather permitting?'

'How do you get to work? Presumably you have a car and petrol to run it.'

'I wish I did, but I cycle. It's only five miles and believe it or not the bike can often get through where a motorised vehicle can't.'

The kitchen was empty but the kettle was boiling on the range and three hot water bottles were waiting on the table to be filled.

'I'm going to make cocoa. Do you want some, George?'

'Absolutely. I'll show you where everything is.'

Knowing how cold it was going to be they were reluctant to leave the warmth of the kitchen. At midnight she had no option. Mum had gone up earlier so George led the way.

'It's a suite – adjoining bedrooms, plus shared sitting room and dressing rooms. Unfortunately, there's only one bathroom and WC on this floor and it's at the other end of the corridor. You might want to use the old-fashioned facilities supplied under your beds.' His voice echoed as he'd not bothered to speak quietly. 'It's fine once you're in bed. Plenty of blankets and a feather eiderdown. Good night.'

A door closed further down the passageway.

'We could always sleep downstairs. I'd rather be uncomfortable than cold.'

Jack all but pushed her into the sitting room. He shone the pinprick of light across to check the shutters were closed before turning on the light.

'I'm surprised there aren't icicles hanging from the mantelpiece. I've a suggestion to make – don't take it the wrong way.'

She knew at once what he meant. 'Yes please. If we snuggle together, I think I could bear it. I honestly think it's colder in here than it would be outside.'

The bedroom they chose had a double to make things easier. 'I'm not undressing and I don't want you to either.'

He laughed. 'Can I take my boots off, ma'am?'

She pulled back the top two blankets – she had no intention of getting between the sheets even if she was fully clothed. Somehow sleeping under blankets didn't seem to be breaking any rules.

As before she tucked herself into his arms and he pulled the blankets and eiderdown over their heads. 'Good idea, my nose is frozen solid. I hope we can breathe like this.'

'And I hope we don't have to get out to use the pot.'

She giggled and fell asleep.

Jack woke first and carefully rolled out from between the covers, making sure he didn't let any of the cold air in or disturb Ellie. There was no light filtering through the wooden shutters so it must be early. He stuffed his feet into his shoes. He didn't untie the laces as it was impossible to retie them with one hand.

He shone his torch on the face of his watch and saw it was a little after six o'clock. He'd use the john and then get the range burning and make tea. He was about to leave when the bed creaked behind him.

'Wait, I'm coming too.'

With their torches on full beam, but pointed to the floor, they hurried downstairs. By the time they reached the hall they were running. They burst through the swing door and thundered down the stairs.

There was no sign of life down here so obviously the servants weren't expected to get up before dawn.

'I'll get the range going. It's easier with two hands and it's similar to the one at home.'

'The only good thing about not having blackouts, apart from the place we ate and the sitting room, is that no one gets up before daylight.'

Ellie removed her greatcoat and draped it over the back of one of the chairs. 'How much snow is there? Are we going to be stuck here for days? I don't know how Mum, George and Fiona can bear to live here.'

'Probably okay in the summer.'

He left her riddling and raking and found his way through the labyrinth of small rooms to the back door. He slid the bolts and pulled it open expecting to see a foot at least of snow. There were only a few inches but it was solid underfoot. His breath caught in his throat. It must be well below freezing. Lethal to fly and even worse to attempt to drive.

The kitchen was empty when he returned but from the sound of it the range was heating up. Where the hell was Ellie?

Eight

Ellie was shocked at how antiquated the kitchen here was. Sir Reginald was supposedly a very wealthy man so why hadn't he updated everything? The range was Victorian, the plumbing little better. She'd almost expected to find she had to pump the water up in the scullery – but there was hot and cold running water.

The first task was to put the kettle on and the next to find something to eat. Fortunately, the pantry was as well stocked as the one at Glebe Farm. It didn't seem fair that thousands of people were barely keeping body and soul together and yet this family of four had enough food in here to feed a village for a week.

There was even a flitch of bacon hanging from the ceiling – why hadn't that been taken to the designated butcher for sale to others? She lifted it from its hook and deftly sliced enough for everyone to enjoy their breakfast. There was a tray of eggs and she collected a dozen in a bowl. What was missing was the dough to make fresh bread as this should have been sitting at the back of the range proving. The loaf that was in the tin was stale but would be perfect for fried bread or toast.

With everything piled onto a tray she was ready to go back into the kitchen and start cooking. Jack yelled her name and she almost dropped the lot. She rushed through to the kitchen.

'What's the matter? What's wrong?'

'Nothing, now I know you're all right. There's not much snow but it's icy – too dangerous to drive.'

'Well, we won't go hungry here – just have a look in the pantry. I'm shocked at how much rationed food they've got here.'

The large clock sitting on the top shelf of the French dresser struck the hour. 'It's seven o'clock – I wonder what time the cook and the other two women start work.'

'It's light enough to see now so I should think they'll be here any moment. Are you going to cook all that or leave it to them?'

'I don't like being waited on. I've got enough here to feed all of us, including them. I'd much rather eat in here where it's warm, wouldn't you?'

'Too right. What do you want me to do?'

'Lay up for seven, put out mugs if you can find them. There's sugar on the dresser and milk and butter in the pantry. There's probably jam and marmalade somewhere as well.'

Breakfast was ready and Jack had gone to fetch her mother and brother. The three missing women arrived as Ellie was dishing up.

'Miss Simpson, you shouldn't be down here. It's not your place to be doing this,' Cook said.

'I know, but it's done now. Sit down and I'll serve you. The tea's freshly brewed, milk and sugar on the table too.'

She was delighted that none of them argued and all sat down eagerly. The plates were piping hot so the food shouldn't get cold even if it had to wait for a bit.

The kitchen door swung open and Jack came in first, closely followed by the other two.

'How delightful, Ellen, to eat somewhere warm. I just wish we could eat down here all the time,' Mum said as she pulled out her chair.

Everything was perfectly cooked and an entire loaf of bread was consumed between the seven of them. At first Cook and the other two women had been quiet but by the end of the meal they were chipping in to the conversation.

'Whilst Sir Reginald is away, Mrs Turnbull, we'll eat in here. If you serve us first and put a tablecloth on even if he does come back I think we'll get away with it.'

'I got the fire going in the sitting room upstairs so it should be warm enough to sit in by now,' Jack said.

'That's the telephone ringing. Excuse me, I'll dash up and answer it,' George said.

Mrs Turnbull solemnly handed them a freshly filled hot water bottle each to make the journey from the kitchen to the sitting room less unpleasant.

'We'll come down for luncheon and dinner but will have coffee as usual in the sitting room.'

She and Jack shrugged into their greatcoats and her mother laughed. 'Now that's a sensible idea. In future I'm going to wear my coat too.'

All three of them ran through the freezing house and burst into the sitting room. George was before them. His face was pinched; his hands were shaking. Ellie's stomach turned over. He'd had bad news.

'What is it, George? What's happened?'

'It's Fiona – she's lost the baby. She slipped on the ice yesterday and had a miscarriage an hour ago. That was her mother ringing from the hospital. I've got to get there. Can I borrow your car?'

Jack shook his head. 'No, only Ellie can drive it. Where's your wife?'

'King Edward VII hospital in Windsor.'

'I'll grab our overnight things; you get what you'll need, George. What about you, Mum, are you going to come with us?'

She hesitated for a moment and then nodded. 'Yes, I don't want to stay here on my own.'

Jack was buttoning up his coat. 'I'll get the car started. We must make sure we take blankets, a couple of flasks of tea, and a couple of shovels. We might well need them.'

Half an hour later they set off. George and her mother were in the back with rugs over their knees and hot water bottles in their laps. Jack had a map and was going to navigate for her.

'It's bloody treacherous, honey – remember, whatever happens don't put your foot on the brake.'

'I was driving a tractor when I was ten, Jack, I do know how to drive in icy conditions.'

They skidded twice going down the drive but she corrected it instinctively and no harm was done. The B road they travelled on initially was like a skating rink but she negotiated it safely and when they got onto the A road she was able to follow the tyre tracks made from earlier vehicles.

They arrived at the hospital at lunchtime. 'Don't get out, Ellie, Jack, no need for you to get cold. I appreciate you bringing us and it was good to see you.' George was out of the car and went around to open the door for Mum as soon as they'd crunched to a halt.

'It might be easier for you to ring me, Mum. I don't want to speak to him.'

'I've got a number for both Hamble and White Waltham. Thank you so much for coming. I just wish the visit hadn't ended on such a sad note.'

'We'll go back via St Albans and see if we can find you somewhere to live. I think it might be sensible to rent initially, then you can decide exactly what you want when you know the place better.'

'That makes sense. You're a good girl and I'm proud of you.'

The door slammed and she and Jack were alone. 'Do you want to find something to eat or shall we have the sandwiches and tea that Mrs Turnbull provided?'

'I don't think it would be a good idea to turn the engine off. It might not start again.'

'Okay – I'm not hungry but I could do with a cup of tea before we leave.'

It was at times like this that Jack resented the fact that he'd lost his hand. Ellie might think she was as good as a guy but as far as he was concerned he should be looking after her and not the other way around. Was he kidding himself to think he'd ever make her a decent husband? Would the ghost of Greg always hover between them? How was it that her brother Neil and his best friend Greg had both died and he'd survived his prang?

'Jack, which way when I pull out of the hospital?'

He checked the map and gave her directions. Despite the appalling weather and sub-zero temperature, they were a couple of miles from St Albans by mid-afternoon.

'I think we need to book into a B&B or small hotel before we go house hunting. We're not expected back until tomorrow at the earliest so there's plenty of time.'

'Here? Not in the city itself?'

'I've seen bus stops and it'll be easier without the car.'

She nodded. 'I'm worried we might be stranded when we should be working.'

'Have you heard any kites go overhead all day?'

'Come to think of it, I haven't. Look, there's a vacancy sign on that house and it's got a space for me to park.'

The landlady was surprised to see them, but delighted to have her two rooms occupied for the night. She took them upstairs and indicated where they would be sleeping. 'There's a nice two-bar electric fire in each. It gets ever so cosy in there with that on. Do you have your ration books?'

They handed them over and she beamed. 'I don't do evening meals but I'll make you a nice mug of cocoa when you come in. I'm sure you'll find yourself something for tea.'

'Do you know when the next bus goes into St Albans?'

'In half an hour. The bus stop's not far. The last bus back nowadays is seven o'clock. Make sure you don't miss it.'

'Thank you. We'll be back before that,' Ellie said. 'Jack, which room do you want?'

'They look the same to me. I'll take the one on the right. It's possible there will be an estate agent open if we go now.'

'Shall we eat the sandwiches and finish what's left in the thermos first? No point in wasting good food.'

He agreed and they sat on her bed, being very careful not to get any crumbs on the blue candlewick bedspread. 'I'll put the flask back in the car. I'm going to ask the landlady if she'll fill our hot water bottles before we turn in tonight.'

Outside the air cut like a knife. 'I'd much rather stay in my room than trudge about in this weather.'

'Stop moaning, woman, and hurry up or we'll miss the bus. We've cut it a bit fine.'

Hand in hand they slipped and staggered along the road, expecting at any minute to see the vehicle go past. They skidded to a halt at the bus stop where a jolly, middle-aged lady was waiting.

'In the nick of time, dearie – the bus is just coming. I heard it a moment ago.'

Sure enough the vehicle trundled up to them and they scrambled in. He was surprised to see it was half full. The woman who'd preceded them onto the bus nodded towards the other passengers.

'Don't matter how bad the snow is, dearie, we still need to eat. The butcher will have offal this afternoon and my Bert likes a bit of liver for his tea.'

They were attracting a fair amount of attention on the bus; no doubt the fact that they were wearing smart navy blue was the reason for this. There was ice on the inside of the window and she was grateful for Jack's bulk pressed up against her.

The bus stopped and started to collect other housewives but they remained the only passengers in uniform. They disembarked in the marketplace. Eventually they discovered an auctioneer and valuer that also acted as an estate agent – however, it had already shut up for the day. They found a decent café before heading back to catch the bus.

'It's a nuisance that place was shut as we won't have time to come here again tomorrow morning. Maybe I can arrange something over the phone.' She'd scribbled down the address and telephone number and had it buttoned safely into her top pocket.

'I think it's getting warmer, not colder, which is a bad sign. It could mean there's more snow on the way.'

'I hope Fiona's all right. How will George and Mum get back after the visit?' She swallowed the lump in her throat. 'I don't know if I'd cope if I lost a baby. Seems so much worse than an adult dying.'

'They can have another one. Just hope this doesn't split them up.'

'I can't think about it now.'

'They'll stay the night, obviously, and find someone to give them a lift tomorrow.' They were back in the marketplace and there was a small queue waiting for the bus. Most of them were housewives with bulging shopping bags but there was a sprinkling of younger women, presumably coming home after a day's work.

*

As promised they were provided with a decent breakfast and at first light they were ready to leave. There was fresh snow but not so much it would make driving impossible. Whilst Jack was busy scraping the windows clear she got in and attempted to start the car.

With plenty of choke it spluttered into life, much to her relief. Jack hopped in, slammed the door, and she moved away from the kerb in first gear making sure she didn't skid.

'We might as well go through the middle of St Albans. The roads will be clearer,' he said.

Just as they reached the market square the engine spluttered and died. For a second she didn't realise the reason. 'We've run out of petrol. Frankie warned us not to go too far. What are we going to do? I don't have any petrol coupons, do you?'

'No, we'll just have to abandon it and face the flak when we get back.'

Fortunately, she'd been able to guide the car off the road where at least it was in no danger of being hit by a passing army lorry. 'What if someone steals it or vandalises it? I suppose we'll have to pay for any repairs or the loss of the vehicle itself.'

'Ellie, there's nothing we can do. We need to get back to White Waltham and explain to Frankie how this happened. He's got friends in high places...'

'So have we – maybe Mainwaring can arrange to have it fuelled and returned.'

'I don't see why he'd do that for us as I've been avoiding his messages.'

'Well, make sure you speak to him when he rings and agree to whatever he says if he'll help us out.'

'I don't think it's much more than forty miles to White Waltham from here. Shall we see if we can cadge a lift from someone?' Jack was looking over her head and grabbed her arm. 'Quick, there's an army lorry just pulled up. If we're lucky they can take us some of the way.'

She turned to look. 'They're Home Guard, not regulars.'

They ran across the marketplace barely managing not to fall flat on the icy tarmac. The Home Guard captain had seen them coming and greeted them with a cheery salute.

'ATA pilots? Good show. Need a lift to White Waltham?'

'We do indeed, Captain. Are you going in that direction?'

'It's not too far out of our way. Hop in the back with my men. Won't be comfortable but better than walking.'

The motley crew inside made room for them on the benches that ran down either side of the lorry. 'Got a day off I expect, have you?' The speaker was a man who must have been in his sixties at least.

'We've just got engaged so came here to celebrate yesterday.' She smiled at him and he nodded.

'It's a blooming marvel what you young ladies do. Never thought I'd see the day when a slip of a girl like you would be flying Spitfires and Hurricanes.'

Jack put his arm around her and she slid back so he could keep her on the narrow seat once they were in motion. He nodded at the old man. 'Not just fighters, they fly bombers as well nowadays.'

There was a grinding of gears and the ancient vehicle moved forward. There were about twenty men in the back with them and their age ranged from spotty youth to someone who looked like an octogenarian. It was unlikely the Home Guard would be needed to defend the country now there was no chance of Hitler invading but they still did a useful job keeping up morale, if nothing else.

Conversation was impossible as they needed all their concentration to remain seated while the lorry lurched from one pothole to another. The journey took two hours but it felt like four. She and Jack thanked the soldiers and stumbled gratefully to the ground.

'Good heavens! They brought us right to the gate.'

The captain leaned out of the passenger window, waved and then the lorry trundled off.

'Right, let's go and face the music. It might be better if I go and see Frankie on my own – after all he's my CO, not yours.'

'No, we go together. I was the designated driver don't forget.'

She was relieved that Frankie had been called away to a meeting somewhere and wouldn't be back until the next day. 'I'm sorry, Jack, I can't stay that long. Do you think he might dismiss you? That horrible Prunella woman was sent packing and all she did was push me over.'

'He won't do that. I'll get a right bollocking but he can't afford to lose anyone. There aren't enough of us to go around as it is.'

'I'm not due back until tomorrow. I suppose we shouldn't keep using the telephone as there are posters all over the place saying we should write a letter or send a postcard instead.'

He chuckled. 'A fat lot of good that would do in our case. But you're right, we should restrict our calls to one a week and write a letter as well. Your letters were what kept me going in the desert and I miss getting them now.'

'I won't ring Hamble. I'm starving; shall we go to the Mess and see if we can find something to eat before I go?'

Nine

Ellie reported at Hamble, but so late in the day she wasn't needed. To her delight she saw her errant bicycle leaning against the wall. She grabbed it and pedalled cautiously the two miles to her cottage. Amanda would stay with her chap tonight and they would report for duty together at eight o'clock tomorrow morning. She'd spent the night alone before, but it was the first time since the homeless man had broken in.

The key turned smoothly in the lock and she opened the door slowly, half-expecting to discover a second intruder inside. That was silly – the doors had been locked so it was unlikely another homeless person would attempt to get in. A genuine burglar wouldn't bother as he would see immediately by peering through the window that there was nothing worth stealing inside.

The cottage was marginally warmer than outside but not by much. Her first task, after changing out of her uniform into comfortable slacks and two thick jumpers, would be to get the range lit. There was no point in lighting the fire in the sitting room when only she was there. They were fortunate that the landlady had arranged for the local farmer to deliver a monthly supply of logs as part of the deal. The ancient range burned happily on wood but stayed in longer if they added half a hod of anthracite as well.

She supposed they were lucky to have electricity, running water and indoor plumbing in so ancient a building. It could only be because there was a large farm a hundred yards down the lane and the farmer would have paid to have both connected.

Judging by the number of tractors and farm vehicles that went past the front garden morning and evening piled high with milk churns it was a very productive dairy farm. She and Amanda took it in turns to go down and buy milk and eggs from the farmer's wife. Occasionally they were also able to purchase a freshly baked loaf, a few slices of bacon and a neatly wrapped package of butter.

The radio crackled into life and she caught the last ten minutes of *The Brains Trust*. She enjoyed the questions sent in by listeners and the answers by the panel of experts were always worth listening to. With any luck, *ITMA* with Tommy Handley would be on next. There was nothing she liked better than sitting curled up in front of the fire listening to him making fun of everyone involved in the war.

Unfortunately, it was a production of *Hamlet* and she really didn't want to listen to that – too depressing and too long. She turned the wireless off and decided to write letters to Dad and Mabel and also to Jack. She was halfway through the first when someone knocked on the door.

They rarely got visitors here. She hurried to answer it.

'Saw you come in a while ago, Ellie; this parcel came for you yesterday and I said I'd give it to you when you got back. The postman didn't like to leave it on the doorstep after what happened before.'

'Thank you, Ada, that was kind of you.' Her neighbour handed over the large, official-looking, brown paper parcel and dashed back to the warmth of her own cottage next door.

It wasn't her birthday, was too late for a Christmas present, was only addressed to her so couldn't be an engagement gift – so what on earth was it? She snipped the string and peeled back the layers of paper.

There was a letter on top of the cardboard box. She opened it.

Dear Miss Simpson,

These items belonged to Squadron Leader Dunlop and have been sitting in our office awaiting collection by Mrs Dunlop. As you were the sole beneficiary of Squadron Leader Dunlop's will we thought perhaps you might like them.

Yours faithfully

Her eyes brimmed. She wasn't sure she wanted to open it. She had nothing of Greg's, apart from his letters and a couple of photographs, and had always regretted this. He'd loved her and they would have been married eventually if he hadn't died so tragically last year.

Her hands were trembling as she opened the flaps. The first thing inside the parcel was a picture of her in dungarees and flying jacket – the frame was antique silver. The next items were too much for her control. There was her engagement ring, the one she'd returned to him after he'd been tricked into marrying that evil woman, but also a box with matching gold bands. These had been meant for her and Greg – he'd obviously not used them in his forced marriage. Her cheeks were wet as she searched for her handkerchief.

How could she ever love Jack in the way he loved her when she was still in love with Greg? She enjoyed kissing him but not as much as she had with Greg. No – that wasn't quite true. Jack made her hot all over and she knew it wouldn't take much to make her forget her determination not to pre-empt any marriage vows.

Maybe that was enough to make a successful relationship but it wasn't fair to him. Mind you, breaking up with him would be so unkind. She would never forget how devastated she was when Greg was forced to marry someone else. She had been prepared to forget his infidelity as long as he'd marry her. Jack loved her enough to marry her regardless of the fact that she didn't reciprocate his deep feelings.

The box was still beside her on the sofa and she wasn't sure she wanted to look at anything else. She replaced the ring boxes and folded the cardboard flaps to seal it. She'd put it upstairs in her wardrobe when she went to bed and forget about it.

The letter to Jack was put aside and she wrote to George and her mother instead. There were five stamps in her stationery folder and she'd only written four letters. The other two were to Dad and the auctioneer in St Albans.

She picked up the letter to Jack and read what she'd already put.

Dear Jack,

I hope you didn't get into too much trouble with Frankie over the car. If we have to pay for it to be recovered, I'll bear the cost because I was the driver. If we hadn't had to go to Windsor we wouldn't have run out of petrol.

I'm sad for George and Fiona and I hope they can support each other and don't grow apart because their baby died. I've written to the estate agents setting out what I want to lease or purchase and hope they'll get back to me soon with what they have available.

Have you heard from Mainwaring? I don't suppose we'll be able to go to London together as Alison has asked me to work my leave days. One of the girls is getting married. I will get an extra day at the end of my next thirteen days, but I have to work until the middle of next month without a break.

I'm not complaining about that but I am sad we won't see each other for ages.

What else could she say? She could hardly tell him about Greg's things. The thought of what might have been with Greg was coming between them. They'd promised to write to each other once a week but she'd seen him yesterday so there was no urgency to finish this. When she got back from her next deliveries she might have something with which to fill the remainder of the letter.

As expected, Amanda didn't return and the following morning Ellie arrived promptly to check in at eight o'clock.

Cycling in the icy conditions when it was barely light hadn't been pleasant but she managed to arrive without going over the handlebars.

Her friend was already there. 'Sorry I didn't get back to the cottage. Was it beastly being there on your own?'

'No, I was fine. Did you have a good break?'

For some reason she didn't tell her about the box – its arrival was still too upsetting. The chits came out. Today was flying new Spits from the factory to Kenley and Debden. The return trips would be to bring damaged fighters to be repaired.

Alison popped her head through the hatch and beckoned her in. 'Everyone here can fly fighters but I've not got enough of you flying twin-engined operational aircraft. I'm sending you back to do the next conversion so you can fly Blenheims, Wellingtons, Dakotas, Hampdens and anything else. You can also take a turn flying the taxi Anson.'

'I thought I needed several weeks flying the light twin-engined kites before doing that.'

'I want you able to fly everything in that class including the trickier ones. By the summer I want you flying the heavy stuff and converted to Class V.'

'I won't let you down. When am I going back to White Waltham?'

'As soon as I can arrange it – probably by the end of the week. As long as the weather holds, you should be able to complete the course and be back the same evening.'

Amanda had been listening to this conversation. 'Lucky you – but to tell you the truth I would rather fly fighters than anything else.'

*

Ellie had posted the four letters but hadn't finished the one to Jack. That night she got it out and her pen flew over the paper as she told him her good news and that they would be able to meet up, if he was around, in a few days.

On the morning that she was to return to White Waltham she and Amanda bumped into their neighbour, Ada, hurrying for the bus that went past the end of the lane.

'Morning, girls, I see you've both got your bicycles back.'

'We have, but we'll walk with you to the bus stop,' Ellie said.

'Must have been a nice surprise getting that parcel. Was it a late Christmas present from someone?'

Amanda looked at her curiously. 'What parcel? You didn't tell me about it.'

They reached the end of the lane; Ellie wasn't obliged to answer immediately as the bus was coming and Ada had to run to catch it.

Ellie was hoping to deflect the conversation, not have to answer, but her friend persisted.

'What was in it? From your expression it wasn't anything good.'

'It was from Greg's solicitors and had some of his personal possessions in it. I only managed to look at couple of things and then shoved it in the back of my wardrobe.'

'Golly, that was a bit of a shock. Did they say why it has taken over a year to get to you?'

Cycling down the rutted lane demanded total concentration and she managed to avoid any further conversation on this difficult subject. The other pool members wished her good luck and she scrambled into the Anson with her chute and overnight bag, glad she hadn't had to talk about Greg anymore.

Ellie had been lucky as an Anson had landed not long after they'd arrived to drop off a couple of flyers. Jack wouldn't see her again unless they got their leave days at the same time. This had happened twice but he doubted it would happen a third time.

Frankie kept him busy. Ellie rang him a couple of times and left messages and he'd attempted to return the calls but they always seemed to miss each other. She could hardly leave personal information so the messages he was given were just to say that she'd rung.

The weather was unpredictable and rarely above freezing. Halfway through February he was caught in another heavy fall of snow after delivering a Spit to Hornchurch. This was the ideal opportunity to go to London as the trains would probably still be running.

He dumped his chute and overnight bag in an empty locker, told admin where he was going, and crunched through the snow to the exit of the base. A lorry pulled up beside him.

'Want a lift, mate? I can drop you at the station.'

'Great, that's where I want to go.' Jack climbed in and settled beside the driver. The vehicle was heavy enough to negotiate the soft snow without skidding and arrived at Romford station just as a train was steaming in.

'Thanks, perfect timing.'

He would have stopped and purchased a ticket but the guard waved him through. As expected, the train was crowded. The lack of heating hardly mattered when the passengers were packed in like sardines. It was only a few stops to Liverpool Street where everyone got off.

The platform was lethal and he almost fell on his arse several times. One of the passengers wasn't so fortunate and he helped the guy to his feet. 'Any damage?'

'No, bloody lucky not to break my neck. Rotten weather, but at least it keeps those bastard Jerries away.'

They slithered their way to the exit. 'You in a rush, mate? There's one of them British Restaurants over there what does a good cuppa and you can always get something to eat.'

'No rush. I've got a fair bit of walking to do today and I'll need something to keep me going.'

The food in one of these government-run cafés was basic, cheap and the portions were small. His temporary companion pushed open the door and unsurprisingly the place was busy.

'Better grab that last table, mate, whilst I go to the counter. What you want?'

'Tea and whatever's available. I'll settle up when you get back.'

Self-service was a novelty but kept the costs down. He was almost resigned to the fact that the lack of a left hand meant he had to accept assistance from strangers. The guy hadn't commented on his empty sleeve but had offered to fetch the food because of it.

All that could be said for what he ate was that it was filling and hot. He offered to pay for both of them but the man took his head.

'No, mate, you've done your bit. I've got a dicky ticker so couldn't fight in case you was wondering.'

'I'm just grateful it was only a hand and that I can still deliver kites for the ATA.'

'Good for you. I better be getting on, I've got two calls to make before I can go home to me missus.' With a cheery wave he left Jack to finish his third mug of tea. It would be dark in a couple of hours so he'd better get a shifty on if he was going to get to Joe's house.

He really should have made more of an effort to find out where his aunt was living. It had been her choice not to give a forwarding address on her last letter so she obviously didn't want to continue the connection. If it had been a shock to him to discover Uncle Joe was a villain, what must it have done to her?

The last place he wanted to go was the house in which he'd lived for a few weeks on his return from America all those years ago. Years ago? Holy cow – it wasn't even four years but seemed like a lifetime. So much had happened – not surprising really that 1939 seemed so long ago.

It occurred to him that it might well have been sold by now; but wouldn't he have been told if this was the case? It was also possible it had been flattened as many of the others in the area had been.

The snow just emphasised the appalling destruction in this part of London. Entire streets had gone, just piles of rubble and the occasional back wall remaining of what used to be people's homes. Where the hell did those who'd been bombed out go to live?

He picked his way carefully down Norton Folgate, avoiding potholes and patches of black ice. Joe's house was in Charlotte Street so he'd have to turn left down Great

Eastern Street and, if he remembered correctly, it was about three down on the right.

The house was a three bedroomed, end of terrace. This particular street had so far been untouched by the bombing. He stopped outside and could see at once the house was occupied. His aunt must have sold the property when Joe died.

He stood for a moment and was about to turn away when something odd struck him. The curtains were the same – surely new owners would have changed them? Something made him knock on the door.

'Jack, what a lovely surprise. Come in.' His aunt stepped aside to allow him to enter. It hadn't occurred to him she would come back here but he supposed it made perfect sense. She had friends and relations in this part of London and now that Joe was gone she was free to do as she pleased.

He'd lived here briefly when he returned from the States in '39 and the place was familiar to him so he knew where to hang his greatcoat and to take off his boots before going into the front room.

She pointed at his sleeve. 'Where did you lose that?'

'Africa – last year. I joined the ATA and can still fly fighters okay.'

'Joe would have been proud of you. I felt bad that I didn't give you a forwarding address, but was that cut up about him dying in prison I wasn't thinking straight. How did you know I was back?'

Should he tell the truth or make up some cock and bull story? He decided on the former. She listened attentively and didn't seem unduly upset that the war office was taking an interest in Joe's illegal affairs.

'They tore this place apart, you know. I had to have it redecorated before it was fit to live in. I'm lucky squatters didn't move in. So many families are homeless I wouldn't blame them if they had.'

'You would have been safer to stay up north with your sister. It's not safe here.'

'I go down the road when the siren goes.'

'You have your own Anderson shelter so why do you go to the one at the end of the street?'

'I prefer the communal one. It's ever so friendly. We keep it neat as a pin and the lavvy is emptied every day by old Bert next door.' She nodded. 'If I'm going to meet my maker, I don't want to do it alone.'

'Fair enough. Now, there's obviously nothing here that would be of any interest to Mainwaring – which reminds me – he obviously doesn't know you're back here. I won't tell him either.'

'I was thinking, Jack love, he had a lock-up somewhere. I have the keys in the dresser. He gave them to me before he was arrested and told me to keep them in my handbag and make sure the bobbies didn't get hold of them.'

Ten

Jack felt a surge of excitement when his aunt told him about the lock-up. 'I'll go down there before it gets dark and have a look, if you don't mind. Where is it, do you know?'

'I'm not exactly sure, but I think it's somewhere round the back of New Inn Yard. It's not far, no more than twenty minutes from here.'

'I'll have the tea when I get back. Hopefully, I'll not be long.'

There hadn't been any raids for a week so they were due a visit from the Jerries and he didn't want to be wandering about in the dark when that happened.

With the keys in his pocket he set off at a brisk pace, keeping his head down so he wasn't obliged to acknowledge anyone. People around here were naturally curious and he reckoned they wouldn't have seen a member of the ATA before.

He glanced at the sky, another hour of daylight with any luck. If there'd been heavy cloud cover it would already be dark. If he'd still been in the RAF they would have been braced for a busy night. Tonight there would be a bomber's moon – not good for civilians on either side of this bloody war. Now the Yanks had finally come to help things should improve.

There was a group of scruffy kids shadowing him. He might as well make use of them and ask where the lock-ups were. Before he turned to confront them, he rummaged through his pockets and found a handful of change. There were three sixpences, a couple of half-crowns and a few pennies. Should be enough to get rid of these urchins.

These children roamed the streets mostly unchecked as parents were doing vital war work and many of the schools were closed through bomb damage.

'Right – a tanner to the boy who can tell me where to find a row of lock-ups.' Strangely it was the smallest who stepped forward with his filthy hand held out. 'Information first, reward second.'

'We'll take you, mister, but it'll cost you a bob not a tanner.'

Jack waited but didn't hand over any money. The boy wiped his nose in his sleeve. 'It ain't far. There's two lots. We'll take you to the first.'

Again, Jack held on to his cash knowing that as soon as he'd paid they might disappear. He followed them down a narrow alley, along the back of a row of privies and across a bombsite.

'There, mister. Where's me money?'

'Here you are. If these aren't the right ones I need you to take me to the second lot.'

'Righto. That'll cost you half a crown.'

'Not likely. You'll be happy with another shilling or you can scarper.'

He didn't wait for the response knowing they would agree to his terms. He wasn't going to be ripped off by a gang of boys. If they didn't hang around he'd find the sheds himself.

The one he wanted would have two padlocks so he didn't bother to investigate the three that only had one. He tried one of the keys and was disappointed when neither of them worked. There was the sound of shuffling behind him and he turned.

'Where's your hand, mister?'

'Somewhere in Africa.' This time he tossed coins to different boys. They appreciated his gesture and beamed.

'Come with us, mister, it's just over the back.'

The "just over the back" entailed climbing over a wall and stumbling across another demolished house. He put his one hand on the top and vaulted over. The diminutive leader of the gang had vanished and he was accompanied by the remaining four.

'No one's bin here for a year or more, mister, reckon this is the one you want.'

The child was right. Three of the four had broken doors; anything of value had been taken. But the final one was intact and brambles had grown over the front. Why had this one been left intact?

The boy who'd spoken sidled up. 'That one belongs to someone what you don't want to cross. That's why we ain't broken in.'

Jack knew at once these children were referring to his uncle – someone he thought of as a benevolent, kindly guy – but he was obviously wrong. Joe had been a dangerous criminal if after so long his lock-up was still sealed.

He gave the rest of his money equally to the boys. 'Bugger off, you lot. You got what you came for now mind your bloody business.' He'd snarled the words and they didn't hang about to argue the toss.

He'd better get a move on as one of the boys was bound to bring back a couple of adults and he'd not bribe them to go away so easily.

As expected, the padlocks opened. He wasted valuable time ripping away the brambles before he could pull open the door. He closed it behind him but had the sense to bring in the padlocks so no enterprising boy could lock him in.

He shone his torch around the assorted boxes. He looked in a couple of them but there were just knick-knacks, nothing of interest. It would take him hours to search this place but he knew if he left without finding whatever Mainwaring wanted it would be gone by the end of the day.

The kids wouldn't hesitate to smash the locks as they had on the other sheds now he'd been in, proving Joe was no longer a threat. The incriminating paper with the names of those who'd joined The Right Club had been kept in a pile of newspapers at the airfield at Glebe Farm. Why would his uncle leave something even more valuable here?

He shone the beam around and his pulse quickened when he saw several piles of neatly stacked newspapers on the shelf at the back. He wasn't sure what he was looking for but thought whatever it was could be there.

The first two piles revealed nothing but the third held a similar brown envelope to the one that had been hidden at the airfield. He slipped it into the inside pocket of his uniform jacket, certain anyone who might have been peering through the cracks in the door wouldn't have seen him do so. He continued to search and when he'd finished, he moved on to one of the boxes that had been tucked away at the back.

His jaw dropped. It was full of expensive jewellery – presumably stolen – and must be worth a king's ransom. He carefully closed the lid, not an easy task one-handed, and tucked it under his arm. Anyone spying on him would think he'd come to recover these valuable items and if he was stopped and robbed, he would hand them over knowing whoever took them wouldn't think to look any further.

Outside the air was crisp and cold. The sun had set and he could barely see enough to refasten the padlocks. Whilst he'd done this, he'd put the box between him and the door and leaned on it to hold it in place.

He replaced the cover on his torch so that would now give him only a pinprick of light – all that was allowed in the blackout – and considered how he was to return to the busier thoroughfares where he would be safe from attack. Climbing over a wall holding a cardboard box would be impossible.

There was a slight scuffle behind him and he braced himself but instead a small hand tugged at his sleeve. 'Quick, mister, come with me. It ain't safe for you. Billy's fetched his dad and a couple of other blokes. They'll do you in if they get hold of you and take what you've got.'

The speaker was the fat boy he'd given a handful of coppers to. 'Keep hold of my empty sleeve and I'll follow you.'

His heart was hammering. He wished he had his service pistol as he feared he might need it. Cold sweat trickled between his shoulder blades. Flying a fighter was a piece of cake compared to this.

The lad took him a different route, in and out of alleyways, up stinking paths, until he heard the sound of traffic ahead of them.

He still had the two half a crowns. He'd give one to this child who might well have saved his life – let alone the valuable items he was carrying.

They emerged onto a road he didn't recognise in the darkness. 'Where are we?'

'City Road, mister. They ain't going to find you here. Where do you want to go?'

'Liverpool Street.'

'Go through Finsbury Square, keep walking and turn left down South Eldon Street. It ain't more than half a mile from there.'

His aunt would wonder where he'd gone but that couldn't be helped, he wasn't going to risk bringing danger to her door. He slipped the boy the coin.

'Ta, mister.'

He had to be back on duty tomorrow so couldn't take the wretched box and envelope directly to Mainwaring, which was what he'd prefer to do. He just hoped no one in authority wanted to look inside the carton as he'd find it difficult to explain why he was carrying thousands of pounds' worth of stolen goods.

He was fortunate to catch a train almost immediately and got out at Romford. He hitched a lift to Hornchurch, collected his belongings from the locker, just as an Anson landed to collect a couple of girls who'd been delivering fighters. He settled into the single seat at the rear of the plane and pretended to be asleep. God knows what he was going to do with these items as he couldn't ride a bike and carry the box. They'd have to go into his locker along with his other personal items.

On her arrival at White Waltham, Ellie discovered there were two men also moving up to Class IV and she wasn't sure if she was offended or pleased they didn't suggest she go first. She couldn't have it both ways – in a man's world she had to take her turn like everyone else.

As it happened the instructor called her name out before them. 'Good luck, but I'm sure you don't need it,' one of them said with a friendly smile.

'Thank you. It took more than a couple of hours last time…'

The instructor overheard her comment. 'Half that time, Miss Simpson, just rubberstamping today. Thought I'd get you done first as the other two don't have so far to go.'

This time there was a bit of technical talk before they took off, but only two circuits and bumps. 'Well done, I'll see you in the summer when you're sent to convert to Class V.' He signed the necessary papers and Ellie scrambled down the ladder, elated that she'd passed so easily.

Then she discovered there wouldn't be a taxi until the evening. 'Is Jack Reynolds likely to be back before I leave?'

The girl checked her list. 'He might be, if you're lucky. He's taken a Walrus to Kent, then collecting a damaged Hurry and will be catching the taxi Anson back.'

Just in case she missed him she decided to write him a note – doing so would keep her busy whilst she waited. She made herself comfortable in the Mess and was surprised when half an hour later the same admin girl told her there was someone to see her.

'Who is it? Did he ask for me by name?' She automatically assumed it was a man.

'No, Frankie's put him in his office and I'll take you there. He must be someone important.'

Her stomach flip-flopped. The only important person she could think of who might ask for her by name was Jack's Mr Mainwaring. She'd not heard from Jack for a week so didn't have any up-to-date information to give him.

Her mouth was dry and her hands clammy. Was this about George? Had this man come to question her? Apart from a brief note from her mother saying that Fiona was staying with her parents and her brother had had his leave extended by a few days there'd been no other communication.

Jack had described Mainwaring and she recognised him at once. 'How can I help you, Mr Mainwaring?'

He looked startled that she knew his name but his smile was friendly. 'Miss Simpson, please come in and close the door. The fact that you know who I am means that Squadron Leader Reynolds has taken you into his confidence.'

She nodded, perched herself on the nearest chair, but didn't reply.

'Excellent, excellent. He's asked me to collect some items but neglected to give me his locker number. I'm hoping that you know what it is.'

Should she reveal she had no idea what items he was referring to or go along with it? 'I do, as it happens, know the combination but I'm not prepared to give it to you. Jack hasn't mentioned to me anything about you collecting things from his locker. He'll be back later today so you won't have more than a few hours to wait.'

His mouth thinned and his benevolent smile vanished. 'Miss Simpson, this is a matter of national importance…'

'In which case, Mr Mainwaring, I suggest you break into his locker and explain to him and everyone else why you've done so. I'm not prepared to tell you as I've only your word that Jack wants you to collect whatever's in his locker.'

His knuckles were white as he clenched the edge of the table. Had she made a grave error of judgement?

'I applaud your loyalty, Miss Simpson, but it should be to your country and not your fiancé.' He stood in front of her and although he was a slight man she flinched and pressed herself against the back of the chair.

His eyes flashed. He'd seen her involuntary reaction and was pleased he'd frightened her. She studied her breathing and forced herself to relax. Nothing untoward was going to happen to her in Frankie's office.

She surged to her feet and stepped forward, making him move backwards to avoid being knocked over. 'You don't intimidate me, Mr Mainwaring. I know nothing about the contents of Squadron Leader Reynolds' locker. Please move out of my way. I have nothing further to discuss with you.'

The matter hung in the balance. They remained a few inches apart. If he didn't move, she would have to back down. She could hardly push him out of the way.

'Very well, Miss Simpson, you may go.'

He stepped aside and she walked past him, managing to appear calm until she closed the door behind her. She leaned against it and her knees almost gave way. What had possessed her to confront him like that? Antagonising a member of MI6, if that's what he was, wasn't a good move on her part.

Jack had obviously found something of great importance if the man had come in person to collect it. What she couldn't understand was why he'd left it in his locker, which was hardly a secure place.

She ran to the ops room and found the helpful girl who'd fetched her a few minutes ago. 'I urgently need to contact Jack. Could you please try and get a message to him?'

'I know where he should be about now and I'll ring there. If you hang about outside, I'll call you if I manage to find him.'

Twenty minutes later he was on the other end of the line. 'Ellie, what's wrong?'

She quickly explained. 'Do you want me to give him the locker number?'

'Yes, I'll tell you what it's all about when I get back.'

She replaced the receiver and thanked the girl. Now all she had to do was find Mainwaring and tell him what he wanted to know. She was about to do so but decided to fetch the things herself. She was curious to know what Jack could possibly have that was of national importance. It had to be something to do with Joe and his connections to the criminal fraternity in London.

Fortunately, the locker room was deserted at this time of day. Inside was a cardboard box – it didn't look very exciting. She would have a quick look before she took it. No one could see what she was doing but her fingers were trembling when she undid the flaps.

She almost dropped the box. Inside were thousands of pounds' worth of diamonds and other precious stones. There was a brown envelope hidden amongst the gems but she didn't want to read that. It was exactly the same as the one she'd found in the pile of newspapers at the aero club a couple of years ago. That had contained a list of names torn from the membership book of The Right Club and Joe had used it for blackmail.

She had no intention of reading this. Whatever was in there, it was none of her business She quickly sealed the flaps. On reaching Frankie's office she barged in without knocking.

Mainwaring was staring morosely out of the window and jumped as if stuck by a hatpin. 'Here you are, Jack said to give it to you. I didn't read what's in the envelope, just in case you were wondering.' She pushed the box into his arms and was back in the corridor before he could reply.

Normally she could wait hours without becoming restless. Today she wandered from the Mess to the restroom and back again several times. She clambered back into her flight suit and went outside.

Eventually the Anson arrived and she saw Jack jump out and race for the admin building. They only had the time it would take to refuel the aircraft before she'd have to leave.

She met him at the doors and threw herself into his arms without hesitation. 'I'm so glad you're here. I gave the box to Mainwaring but I don't know if he's still here.'

They were blocking the entrance and he guided her to a quiet corner before answering. 'Ellie, I can't tell you how glad I am to get rid of that stuff. Did you read what was in the envelope?'

'No, did you?'

'No, let the spooks sort it out. Not sure what they'll do with the jewellery – no doubt it's on a stolen list somewhere and they can return it to the owners.'

'Is that it? Will they leave you alone now?'

'I bloody well hope so. I should have asked – are you now converted?'

'I am, and will also be promoted to second-class officer and get an extra stripe. I've got to go – I don't want to miss my taxi.'

For the first time in their new relationship she initiated a kiss. She stood on tiptoes and pulled his head down so his mouth met hers. By the time they'd finished she was glowing all over. She was breathless and there was hectic colour across his cheekbones.

'Before you leave, tell me, have you heard from the estate agent?'

'Not yet, but hopefully there'll be something waiting for me when I get home tonight. Take care, Jack, I'm beginning to think that I couldn't live without you.'

She slung her chute over her shoulder, grabbed her overnight bag and dashed for the Anson. Had things turned a corner with him? Could she finally put her feelings for Greg aside and move on with her life? Then an image of the cardboard box filled her head and her eyes filled. Things hadn't really changed at all.

Eleven

Jack was relieved he didn't have to face a grilling from the spook but wished Ellie had been able to stay. As she was now qualified to fly twin-engined bombers this meant it was unlikely they would be going to the same places anymore.

He stowed his flying gear and went in search of his bicycle. Someone from admin yelled his name and wearily he turned back, expecting to be given a priority chit and be on his way again.

'Jack, glad I caught you. Your young lady left you a letter. I meant to put it in your pigeonhole but forgot.'

'That's odd, I've just seen her.'

'She didn't know if you'd be back before her taxi came.'

'Thanks, mate, you've made my day.' He stuffed the envelope into his greatcoat pocket and retreated hastily before Frankie could find him something else to fly.

Pedalling in the dark was fraught with unseen hazards but the worst that could happen was he'd go headfirst into a ditch. Fortunately, his ride was uneventful and he shoved his bike out of the way in the pub yard and ducked into the kitchen. He was greeted by his landlady who took one look at his weary features and shooed him out of the door.

'You get on upstairs and I'll bring you up a bite of supper, love. There's still some soup left that the kiddies didn't eat and I'll make you a nice spam sandwich to go with it.'

'That would be great. I'm knackered. Don't suppose there's any hot water for a quick bath?'

'Sorry, it won't be hot enough. You get in there first tomorrow morning, why don't you?'

The racket from the bar meant the guys were back as well but he didn't have the energy to join them in a game of darts or a pint of mild.

He dumped his garments on a chair and pulled on his dressing gown. Whilst the place was quiet, he'd go into the bathroom and have a strip wash. It didn't matter if the water wasn't hot for that.

He was just buttoning up his pyjama jacket when supper arrived on a tray. Vera was used to seeing him like this. 'Here you are, Jack love, piping hot. You look done in – you need to get some sleep.'

'I will after I've eaten this. Thanks, I really appreciate everything you do for me.'

'Get away with you, love, it's my duty to take care of you boys.'

She bustled off and he sat at the small table and devoured his food. After a final slurp of tea, he picked up the letter.

If he'd been expecting a love letter, he would have been disappointed – it was the usual chatty, friendly note that she always wrote. He put it with the others she had sent him over the years and climbed into bed with his latest Agatha Christie murder mystery.

With the Yanks over here at last things should get easier and maybe this bloody war would be over in a few months. Until then he would do his bit and hope that he and Ellie came out of it unscathed.

The weeks passed, the weather improved and he was so busy he scarcely had time to worry about the lack of contact from Ellie. He heard no more from Mainwaring and decided the matter was now closed. Her weekly letters had stopped. He hoped this was because, like him, she was too busy to correspond. He was determined to see her as soon as he got sufficient consecutive days' leave to visit Southampton.

Had she managed to relocate her mother? Were her brother and his wife still together? Neither of these subjects had been mentioned in the last letter – but that had been a month ago. He rang Fred and was told Ellie hadn't been in touch with him either.

'To tell you the truth, son, my Mabel and I are worried. Last time we got a letter she said she was flying bombers as well as fighters and was too busy to visit.'

'I'm going to see her next leave, but don't know when that will be.'

'Give her our love if you do, Jack.'

He put down the receiver and stepped aside to allow the next guy to use the one pay phone available to them at White Waltham. Ellie's passionate kiss was a distant memory and he was certain she was having second thoughts about him. Only one way to find out and that was to speak to her in person.

Frankie called him over. 'You've not taken your free days for several weeks, old thing, so I'm giving you four days starting tomorrow. You need a break. No argument.'

'Thanks, I'll use it to see my fiancée. Hopefully she won't be away from base overnight. I'll give Hamble a ring before I go just to be sure.'

'Good show, give her my regards. Splendid filly. Heard she's flying bombers now.'

'Outranks me. Don't envy her though – I'm happy to just fly fighters.'

'I can't believe it's April already, Ellie, and you still haven't told Jack that you've changed your mind about this engagement,' Amanda said as they waited to collect their chits.

'I've been so busy these past few weeks I've not really had time to think about it. I feel bad that I haven't answered his last two letters but I need more time to come to a decision. I do love him – sort of – but not the way I felt about Greg.'

'At least you've managed to get your mother settled in St Albans. You ought to take your leave and go and see her.'

Ellie picked up her day's duties and saw that she was to fly the taxi Anson. This was her least favourite job as it just involved delivering and collecting flyers all day. Necessary but boring.

Alison beckoned her into the office as she walked past. 'You've not taken your time off for two months. I've pencilled you in for four days starting tomorrow. Your last drop is at Hornchurch and someone else will bring the Anson back. Why don't you spend Easter with your family?'

'Actually, I was planning to visit my mother who has recently moved to St Albans. However, I'll take the opportunity to spend some time at Glebe Farm as I'm going to be so close.'

'It's Wednesday today, I don't want to see you again until Monday. The Met office forecasts unsettled weather and heavy rain so I doubt we'll be very busy over the next few days anyway.'

'More of the same, then? It's been miserable since January. Flying's no fun in bad weather.'

'An instructor once said this to me: Flying is safe so long as you remember that it is dangerous.'

Ellis nodded. 'I'm cautious and try not to take risks like some of the men do.' She smiled and turned to her friend. 'I hadn't realised this weekend was Easter. It's late this year.'

Amanda laughed. 'You might not be a churchgoer but I hardly think you would have missed Good Friday and Easter Sunday.'

They were the only two inside – everyone else was already in the locker room getting on their kit.

'I hadn't planned on being away for so long – it's a good thing I've got spare clothes and things at home as I'm going to need them.'

It was bad form for the pilot of the taxi to arrive last and she apologised to the girls waiting patiently to be ferried to collect their first delivery of the day. Her friend was taking a new Spitfire to Debden and returning with a damaged one, so wasn't one of her passengers.

The only good thing about flying the taxi was that she didn't have to fill in countless forms or hang about for hours. The rule was that if those she was designated to collect weren't waiting, she had only to give them a quarter of an hour's grace before departing. They then had to wait for the next taxi or make their own way to wherever they had to be next.

It continued to drizzle all day but the visibility was good enough to keep airborne. The clouds cleared late afternoon to everyone's delight. She landed at Hornchurch with still a couple of hours of daylight left in the day and she jumped to the ground. She headed for the locker room to stow her flight gear. To her astonishment she found Jack waiting to greet her.

'Hi, honey, I couldn't believe my luck when I discovered you were going to see your folks too. I'm coming to Glebe Farm and I've got transport for us.' He made no move to embrace her but his smile was as friendly as ever.

'It's good to see you. I'm sorry I've not written recently but now I'm able to fly the twin-engined bombers as well as the Anson I've been working flat out. The next four days will be the first ones I've had free since February.'

'Same here – we're shockingly bad correspondents. Shove your gear into a locker. Keep your flight jacket, helmet, goggles and boots on – you're going to need them.'

She did as he suggested, hoping she wasn't going to have to ride a bicycle all the way to the farm. He placed his arm around her waist for a moment and turned her towards the perimeter. 'Your carriage awaits, my lady.'

He was treating her as he had before they'd become engaged – before he'd lost his arm and she'd lost Greg. The knot in her stomach uncurled. He was still the man she'd known and loved for the past two years; if they weren't going to get married, they could still be good friends.

'Good heavens! A motorbike and sidecar – thank goodness it's not raining anymore. I understand why you wanted me to keep this on.' She tossed her overnight bag into the sidecar to join his. 'I'd much prefer to sit behind you, that contraption doesn't look at all safe.'

'Fine by me. I've got a full tank of petrol so no danger of being stranded like we were last time.'

He kicked the bike into life, straddled it and she hopped on behind him. Even if she'd wanted to, the noise from the engine and the air whipping past her face made conversation impossible.

They had travelled a few miles before she remembered that he had only one hand. How on earth was he managing to control a motorbike safely? Her grip tightened – as if that would make any difference if they crashed.

He felt her tension and slowed until it was possible to talk. 'You change gears with your foot and the sidecar makes a motorbike the safest thing on the road.' He turned his head and laughed at her. 'Left hand's for signals, right hand's for breaking.'

'That's a relief,' she yelled and he turned the throttle and the bike thrummed back to its previous speed.

They arrived safely fifteen minutes later to be greeted by the two dogs. Even the cats came to curl around their feet as if they too were pleased to see them.

The front door flew open and Mabel ran out, her wraparound pinny and hands covered in flour. 'What a treat to have both of you here. Fred's ever so excited. He'll be back any minute.'

Ellie rushed over and hugged her stepmother and then Jack followed suit. The front door was rarely used and it seemed strange to be going in that way.

'I'll take my things up to my room and get changed, Mabel. Do you need me to make the beds up?'

'Bless you, lovey, that's all done. Jack, you know which room's yours. I'll have a lovely pot of tea on the table and a nice bit of cake to go with it when you come down.'

Jack let Ellie go ahead. He wanted to speak to Mabel and Fred on his own. He followed her into the kitchen and pulled out a chair.

'Things are not going well between you then, love?'

'Is it that obvious? We were getting on so well and then everything changed. Has she said anything to either of you about breaking off the engagement?'

He addressed this last remark to Fred, who'd just walked in. 'Not heard a dicky bird from her, son, not for several weeks.'

'Pity, I hoped you might know something. I don't want to push her for an explanation and force her to break it off officially. Things changed after we met her mother and George so I think maybe it's something to do with that.'

'Don't worry about it, Jack love, it'll all come out in the wash. You get yourself settled in and stop fretting. Our Ellie will realise how much she loves you one day – you just have to wait.'

When he returned to the kitchen she was already there, out of uniform, and looking just like the girl he'd fallen in love with. 'I haven't got anything else to put on or I would have joined you in mufti.'

'You're the same height as Neil was, son. Wardrobe in your room is full of his clothes. Didn't like to get rid of them,' Fred said.

'Thank you, I'll go and change now.' He wasn't sure how he felt about wearing a dead man's things, but better they were in use than hanging about in a wardrobe gathering dust and moth holes.

Ellie was worried about telling her dad and Mabel about Mum and her brother. She didn't want to hurt dad's feelings.

'Jack and I went to see Mum. I wanted to see how they all were. I never got on with either of them but things have changed. Any of us could be killed by a bomb or something.'

'There's no need to explain, Ellie love,' Dad said. 'Blood's thicker than water. How were they?'

'Not enjoying living with Sir Reginald. The house is huge and freezing. Mum was quite different and was pleased to see me. Although we're not close, we're now on good terms.'

'That's how it should be, Ellie. Me and Fred are glad you made the effort.'

Their reaction was so much better than she'd expected. Jack returned and she smiled at him and waited until he was seated at the table.

'I've got more to tell you, but I wanted to wait until you were here, Jack, so I didn't have to say it all twice.'

'I am all agog. Fire away.'

'Well, my first bit of news is that I've leased a house by the cathedral in St Albans for Mum, George and Fiona. They moved in last month. The place is furnished, which made things easier.'

'Don't suppose Sir Reginald was best pleased,' Fred said.

'He wasn't, but there's nothing he can do about it as none of them are financially dependent on him anymore.' She paused and looked at Jack. She knew he'd guessed what the next topic of conversation was going to be.

'Dad, Mabel – George was under suspicion for being a traitor. Don't look so horrified. He isn't a spy. Jack and I went there specially to tell him and he was appalled but thought he knew exactly who it was.'

'Was it that the bloke he mentioned to us? The last one who was getting leave of absence?'

'It was and the man was arrested and George is in the clear.'

'What about his poor wife?' Mabel asked. 'Has she got over the loss of her baby? We were so sad to hear that news when you wrote to us.'

'As far as I know she's fine. Mum said that they seem much happier now they're away from Sir Reginald's influence. I'm going to see them whilst I have the chance as I doubt that I'll get four days in a row again for a long time.'

'I hope you don't intend to drive all the way to St Albans on that old motorbike, my girl.'

'I certainly don't, Dad. The bike will be returned to whoever Jack borrowed it from and then we'll go to London and get the train from St Pancras.'

'There won't be any running on Good Friday, lovey, so you'd better go tomorrow. Shame you can't stay any longer, but it's been a pleasure to see you both.'

'I doubt there'll be any on Easter Sunday either and we both have to be back at work on the Monday. That means we only get one night in St Albans as well,' Jack said.

'I'm hoping I can get a lift from Hornchurch back to Hamble on the Sunday. I'm sure you'll get one to White Waltham too.'

Jack made no attempt to kiss her when they headed upstairs later that evening. He didn't want to rock the boat as things had gone better than he could ever have hoped. She'd not made any mention of breaking the engagement and he had been overjoyed when she'd included him automatically in her visit to see her mom.

'Good night, honey. What time are you getting up? We don't have to leave until lunchtime tomorrow.'

'I don't want to miss a minute with Dad and Mabel so will get up when they do, but you can have a lie-in if you want.'

'Not a chance. I'd like to check the airfield – have a look at the Tiger Moth and see if it still functions. I want you to be able to fly again as soon as this bloody war's over.'

Her smile was radiant. 'I'd like that too. See you in the morning.'

He stood alone in the passageway staring at the closed door, wondering if he would ever have the right to walk through it with her.

Twelve

Ellie had expected to spend a sleepless night after seeing Jack again. If he had tried to kiss her then things might have been different but he'd treated her like he was an affectionate brother and not her fiancé. However, she had come to a decision and not the one she'd expected. As long as he didn't try and move things on to a more intimate footing she was prepared, no – happy – to continue to be engaged to him. Who knows what might happen in the future?

She wished she reciprocated his love as it would make things so much easier. Maybe in a year or two, when she'd managed to put her feelings for Greg to one side, she would be ready to move on with him.

She was woken by the sound of heavy rain battering the windows. She scrambled out of bed and pulled on her discarded uniform. There wasn't much point in dressing in anything else and then having the bother of changing before she left.

He must have heard her moving about as he tapped on her bedroom door. 'It's tipping it down, Ellie; we're going to get soaked if it doesn't stop before we leave.'

'Come in, I'm decent.'

The door opened but he remained in the passageway leaning against the doorframe. 'Neither of us have spare uniform with us. Fred has offered to drive us to the station and then get someone to take the bike back to Hornchurch when the weather improves.'

'Golly! We mustn't do that. We'll just have to get wet and dry out when we get to St Albans.'

'I'm okay with that if you are. I can smell bacon – the last time I had any was when we visited Herford Hall. I hope Mabel's done plenty.'

They were lucky and the rain stopped mid-morning. 'We'd better go now, Ellie, we don't know how long this break in the weather will last.'

She embraced Mabel. Dad wasn't keen on physical contact but today he stepped in and gave her a hug. 'Take care of yourself. Don't do anything dangerous. Give my regards to your mum and George and his wife.'

The dogs followed them to the end of the drive and their barking was audible over the sound of the engine as they turned onto the lane.

'Look, this is Sopwell Street and you can see the cathedral from here,' Ellie said when they turned into the narrow street.

'I think it's only a stone's throw from the abbey and the park as well.'

'It's an ideal position for all of them. No more than a quarter of an hour's walk to anywhere.'

These houses were timbered, probably Elizabethan, but most of them were in good condition – no crumbling plaster or peeling paintwork as far as she could see.

'This is the one. We're just in time as it's starting to rain again and in half an hour it will be too dark to see.'

She knocked and the door opened immediately. She scarcely recognised her mother as this smiling, happy person who immediately embraced her.

'I'm so glad you got here before the blackout. Are you horribly wet? Come in, drop your bags on the stairs.' Jack bent down to unlace his boots but she stopped him. 'No, just wipe your feet, that's sufficient. These wooden floors are so easy to keep clean.'

Ellie draped her greatcoat and other outdoor garments over the banisters and waited for Jack to do the same. The house was quiet, no sign of either George or his wife.

'I expect you're wondering where Fiona is. She's gone in search of something for supper. She won't be long. George will be back at six unless he's asked to do something important and has to stay behind.'

Jack had to duck his head to enter the sitting room but once inside it was safe for him to stand upright without fear of knocking himself out.

'This is a lovely room, Mum, and considering it came fully furnished I'm impressed. Have you settled in, made any new friends?'

'The ladies at church seem pleasant enough and I've made myself known to the WRVS and the Women's Institute. I'll be attending my first meetings next week.' She gestured to a comfortable buttoned sofa. 'Sit down, you must be exhausted after all the travelling.'

Ellie exchanged an amused glance with Jack but didn't correct her mother. 'I seem to remember there are three reception rooms and four bedrooms, plus the kitchen and scullery. What I'd really like to do is have a look around if you don't mind.'

Immediately her mother's expression changed to one that was more familiar. Tight-lipped and sharp-eyed. 'Of course, I was forgetting for a moment that this is your property. You're paying for everything so are entitled to a go anywhere you want.'

'Mum, don't be like that. Dad would have been more than happy to make you an allowance but you wouldn't let him. This is your home. I'm not paying for it, not really – it's Greg's money.'

Jack touched her arm and nodded towards the seat and she subsided. 'Mrs Simpson, it's very kind of you to allow me to accompany Ellie. However, if you would prefer it, I can find myself a B&B for the night.'

Her mother's face crumpled. 'I'm so sorry, my dear, I'm not very good at being gracious.'

'It's all right, Mum, I understand. Please don't be upset.'

'Thank you, Ellen, for being so forgiving. Now – where was I? Ah, yes. We are all very happy here – in fact, I think that George and Fiona are thinking of trying for another baby. The consultant told them they only had to wait three months and that there was no medical reason for anything dreadful to happen again.'

'That's good news. Is Sir Reginald making things difficult for you?'

'Strangely I've not heard anything from him. I left him a note thanking him for his hospitality and saying that we were moving somewhere more convenient.' Her mother's laugh was almost girlish. 'Mind you, as I didn't give him this address, I suppose it's hardly surprising he hasn't been in touch.'

The bang of the front door opening and closing interrupted the conversation. A cheerful voice called from the hallway. 'I managed to get half a dozen sausages and some liver, Ma, hope that will be enough.'

Fiona stepped in, waving her shopping bag triumphantly. Ellie and Jack were on their feet to greet her. 'Gosh, I didn't realise you were here already. I'm so pleased to meet you. George told me what you did for him.'

'What did they do for him, Fiona?'

Jack averted a possible disaster. 'We drove you all to the hospital, remember, Mrs Simpson?'

'Of course you did. I try and put that day out of my mind. I'll take that, my dear, whilst you get to know my daughter and her fiancé.'

Mum took the bag and vanished through the door at the end of the room – presumably it led to the kitchen.

Ellie could see that Fiona was several inches shorter than her and certainly plumper. Her hair was an indeterminate colour between blonde and mouse and her eyes were blue. An unremarkable combination but her face came alive as she smiled.

'I nearly let the cat out of the bag just then. George didn't want Ma to know anything about it. Good thing you covered up for me, Mr Reynolds – or should it be Squadron Leader Reynolds?'

'Neither – please call me Jack.'

'Right ho. I see your bags and things are still on the stairs – shall I show you your rooms so you can get settled? Ma doesn't like to be disturbed in the kitchen, which is a good thing as I'm a shockingly bad cook. I do the shopping and washing up.'

They followed Fiona out of the room and grabbed their belongings from the stairs. 'Do you have a daily?'

'Absolutely. George was most insistent that neither Ma nor I could do any of the heavy stuff.'

The stairs creaked as they ascended, which was only to be expected. There was a small landing and the long corridor with a window at the far end, which let in welcome light. 'The house is narrow but goes back a long way. George and I have the back bedroom; Ma sleeps in the front. Your rooms are the two in between. That is, I mean to say...' She paused and her cheeks turned scarlet.

Jack once again stepped in. 'Yes, separate rooms for us, of course.'

Fiona galloped back down the stairs, leaving them alone. 'She's very sweet, not at all how I expected her to be. I think I might adopt her way of addressing Mum. Not quite as formal as calling her mother or as informal as mum.'

'Which room do you want? She neglected to say which door is the bathroom – do you think they have indoor plumbing?'

'Good grief! I should think so. In fact, one of the stipulations to the estate agents was that there should be a WC and bathroom. I'll take the room next to Ma; you have the other one. I think the bathroom must be downstairs, which is a bind.'

'More so for me than for you, sweetheart. Let's get sorted and downstairs. I'm hoping there might be a cuppa available before your brother gets home.'

Jack hung his greatcoat on the hook behind the door but didn't bother to unpack his overnight bag. Although they were staying two nights here, it didn't seem worth the effort. Doing even something so simple one-handed was more difficult for him.

George and he discussed the Japanese attacks in the Pacific and the perilous position of Malta but the ladies were more concerned about the rise of conscription age for both men and women to forty-five.

'If I'm expecting then I won't be called up,' Fiona said, 'which is why we've decided to try again so soon.'

Ellie nodded and smiled but clearly thought this a poor reason to start a family. Her sister-in-law should be eager to help with the war effort, not looking for a way out. 'Have you joined the WRVS or volunteered for fire watching?'

'I'm considering the WRVS but certainly not fire watching. Mummy and Daddy wouldn't want me to do anything dangerous.'

'Surely, Fiona, it's up to you and George what you do?'

Jack exchanged a grin with George and they rejoined the conversation before things got heated.

'Ellie, did you tell them about your intruder?'

His change of subject averted a disaster and the remainder of the evening went smoothly. His relationship with Ellie hung by a thread. He wasn't going to do anything, ask her difficult questions, just in case it pushed her in the wrong direction. Not an ideal situation, but better than the alternative.

The visit was a resounding success and when they left to walk to the station on Saturday afternoon, he now considered George a friend. Ellie got on well enough with Fiona, but they didn't have a lot in common. Mrs Simpson was a changed woman and her vinegary disposition appeared to have been replaced by something more pleasant.

'That's the best break I've had in a long time. In fact, it's the only leave I've had for three months.' He rubbed his chin, which he'd failed to shave as closely as usual that morning. 'I know we're supposed to have two days off and thirteen days on duty but I'm not the only one who doesn't take their free days. Only fair that the blokes who are married get to see the wife and kiddies when they can.'

'Same for me, Jack – I'd rather be working, doing my bit, than sitting around twiddling my thumbs. I'm happiest when I'm on my own in a Spitfire – the world and the worry just fall away.' The train lurched and she fell against him. He steadied her with his good arm but didn't take advantage. Her smile told him he'd made the right decision.

'Have you been forced to land at any of the American bases?'

'I don't think there are any that are fully operational. Must be a bit overwhelming for the villages in East Anglia that suddenly find themselves inundated with GIs. Debden already has the Eagle squadron – you know – they're part of the RAF but made up almost entirely of Yanks. The RAF are moving out and soon it'll be all Yanks.'

'I've not delivered or collected from there very often and didn't meet any Americans. As they only started coming over in the New Year I don't suppose we'll see much evidence of them yet.'

London was relatively quiet and for once the air wasn't full of smoke and the smell of burning. 'Where are you staying tonight? I've got to get a flip to White Waltham but you have to stay at Hornchurch.'

'I'm sure there'll be a bed in the WAAF's accommodation – there usually is.'

'I know you're busy but if you can, please find the time drop me a line every now and again.'

'I will, I promise. Shall we try and get together sometime in May? Perhaps we could go to a show in Town, make a night of it?'

'That would be swell. I'll speak to Frankie as soon as I get back. If I agree to forego my days off until then I'm sure he'll agree.'

'I'll do the same with Alison. It was she who insisted I took some leave. She doesn't like any of us to overdo it. She doesn't want the ATA to lose any more pilots. There have been fifteen killed so far this year and two of them were women.'

'I don't know that any of them were due to fatigue, but I think she's right. The Argus going down at White Waltham was hideous. It just stalled and crashed. Made it worse that there were two girls on board.'

'Amy Johnson was the first and that was over a year ago. We still talk about her.' She smiled sadly. 'Let's not think about it anymore. Brings back too many unpleasant memories.'

Bugger it! Now he'd reminded her of Greg and probably her brother Neil as well. 'As soon as you can confirm your days off, I'll organise mine.' This meant she had to contact him either by post or telephone.

'Okay. Then I'll ask for the same time; I'll book the hotel and the theatre. Unless you want to do that?'

'We can decide nearer the time. I'd like to visit my aunt, if that's okay with you.'

'I was fond of Joe – although I doubt I'd have felt like that if I'd known who he really was – I'd like to meet her.'

'Great, as soon as we've got our leave finalised I'll get in touch with her.' The train lurched to a halt at Romford. 'Come on, we'd better make a move or we won't get off before the train leaves again.'

They hitched a ride to the base and to his dismay he discovered there was an Anson about to depart for White Waltham and there was a spare seat. He'd hoped to spend a few more hours with her.

He hugged her briefly and then with what he hoped was a cheerful grin and a wave he raced across the tarmac and just managed to scramble in before the door closed.

He knew most of the other passengers but wasn't in any mood to attempt a conversation over the racket of the engine and the rattle of the fuselage. He wasn't on duty until the following morning so found his bicycle and, with his overnight bag slung over his back, pedalled back to the pub.

That night he got plastered. At least he slept well, although he regretted the hangover the next morning.

When he broached the subject of saving up his leave Frankie slapped him on the back. 'Just the ticket. If you're prepared to forfeit two days then I'm happy to let you take the other four in a block. Middle of May? Should be tickety-boo.'

Thirteen

Southampton, where Hamble was situated, was regularly bombed and surrounded by a circle of barrage balloons but so far no one had become entangled with the wires. Ellie thought with her skill at aerobatics she should be able to avoid a disaster of that sort.

She was determined to ask Jack to teach her more about flying with instruments next time they were together. It was ridiculous that the ATA in their wisdom decided none of the pilots needed this ability because they only flew in good conditions. This was patently untrue as the weather could change once you were airborne and it really wouldn't take all that much time to give all the pilots sufficient knowledge to fly safely in poor visibility.

Good grief, they were expected to fly an aircraft they'd never seen before with only the help of their manual. Doing this was far more technical and skilled than being able to read the instrument panel in order to fly safely in adverse conditions. She was dwelling on this when her friend called her name.

'Ellie, have you seen what you've got today?' Amanda asked as she collected her chits. All this information was also written on a blackboard but the girls needed the details on paper to take with them.

'A Moth, two Spitfires and a DB7. I've not flown one of those before, I hope it's one of the big ones as that will be much more interesting.'

'The name for the night fighter version – Havoc – doesn't fill one with confidence. Why don't they stick to calling it the Douglas DB7 or Boston?'

'Haven't a clue. It's an American kite. If they've given it to us it's probably not much use. Anyway, it's my first twin-engined light bomber and I'm going to enjoy it.'

She had to take a Moth to Brize Norton in Oxfordshire and then collect the DB7 and take it to Middle Wallop in Hampshire. From there she had to make her own way to the Spitfire factory in Southampton and take a new plane to Debden and collect a damaged one and return it to be repaired. It was going to be a busy day and it was perfect flying weather, which was fortunate as her first ferrying job today would be in an open cockpit.

She landed the Tiger Moth smoothly and taxied to the perimeter. A man in overalls approached her with a scowl.

'I don't believe it. A bloody girl sent to collect the DB7. Don't hold with females flying at all and certainly not bombers.'

She nodded a greeting, but ignored the comment. 'Here are the necessary forms, sir. You will find them in order. I have a lot to do today so I would be grateful if I could have them signed and get off as soon as possible.'

Her brisk, matter-of-fact attitude did the trick. The man shrugged and held out his hand. He scanned the papers, signed those he had to and handed them back.

'Good thing it's not raining or you'd be stuck here.'

With her parachute over one shoulder and her overnight bag in her hand she headed for the bomber. A couple of ground mechanics closed the door behind her and she made her way forward to the cockpit.

This was palatial compared to the Spitfire with double the number of dials and knobs to become familiar with. She took a deep breath and sat in one of the two pilots' seats and got out her book of notes. She flicked through and found the specifications for this aircraft and there was nothing there she didn't understand.

The only thing that was new to her was the tricycle undercarriage. From what she'd been told this meant take-off and landing would be straightforward. The only drawback was that the brakes were wheel brakes and the manual said they could be fierce. She did her preflight checks, taxied forward and waited for the green light to tell her she could go.

The short flight was uneventful and when she made her approach there was no wind to cause her any problems and not a cloud in sight. The runway was grass – but that shouldn't be a problem if it was dry.

Her approach was textbook and she applied the brakes as soon as they touched the grass. The wheels locked. The plane continued to slide forward – fast. Her heart was pounding. She took a steadying breath and released the brakes and tried again. It happened a second time.

She tried repeatedly. Nothing she did halted her progress. Was this it? Rapidly approaching was a sunken gun emplacement, a lorry and a brick wall. She had two choices and neither of them good.

One, opening up an engine to full power and hope it would swing her off course but if this failed she would die. Two – retract the undercarriage and drop the DB7 on its belly.

Instinct told her the second option was the best and she heaved on the lever. The kite continued to slide, eventually skidding to a halt twenty-five yards from the gun emplacement. Seeing the gunners dive headfirst from the door a few moments before she stopped would have been funny in any other circumstances.

For a few seconds she was unable to move, then the world righted and she was once more in command of the situation. When she emerged she was greeted by a round of applause from the men gathered at the foot of the ladder.

'Bloody hell, miss, that were a close call. Thought we were all going for a Burton,' one of the gunners said with a grin. She smiled at him but spoke to the officer who was approaching her.

'I hope I haven't damaged your kite. I didn't know the grass was wet…'

'How could you? You did damn well, young lady, most impressed, I must say.' He offered his hand and she took it to have her arm pumped. 'Wing Commander Battersby, delighted to make your acquaintance. I'm not sure how many of my chaps would have had the foresight to retract the undercarriage.'

'Ellie Simpson, second officer, ATA.'

'Jolly good show, Miss Simpson. Come to the Mess and I'll sign your papers. Where are you off to next?'

'Back to Southampton to collect a Spit.'

'One of my blighters can give you a lift. Least we can do in the circumstances.'

An hour later she was on her way in the staff car, being driven in style to the factory. Battersby had insisted there was no need to inform her CO, Margot Gore, of the near miss as the aircraft had suffered no serious damage by her unconventional landing.

On the short drive she had time to consider her brush with death. She wouldn't have done anything differently and all she'd learned was that it was dangerous to land the DB7 on a wet, grass runway. American runways wouldn't be grass – she hoped the powers that be would make sure no bombers were expected to land on anything but hard surfaces. Grass was fine for fighters but not anything bigger.

The Spitfire was waiting and the paperwork ready to sign. 'Ellie, lass, I've just checked with the Met office and there's more rain coming in from the north-east. I doubt you'll get to Debden today.'

'Thanks, Bill, let's hope it holds off until I get there.'

A brief letter arrived a week after Jack had seen Ellie, saying she had arranged to take her leave from Wednesday, 13th May. This was five weeks from today so with any luck there wouldn't be any problem getting the same days. That night he wrote to her with the good news.

His life was comparatively uneventful as the weather was excellent for the remainder of April. Then he and a dozen others were to deliver Spitfires to Scotland. These had already arrived from Southampton and were waiting on the apron.

Frankie took him to one side. 'Look here, Jack, I've put you forward to do something I don't think many of the chaps could do.'

'Right – fire away.'

'What I'm going to tell you mustn't be shared. It's all very hush-hush. Fifty-seven Spits are being shipped to Malta on the *Wasp* – a US aircraft carrier. There are two airfields near the Clyde where the *Wasp*'s berthed – one has an excellent runway but the other at Renfrew is a trifle short.'

'Go on – tell me why we're using Renfrew.'

'If they go to Abbotsinch the buggers will have to be more or less dismantled in order to get them through the narrow streets to the docks. If they land at Renfrew only the wingtips will have to be unscrewed.'

'Just how short is this runway?'

Frankie grinned as if it was a great lark. 'It's 590 yards.'

'Bloody hell! The manual says a Spit needs a minimum of 800 yards.'

''Fraid so, old chap. These are long-range kites with extra fuel tanks so it will be a bit tricky.'

'All of these are categorised as P1 (W).'

This meant pilots had to go immediately and wait day and night until they were ready to fly. 'Let me get this straight – I'm to take one of these to Prestwick and then have to hang around and ferry each of them to Renfrew?'

'I knew you were a bright chap. Got it in one. You're one of a select band of senior pilots doing this. You might well be stuck up there for a while – weather's less reliable in Scotland. I guarantee you'll be home in time for your leave.' His expression became serious. 'Remember, no one else knows what's going to happen to the kites once they've delivered them to Prestwick.'

Frankie slapped him on the back and Jack grabbed his gear from the locker room and made his way to the runway and the fighter he'd been designated to fly. It occurred to him that possibly Ellie might be taking a Spitfire directly from the factory at Southampton and that they would meet at Prestwick. Unlikely, but not impossible.

They took off one after the other, but from that point each guy made his own way. Flying in formation had been abandoned, even by the RAF, some time ago. At the allowed cruising speed of 200 mph and with decent weather all the way north, he completed the journey in just over two hours. Of course, they all flew around Birmingham and Manchester – too many balloons.

He landed and taxied to join the other fighters parked around the perimeter. He was the first of his group to arrive but that was hardly surprising as he'd ignored the ATA stipulations of flying no higher than 2,000 feet above ground level for a good deal of the journey.

A guy in similar uniform climbed up on the wing and offered him an arm. 'You must be the one-armed chap, Reynolds isn't it? I'm Geoff Murray, pleased to meet you.'

'You're expecting me?'

'We are indeed. Come and meet the others. We're going to be seeing a lot of each other over the next few days.'

Jack discovered during the conversation that Frankie had recommended him for this highly skilled operation despite his disability. For the first time since he'd lost his hand last year he felt whole, as if he was equal to any other flyer.

Over the next hour or so the remainder of the blokes from White Waltham turned up safely. He and the other handful of senior pilots had been given a small office to wait in, segregated from the others bringing in the Spitfires. The powers that be obviously didn't want them to inadvertently mention what was actually going on.

Geoff handed him another mug of tea. 'You expecting any more? I thought all those from your pool had arrived.'

'My fiancée is based at Hamble but I was hoping she might be coming here as well.' He took a slurp from his tea. 'She's recently converted to Class IV and is now flying small twin-engined operational bombers all over the shop. She's probably busy doing that but I expected to see some of the women from her pool. After all, they were put there to deliver fighters from the factory.'

'You're in luck – if I'm not very much mistaken that's a popsy who's just arrived.'

Jack turned and it wasn't Ellie, but the next best thing. It was her friend Amanda. 'Thanks, I know her.' He turned to leave but Geoff grabbed his arm sending the contents of his mug all over his trousers.

'Sod me! I'm bloody soaked now.'

'Sorry, old chap, but I've been put in charge of this lot and have strict instructions not to let anyone fraternise with the other pilots delivering here. *Loose Lips* and all that.'

Jack's fist bunched. Then he forced himself to smile. 'Forgot about that. Good thing Ellie isn't here because I would have gone to see her regardless of the rules.'

Transferring the kites proved to be tricky but doable. His aerobatic experience perhaps made things a little easier for him than the others – but his lack of a hand no doubt balanced the equation. All aircraft were safely delivered. He didn't envy the RAF bods who would have to fly the Spitfires from the aircraft carrier when they eventually arrived in Malta.

An Anson was laid on to return the select band of pilots who had successfully completed what might have seemed an impossible task. He eventually arrived at his base two days before he was due to take his leave.

'What show are you going to see and where are you staying when you meet Jack?' Amanda asked as she wandered into Ellie's bedroom.

'I haven't got around to booking anything – there's plenty of time.'

Her friend raised her eyebrows. 'It's the day after tomorrow. I doubt that you'll get anything decent at such short notice.'

'I'm sure I'll get a suite at the Ritz or the Savoy. We can go to the pictures instead of the theatre. I'd really like to see *Jungle Book*. I know it's for children but I've heard it's very good.'

'I'd forgotten you're a woman of means. I'm sure Greg would want you to spend the money he left you on yourself.'

This was hardly time to remind her about her lost love. 'I've not looked through that box. I think I'll do it now. It might help me make up my mind about Jack.'

'Do you want me to go away?'

'No – it'll be a lot easier with you here. I really should have done this before. There might be things in there that need to be dealt with.'

'I doubt it – everything like that was done by his solicitors.'

Ellie rummaged on top of her wardrobe and brought down the cardboard box. She had been too overwhelmed with grief when she'd opened it last time, but things had moved on and she was stronger now. Other people had lost loved ones and they didn't mope about dwelling on the past.

She put it on the bed and looked at it, her heart thudding. Her fingers refused to move and the box remained closed.

Her friend pulled back the cardboard and upended the contents onto the candlewick bedspread. 'There – doesn't look like anything too upsetting.' Amanda picked up the small velvet box with the wedding bands. 'Why don't you sell these? They must be worth a small fortune.'

She was about to protest but then said something else entirely. 'You're right. I can hardly ask Jack to use them for our wedding.'

Amanda flung her arms around her. 'At last. You've finally come to your senses. Do you want me to go through this for you?'

'No – we'll do it together.' She couldn't stop smiling. The decision had been made – she was going to marry Jack. Greg was no longer a barrier to their love. It must have been her brush with death in the DB7 that had changed her mind.

'This photograph of you in your dungarees is too good to be left in this box. We'll put it on the mantelpiece in the sitting room.' Amanda held up a bundle of letters tied with a ribbon. 'These will be yours – do you want them or shall I burn them?'

'The fire, please, I want to forget and move on with my life.' She swallowed a lump in her throat. 'No, I've changed my mind. I'll always love Greg and when I'm old I might want to remember him by reading these letters. I've still got the ones he wrote to me on the top shelf of the wardrobe. I'll put them together.'

'There's a couple of photographs of Greg in his uniform, cufflinks, his watch and a few other odds and ends. What do you want to do with those?'

'Hang on a minute, I'll get the box with the other things and then I'll put it all in together. Maybe when I'm gone my children will be interested and enjoy looking at them.'

Ellie removed the wooden writing case in which she'd stored the letters and put the others in with them along with the photographs and all the jewellery.

'I'm surprised you didn't burn those after he married someone else.'

'I was too upset at the time to even think about doing so and then I forgave him so was glad I hadn't destroyed them. I wonder if Jack's kept anything from his time in America?'

'I shouldn't think so – men are less sentimental than us.'

'Does this mean that you'll be planning your wedding for this summer?'

'Absolutely not. We're both far too busy to think about getting married at the moment. If things calm down then possibly next year but certainly not before that.'

The following morning as soon as she got to the base and had the use of the telephone, she booked a suite of rooms at the Ritz the cost of which made her eyes water. Although she had booked two rooms with a sitting room and shared bathroom Ellie had a strong feeling that only one of the bedrooms would be in use.

Several people remarked that she looked happy and she just told them she was spending a few days with her fiancé and they nodded and smiled understandingly. She couldn't wait to get to London and tell Jack the good news.

Fourteen

Jack needed more than his overnight bag for this four-night stay in the grandest hotel in London. What had possessed Ellie to book a suite in such a snobbish place? He wasn't comfortable mixing with the toffs, politicians and royals who now lived there permanently.

He had his uniform, a lounge suit and a tux as well as the necessary shirts, braces and so on needed to complete each outfit. What he didn't have was a respectable suitcase – he was damned if he was going to walk into the Ritz with his gear in his old kitbag.

'What's up, you look as if you've lost a quid and found a farthing,' one of the locals, drinking his mild and bitter in the public bar of his digs, said to him.

Jack explained his problem and the guy shook his head. 'Wear whatever you bloody well like, mate, who gives a toss what that lot think? You're a blooming hero not some waste of time like one of them.'

'It's not then I'm worried about, it's my fiancée. I don't want to let her down.'

'Ain't she in the ATA like what you are?'

He nodded. 'She's flying the smaller bombers and outranks me now.'

'Then she's a sensible girl and won't care what you wear nor nothing else neither. You go and have a good time – you deserve it.'

Jack finished his drink and refused a refill. 'No, thanks, I want an early night.'

The next morning he rolled his dinner jacket and suit and stuffed them into his old RAF kitbag. Then he put everything else he needed on top, tightened the drawstring and slung it over his shoulder. He was catching an Anson to Hornchurch and then hoped he'd get a lift to the station from there.

He was looking forward to seeing his lovely girl again after a break of more than six weeks. Two phone calls just weren't enough contact as far as he was concerned. How the hell the guys posted overseas managed he didn't know. His mouth twitched. He'd been one of them before his accident.

They'd agreed to meet at the hotel in Piccadilly as neither of them knew exactly when they would be able to get a flip from their base to the capital. He arrived just after lunch and was amused by the smart doorman wearing a flat, gold-braided cap, tailcoat leaping about in the road and waving a cane in an attempt to flag down a passing taxi for a departing guest. Jack strode past him, through the rotating door and into the impressive foyer. Most of the men were in uniform but the ladies milling about in the vast space were dressed to impress. He decided then he would only go out in his uniform – his mufti wasn't up to scratch when compared to those he could see.

Despite the fact it was the middle of May several of the women wore mink coats and were dripping with expensive jewellery. Their tinkling laughter and plummy voices got on his nerves. He moved towards the reception and the supercilious young lady in twinset and pearls looked at him from behind the desk. To his astonishment she smiled warmly.

'How can I help you, sir?'

'My fiancée, Ellen Simpson, has booked a suite for us. Do you know if she's arrived already?'

'She arrived half an hour ago, Squadron Leader Reynolds, and has gone up.' She snapped her fingers and a bellboy rushed over and picked up his kitbag from the floor.

'This way, sir, if you would care to follow me.'

He'd much prefer to carry his own stuff but supposed this was how things were done in places like this. No doubt he'd be expected to tip the boy a couple of bob as well. There was also someone in charge of the lift – what a ridiculous waste of manpower, well, boy power – when there was a war on.

If he was expected to give the lift attendant something every time he went in it he was going to use the stairs.

He stepped into a palatial sitting room with half a dozen chintz-covered armchairs, a sofa, occasional tables, bureaus and gilt-framed mirrors. He scarcely had time to take in such luxury when Ellie exploded from a door at the far side of the room.

'Jack, I'm so glad you're here. Isn't this absolutely spiffing?' To his astonishment and delight she flung herself into his arms. By the time they both came up for breath his kitbag had been dumped unceremoniously on the carpet and the bellboy had vanished.

'Sweetheart, why here? Couldn't you find anywhere more our style?'

She wasn't put out by his criticism of her choice. 'I completely forgot to book rooms, theatre or dinner and if Amanda hadn't reminded me yesterday, I probably wouldn't have got this suite either. I'm not paying for it, not really, I'm using the money Greg left me.'

He was unable to hide his dismay but she laughed up at him. 'Don't look so cross, darling, he would have wanted us to be happy together and what better way can you think of to spend my inheritance?'

'Something's changed since I last saw you. I thought you wanted to just be a friend – I'm not sure what's going on.'

She pulled him to the sofa. 'Sit down – I've so much to tell you. But first I want to say that I love you, that I want to marry you and Greg's no longer an obstacle to that. I'll always love him but he's dead and we're both very much alive.'

He ran his finger around his collar, which felt as if it was choking him. 'I've been waiting so long to hear you say that you returned my feelings and I can't quite believe it's true.'

'It is – I don't want to get married this year but next summer would be absolutely perfect. Hopefully, with the Yanks here, things will be easier for both of us.'

'I don't care when we get hitched, as long as I know that one day we will. Actually, I reckon things will be busier not quieter until this bloody war's won.'

She settled back in his arms and told him about how she'd almost gone for a Burton and he told her about delivering Spitfires to Renfrew.

'For God's sake don't mention any of this to anyone. Top-secret information.'

'You know I won't. Which reminds me, have you heard anything from Mr Mainwaring? It seems rather odd to me that he went off with all that jewellery and the envelope and didn't contact you again.'

'Suits me perfectly well. I'm not eager to be involved with the spooks. I'm a straightforward sort of guy.'

'I've booked afternoon tea in the Palm Court. Amanda told me it's terrific. That's in an hour, which gives us plenty of time to unpack.'

She showed him around the luxurious suite. 'There's room for two of us in that bath,' he said with a wicked smile.

'I might have considered such a scandalous proposition if we were allowed more than five inches of water.'

'We could fill it up...'

'Jack, you're making me blush. I'm still not sure I want to... well you know what I mean. It's not that I don't love you, but I would much rather wait until we're married. I absolutely won't risk becoming pregnant whilst the war's on.'

He dropped a kiss on top of her head. He could have explained to her that prophylactics were available but didn't want to ruin the moment. 'Then I suggest you lock your bedroom door tonight if you don't want an uninvited guest. You're too damn beautiful and I love you so much that not being able to make love to you when you're so close is going to be torture.'

'Abstinence is good for the soul – at least that's what we were told at school.'

'Bugger that! And I think it refers to alcohol not sex.'

Ellie realised it wouldn't take much persuasion from him for her to change her mind and tumble into bed with him. She hastily returned to the safety of the sitting room. 'I wonder why the furnishings are so old-fashioned. It's like something out of Versailles – not at all what I expected.'

He took her cue and stopped flirting with her. 'A posh bloke said to avoid the basement bar – it's for a different kind of customer.'

'What do you mean?'

'If I said it's known as the "Pink Sink" does that give you a clue?' He was trying hard not to smile.

'Is it where the prostitutes go to pick up men?' She'd hoped to shock him by her risqué reply but he nodded.

'Close – it's where men go to pick up other men.'

Her eyes widened. 'Good heavens! I thought that sort of thing was illegal.'

'It is, but one law for the poor and another for the rich.'

'I wish you hadn't told me that. It makes the whole place seem rather sordid and I was enjoying being somewhere glamorous for a change.'

'Okay – forget that I told you. Something else I learned was that foreign politicians and royals have moved in here permanently. I reckon this hotel must be full of spooks and traitors.'

'If that was your way of making me feel better then you failed miserably. I wish I'd found somewhere else...'

He laughed and hugged her. 'I was looking at any guy on his own and wondering if he was going to the basement. They all sound as if they've got a spoon in their mouth and I'm just not comfortable somewhere so grand.'

'Too bad, Squadron Leader Reynolds, this suite has been paid for as well as our afternoon tea and breakfast. However, I only reserved for one night so we can go somewhere else for the other three. Has your aunt any spare bedrooms?'

'Yes – but you wouldn't want to stay in the East End. We'll visit, but not stay.'

'I suppose we'd better get changed.'

'No, let's not. I'm proud to be in this uniform and so should you be.' He grinned and pointed to his discarded kitbag. 'Anyway, I doubt my dinner jacket or suit is good enough for such grand company.'

'I don't want you to feel uncomfortable so I won't change.' She pulled a face. 'Although, to be honest, I was looking forward to wearing something other than this. My uniform is very smart and well cut but not very glamorous.'

His eyes darkened. 'Don't you believe it, honey, you look stunning. I suppose all we'll get to eat are dainty sandwiches and cakes. We might have to go in search of fish and chips later on.'

'Actually, with rationing and so on, I'm intrigued to know how they can make their famous tea acceptable. As a three-course dinner mustn't cost more than five shillings nowadays I don't see how they can cater for the sort of guests they get here.'

'Luxury foods like lobster and caviar aren't regulated. If you can pay then you can still have whatever you want.'

He held open the door and stepped out into the luxuriously carpeted passageway. There were mirrors everywhere, making the space appear larger than it really was. 'Then I'm sure we'll get something delicious as everything costs an absolute fortune.'

She looked around with interest as they made their way down the stairs and through the hotel to the famous Palm Court where afternoon tea was served. 'Have you noticed that most of the male staff are either incredibly ancient or very young?'

'Hardly surprising.'

Ellie was carrying the key to the suite prominently so they were bowed ceremoniously into the elegant space. 'It's beautiful but not my taste. I prefer something simpler. Too much gold and fuss for me.'

As always, she was walking on his right side and he was holding her hand. He raised it to his lips and pressed a kiss on her knuckles. Her stomach somersaulted. How could she ever have thought he was second best to Greg?

'Squadron Leader Reynolds, Miss Simpson, if you would care to follow me, I will take you to your table.'

'Good God! Everyone's in evening dress – I don't understand why anyone would want to change just to eat tea.'

'This isn't just any old tea, Jack, it's afternoon tea at the Ritz in the Palm Court. I only got a table because I'd booked a suite. Smile and enjoy yourself. We're in uniform so we can look down our noses at them – not the other way around.'

Everything they were served – from the dainty crustless cucumber sandwiches, the delicious warm scones with real strawberry jam and the tiny delicate pastries – was delicious. Even Jack was silenced and enjoyed every morsel as much as she did.

'Let's raise our cups to Greg, after all he paid for this.' For a moment he hesitated then he nodded and picked up his tea and they clinked cups.

'To Greg.' He put his drink down and stretched across to take her hand. 'He asked me to take care of you if he bought it. He knew how I felt about you and wanted us to be together.'

'Then wherever he is, he'll be giving us his blessing. I know it's taken me a long time to get over him and realise how much I love you – but I got there in the end and I'm so glad that you were prepared to wait.'

'I know you don't want to get hitched until the end of the war but I don't see that being married will make any difference to our work with the ATA. A lot of the women pilots are married and I think some of them even have families.' She tried to remove her hand but his grip was too firm. His eyes blazed into hers and she knew exactly what he was thinking.

A wave of heat spread from her toes to her crown. 'Stop it, you know why I don't want to get married.'

'Amanda sleeps with her guy and she hasn't got pregnant. Why don't you speak to her? I'm not sure I'm the best person to explain how this works.'

'Excuse me, sir...'

Jack, startled by the unexpected interruption, released his hold so suddenly her hand flew sideways and caught the half-full teapot sending it crashing to the floor. The unfortunate waiter who had come to enquire if they required anything further was drenched.

In the pandemonium that followed the very personal conversation was forgotten. When eventually they returned to their suite it was to find a complimentary bottle of champagne waiting on the coffee table.

'There's a card. Look, they're apologising for the incident downstairs and the management hope this will compensate.'

She viewed the champagne cork with apprehension. 'I've never opened one of these. Do we have to call someone to do it for us?'

'I don't think we should open it at all. We'll both do something we regret if we drink a bottle of fizz between us.'

'Then I'm going to put it in my suitcase and we can have it another time. I hope they don't ask where the empty bottle is.'

'I'm sure they don't care. It's still light. Shall we go for a walk in Green Park before we turn in?'

After an enjoyable stroll they returned to the hotel and she wasn't sure if she was relieved or disappointed that he didn't come to her.

Next morning, they caught a bus to the East End and got off at Liverpool Street from where they intended to walk to Charlotte Street. Everywhere she looked there were signs of damage – craters, sandbags, broken windows. 'Look at that.' She pointed at the empty space between the rows of houses. 'I can't believe how quickly nature has taken over and covered the debris with grass, brambles and wildflowers.'

She moved closer to him and he tightened his hold on her hand. 'Despite everything people here seem cheerful.'

'Life goes on and you just have to get on with it however hard things are. We turn down here. It's a pity she didn't get the phone reconnected so we could make sure she's actually there when we turn up.'

'She must have thought it a bit odd when you went off to find Joe's lock-up and never came back.'

'I wrote to her explaining what happened but now you come to mention it I never got a reply.'

He increased his pace and she lengthened her stride in order to keep up with him. 'There haven't been any air raids on London recently, Jack, I'm sure everything's fine.'

'I wasn't thinking about bombs but the bastards who might have been incriminated in whatever was in that envelope.'

A prickle of fear ran through her. 'Surely they wouldn't do anything to your aunt? She knows nothing about it and your uncle's dead so I can't see that hurting her…'

'For Christ's sake, it's me they would want to hurt. They know I came here a few weeks ago and that I gave the information to the authorities.'

He stopped so suddenly she tripped over her feet. Only his quick reactions saved her from falling to the pavement. Before she could protest he turned and began to run back the way they had come. His grip on her hand was relentless and she had no alternative but to pound along beside him.

Heads turned in astonishment as they raced past but nobody attempted to stop them. She'd no need to ask what the urgency was – he thought bringing her here had put her in mortal danger from the criminals who ruled the darker side of the East End.

The entrance to the station was just ahead and as luck would have it there were two police constables walking towards them.

Neither of them was out of breath despite their mad dash down Norton Folgate. Once inside the safety of Liverpool Street they stopped running.

'I've got Mainwaring's phone number somewhere. Do you have any coppers?'

She put her hand on his arm. 'If anything had happened to your aunt surely you would have heard about it. The Secret Service, or whatever they are, wouldn't deliberately put her in danger.'

Suddenly he pushed her almost roughly behind him. She didn't recognise him. His eyes were hard – his mouth thin. He looked dangerous.

Fifteen

Jack scanned the people entering the station. He was looking for a couple of blokes on their own with their hands in their pockets. He couldn't breathe – they'd have to come through him before they touched his girl.

He watched for a minute. Nobody suspicious walked through the arch. They were safe – for the moment. 'Sorry, honey, I wanted to be sure we weren't followed. There's a telephone kiosk over there – I need to make that call pronto.'

She didn't argue, just nodded and moved closer to him. He smiled ruefully. He rather thought she was protecting him and not the other way round.

He dialled one hundred and gave the operator the number. He had his coins ready to drop in the slot when asked. Someone picked up the receiver at the other end and he pressed button A. The money dropped into the box and he was connected.

'Mainwaring?'

'Reynolds – thank God. I've been trying to contact you but no one bloody well knew where you were.'

Jack explained. Mainwaring swore.

'The information in that envelope was far more valuable than the other one your uncle was holding. It listed the names of the villains involved in several unsolved murders and gave details of their involvement. Scotland Yard has used this to build a case against the perpetrators. They were arrested yesterday.'

'What about my aunt?'

'She was advised to return to her family in the North and she packed her bags and left several weeks ago. That's why you couldn't get in touch with her.' He cleared his throat. 'Now, I have to tell you that you and your fiancée were in real danger as soon as you set foot in the East End.'

'I should have realised this might happen. Someone would have recognised me when I was looking for the lock-up. God – I hope the little lad who kept me safe hasn't been harmed.'

'No reports of children being murdered in that locality. Mind you, it's quite possible we wouldn't hear anything about it. Easy to dispose of a small body.'

Jack swallowed bile. The beeps went and he hastily dropped another couple of coins into the slot. He didn't want to be cut off in the middle of this conversation.

'What should we do know?'

'Return to your ferry pools pronto. You'll both be safe as long as you stay within the bounds of the places you fly. I think it highly unlikely they'll pursue you, but it would be wise to stay away from London for the foreseeable.'

'We've left our kit at the Ritz.'

'I'll have your belongings brought to you.'

'What about Ellie's parents? Can they be protected? It's a short hop from Romford to Glebe Farm.'

'The matter's in hand. Don't attempt to visit them at the moment.'

The beeps went again warning him he was running out of money. 'Swell! I've no more change.' Ellie touched his arm, pointed across to the train getting up steam on platform nine and raised her eyebrow. He nodded. 'I've got to go – there's a train we can catch. This is a goddamned nightmare and I wish I'd never agreed to help you.'

He slammed the receiver down. 'I'll explain everything on the train.' He grabbed her hand and together they hurried across the station and joined the queue of businessmen, service men and women queuing to get into the nearest carriage.

All compartments were occupied and they had just jammed themselves into the nearest corner when the guard blew his whistle and waved his green flag. The train lurched into motion.

There were two brown jobbies crushed against them so it was impossible to talk about what had just happened. He positioned himself between the two soldiers and Ellie using his bulk to protect her from being squashed. Having his back to them meant they didn't have to talk to them.

As they were next to the exit, getting off was easier than getting on. They were waved through the barrier by the ticket collector and went in search of a lift to Hornchurch. She didn't have to be told they were in danger here as well as in London.

They walked close together, keeping their heads down but with eyes swivelling from side to side on the lookout for anyone who might be dangerous. They had been walking for no more than a quarter of a mile when an RAF staff car pulled up beside them.

'Going to Hornchurch?' The driver was a WAAF who nodded towards the empty back seat. 'Just dropped a bigwig at the station. Hop in – as far as I'm concerned ATA are entitled to the same service as the RAF.'

They scrambled into the rear of the vehicle. Ellie looked at him and her smile said it all. She was as relieved as he was to be safe. The vehicle was waved through the checkpoint at the base and pulled up outside the adjutant's office.

'Here you are. I hope there's an Anson to take you home.'

The car drove away. This was the first opportunity they'd had to talk privately about what had just happened.

'What a bloody shambles – I'm sorry I've dragged you into this mess.'

'It's not your fault, neither of us had any idea that Joe was such a hardened criminal. We mustn't tell my family about this.'

'Your mom doesn't have to know but Mainwaring said that Fred and Mabel have been informed. Those bastards are well aware that Joe owned the airfield.'

'No, I don't think they do. It was the fascists who came to the house. Why should the villains in London know about the airfield? After all, it's registered in your name not his.'

He hugged her and was finally able to swallow the lump in his throat. 'Stupid of me. I've been in a blind panic the past couple of hours.' His relief was short-lived when he recalled what Mainwaring had said.

'Let's ask if we can use the telephone and find out when the next taxi will be here. It's a damned nuisance having to leave our kit behind.'

'I'm wearing all I need – I doubt I shall want a smart outfit until the war's over. From now on we should stay in uniform. It makes us a bit more anonymous.'

Jack's grin was infectious. 'My carrot top and missing arm make me conspicuous whatever I'm wearing. However, I get your drift. Mainwaring said not to wander about in public if we can avoid it.'

'That's all very well, but both of us live a couple of miles from our ferry pool and we can't always get from place to place by Anson.'

'I don't know a lot about London villains but I'm pretty sure they wouldn't send anyone looking for either of us any further than Romford. As long as we stay away from London as well, I'm sure we'll be in no danger.'

'We're getting strange looks standing about out here so let's go in and make that phone call. I can't tell you how sorry I am that we didn't have our three nights together. It might be months before our days off coincide again.'

He brushed a stray curl from her cheek. 'Neither of us are due back on duty for another three days – we could spend it at your cottage if you like.'

She didn't hesitate. 'Yes, that's a splendid idea. I don't know why I didn't think of it myself. Amanda might be there some of the time but she's very broadminded.'

His eyes darkened and his smile was dangerous. She stepped willingly into his arms and they kissed passionately. When she finally raised her head, her cheeks were glowing and her lips tingling; she was horrified to see a row of grinning faces watching through the window of the office.

Jack ignored them. 'They're just jealous that we're in love. I suppose we'd better go in and see if there's a taxi going to Southampton sometime today.'

Eventually they arrived at Hamble just as the sun set. She was delighted to see her bike and Amanda's propped up in the rack. 'I'll just find out when she's back.' She emerged a few moments later with the good news that Amanda had just started her two days off and was away somewhere in the country. 'You can use her bicycle as she won't be here before you have to go.'

The two-mile cycle ride was accomplished without incident. Neither of them wanted to talk, they both enjoyed the birdsong and sweet scent of early honeysuckle in the hedgerows.

'We leave the bikes just inside the hedge,' she said as she jumped nimbly from their saddles.

'Okay. I don't suppose Amanda's guy leaves any shaving stuff here, does he?'

'If he does it will be in her bedroom. You haven't even got a clean collar let alone anything else. It's so warm that if you wash out your smalls they'll dry overnight.'

His laughter followed her to the front door. 'Sweetheart, I can do most things, but laundry ain't one of them.'

She turned. 'I don't even notice the lack of your hand anymore. I suppose in the circumstances I might be persuaded to do your washing. However, I shan't make a habit of it.'

He arrived at her side. He stood so close his hot breath tickled the back of her neck. An involuntary shiver rippled through her. She wasn't sure if it was fear or anticipation. Was she really going to go to bed with him?

Her hand was trembling. She couldn't put the key in the lock. He reached round and did it for her. The door sometimes stuck, but this time it opened smoothly. She tried to put distance between them but he prevented her from escaping by taking her hand.

'Darling Ellie, whatever you want to do is fine by me. I'll wait until we're married if that's what you want to do.'

'It's just that I'm terrified of getting pregnant. I do want to have babies with you but not until we're married and the war's over.'

He said something extremely rude then ran his hand through his hair. 'Sod me. What we need is in my kitbag.'

'Then you'll have to sleep in Amanda's room. If you lie on top of the bedspread, I'll find you a spare blanket and then I don't have to change the sheets.' He nodded but she knew he was disappointed. She threw herself into his embrace. 'I love you so much…'

'No, honey, we won't risk it.'

'What about if you're beside me but not inside the sheets? Would that be too difficult?'

'That would be swell. Just holding you, lying beside you all night, even if we can't make love, is enough for me.'

They were interrupted by a tap on the front door. Jack moved swiftly out of sight before she opened it. Her neighbour greeted her with a friendly smile.

'Thought you were away with your young man, Ellie. I've got some milk and a nice tasty Woolton pie for your tea. I expect you'll need to keep your strength up.'

The jug and pie dish were handed over without comment. She barely recovered her composure in time to call out her thanks.

'There's no need to lurk in there, she obviously saw you come in with me.'

He sniffed appreciatively. 'That smells tasty. I was wondering what we were going to eat. We really didn't think this through very well, did we?'

'I'm a fallen woman – everyone in the neighbourhood will know you stayed here.'

He laughed. 'If she's not bothered, why should we be? Come on let's eat that whilst it's still hot.'

The pie, named after the man who invented it, contained no meat but was tasty nonetheless. They drank several mugs of tea and devoured the lot. Now she was comfortably full and safe in her own cottage she felt ready to discuss what had happened.

'Do you really think we were in actual danger in London and Romford?'

'I'm certain of it. I could have got us both murdered. I should have thought it through.'

She shuddered at his vehemence and his use of the word *murder*. This wasn't a game – it was reality.

'I suppose this means we can't go to see my parents again for a while. I don't want to put them at risk.'

For a moment he didn't answer, looked down at the cracked oilskin tablecloth. He raised his head and his expression was bleak.

'Ellie, I don't think you quite realise what's going on. Until those under arrest are tried and convicted, we can't go anywhere near the farm. We'll know just how bad things are after I've spoken to Mainwaring.'

'That could be months. I blame that Mainwaring person for forcing you to go there. I'm sure that if he'd asked nicely your aunt would have given him the key to the lock-up and you could have stayed out of it.'

'There's nothing we can do about it now, sweetheart, we just have to accept this is how things are. You can write or telephone but that will have to do.'

'It's all very well for you to say so but they're not your parents. The thought that they might be harmed because of your uncle...'

He stood up. 'I know it's all my bloody fault. You don't have to rub it in. I'm going for a walk – I need to clear my head.'

She should have called him back, apologised, not let him go away angry, but she didn't. She sat silently until she heard the front door bang, stunned by his outburst. Only then did she move. She washed up and tidied the kitchen, hoping he would be back so she could make things right.

An hour passed but still he hadn't returned to the cottage. She decided to make up his bed in Amanda's room as she didn't want to sleep with him, however innocently, at the moment. He was right to say that she blamed him. Although she'd said it was Mainwaring, they both knew if he hadn't been seen collecting the incriminating evidence Dad and Mabel wouldn't be in danger. She wasn't bothered for herself or Jack because they were safe as long as they stayed away from Romford or London.

At ten o'clock she decided to go to bed. He'd probably walked to the village and was drowning his sorrows with a pint or two of beer. She had a good mind to bolt the front door so he couldn't get back in but decided against it.

She left the door to her friend's room wide open so he would know not to come into her. Her initial annoyance at his desertion had dissipated but she was cross that he'd stayed out so long. Hopefully he had his torch with him as it had been pitch dark for the past hour.

She undressed and was tempted to put a chair under the door handle but decided that would be silly.

Jack regretted his childish exit by the time he'd reached the village green. When he saw the pub he decided to have a swift half before returning and apologising to Ellie.

The bar was busy and his uniform was immediately recognised. The locals plied him with drink and he was too polite initially to refuse and then too drunk to care.

He was ejected from the premises along with the others into total darkness.

'Hope you've got your torch, Jack, you'll never find your way back if not.'

'Never travel without it, mate. Good night and thanks for a great evening.'

Their voices echoed across the green, no doubt annoying the villagers who had retired early. He was tempted to sing as he staggered to the cottage but decided against it. Halfway back he needed a pee, so relieved himself in the hedge.

He pushed open the front door and then carefully closed it behind him. His head had cleared a little but he was still decidedly pissed. He negotiated the stairs with difficulty as he couldn't hold on to the banister and his torch at the same time. He dropped the bugger halfway up and swore loudly.

He remembered that Ellie's door was on the right. He fingered his way along the landing and found the door latch. He didn't want to wake her so decided to strip off where he stood. He was as quiet as he could be but removing his clothes one-handed was always tricky – doing it now was almost impossible.

He vaguely remembered agreeing to sleep on top of the covers and was a man of his word. He opened the door and stepped in, blinking in the unexpected brightness.

'Jack Reynolds. Not only are you naked you are also horribly drunk. Go away – I don't want you being sick in here.'

For a moment the words didn't register. Then his head cleared. Without a word he spun and closed the door behind him. What had he been thinking? Then his legs gave way and he slid down the door. It was bloody funny – in fact it was the funniest thing that had ever happened.

He started to chuckle then laughed out loud. The more he thought about it the funnier it seemed. Then he was flat on his back. Mysteriously the wall had vanished from behind him.

Never mind. He could sleep just as well on the floor as in a bed. He closed his eyes and ignored whoever it was who was shouting at him.

Sixteen

Ellie heard Jack stumbling up the stairs and guessed that he'd drunk more than was good for him. She pushed herself up on her elbows praying that he didn't miss his footing and tumble backwards. Although he insisted that having only one arm didn't affect his balance, she was sure that it did – especially when he was already unsteady.

She waited to hear Amanda's bedroom door close but instead she heard him banging about outside her room. What on earth was he doing? With a sigh she got out of bed and switched on the bedside light.

The door swung open. Her eyes widened. A wave of heat travelled from her toes to her crown. He had no clothes on at all. She told him in no uncertain terms to go away. He blinked and then stepped back and slammed the door.

She was about to clamber back into bed and switch off the light when there was an ominous thud and to her astonishment she heard him laughing. Forgetting he was in no state for a lady to see him she pulled open the door and his top half crashed onto her floor leaving the rest of him spreadeagled in the corridor.

'Get up at once, you can't sleep here. You're disgustingly drunk and I'm very cross with you.'

With a sigh he closed his eyes and was instantly deeply asleep. Snores reverberated down the passageway. She prodded him with her toe and got no response. Hastily she snatched the candlewick bedspread from the chair and spread it over him. She'd seen more than enough of his nether regions, thank you very much.

She fetched a pillow, pushed it under his head and then folded up his discarded clothes and placed them neatly by his feet. He was going to be horribly embarrassed when he woke up and it served him right.

With him half in and half out of her door she wasn't going to get much sleep. She might as well use Amanda's bedroom and leave him in his drunken stupor where he was. With everything she needed for the morning under her arm she stepped over him.

Perhaps it would be wise to leave him a basin in case he was sick. His colour was good, and apart from his snoring she would have thought him sober. His shock of red hair flopped endearingly over one eye and her heart filled. Why had she not realised sooner how much she loved him?

No doubt he'd have a horrible hangover in the morning but with luck would be better by the evening. If he was then he could spend the night with her and not on top of the bed covers but between the sheets with her. She wanted to know what it was like to make love, to become part of the man she loved.

Her euphoria lasted until she was settling down to sleep. Then reality took over. Nothing had changed – she had a job to do and wasn't going to risk getting pregnant however much she wanted to take the next step.

She half expected to be kept awake by his snores, or the sound of him being ill, but she didn't stir until there was a tentative knock on the door the following morning.

'I've got tea here, I'll leave it outside the door.' There was the sound of a tray being put down and then of his footsteps on the stairs as he descended.

She tumbled out of bed and flung open the door. 'Don't you go anywhere, Jack Reynolds, I want to talk to you.'

He paused halfway down and turned to face her. He looked decidedly unrepentant after his disgraceful behaviour last night. 'Yes, my love, how can I be of assistance?'

'You came into my room in your birthday suit and then passed out on the floor and kept me awake with your snoring.'

'Think of it as an education – it will make it less of a shock next time.'

'The way I feel about you at the moment, I doubt there'll be a next time.'

'If that's the case, honey, you might want to adjust your nightie.'

She glanced down. One breast was almost entirely visible as the garment had slipped sideways during her hasty exit from bed. 'Would you prefer the full reveal? I saw everything you've got so that would only be fair.' She had no intention of revealing anything and his shocked expression was absolutely priceless.

'Thanks for the tea, I'll be down shortly.'

There was a strange fluttery feeling inside, which increased whenever she thought about seeing Jack naked. It was going to be difficult saying no when she felt like this.

Whilst she scrambled into her clothes, she compared her feelings for him to those she had had for Greg. There was no doubt in her mind that she'd loved him but it had been different – purer, less earthy and certainly a lot less urgent.

The next time she saw her friend she would ask her how she prevented unwanted babies. Amanda had been sleeping with Nigel on and off for almost a year with no unwanted side effects.

If they hadn't been obliged to abandon their belongings at the Ritz yesterday, she was certain things would have happened. She was smiling when she walked into the kitchen, thinking that her honour had been saved by a villain in the East End of London.

'Thank you for the tea...' The delicious aroma of toast filled the room. There were also four eggs boiling on the stove. 'Where did all this come from?'

His smile melted the last of her reserve. 'I sweet-talked the farmer's wife and she gave me half a dozen eggs, some butter and the bread.'

'Gave? Do you mean you didn't have to pay?'

'She refused to take any money. Mind you, I did lay it on a bit thick and waved my stump around. She's a good sort and seems fond of you and Amanda.'

She poured herself a second mug of tea. 'I was going to be very cross with you but I can't be angry with the man who made me toast and freshly boiled eggs.'

He was remarkably dexterous and was able to deposit the eggs neatly into the egg cups. 'Here you are, I did them for five and a half minutes. I managed to cut the bread but I think you'd better butter it yourself.' He joined her at the table. 'I'm sorry I walked out last night.'

'But you're not sorry about the rest of your appalling behaviour?'

His smile made her drop her spoon.

'Course I am. I don't do it very often – in fact I can't remember the last time I got plastered. Blame it on the locals for buying me so many refills. It would have been impolite to refuse.'

'Then shall we forget all about it? We could catch the bus into Southampton later but I want to catch the van when it comes this morning. I don't suppose you've got your ration book in your pocket?'

'I gave it back to my landlady. She uses my coupons to buy extras for her kiddies.'

'Not to worry, as long as there's bread and something to put on it we won't starve. Good thing I can get milk, butter and eggs from the farm every now and again.'

'Could you ask your neighbour to buy what you need from the van? Then we could catch the first bus and have a whole day in town.'

'No harm in asking. Have you any idea when our belongings are going to arrive? Mainwaring won't know to send your kitbag here. We need to get to a telephone box and tell him to leave everything at Hamble.'

Jack made the call without her standing beside him. The interior of the red box smelt of pee and she'd refused to come in. He didn't blame her – it certainly smelt rank in there.

'All done, Ellie, our stuff should be at Hamble later today. We can collect it on the way home.'

'What a relief. I wasn't looking forward to washing your underpants and socks tonight.'

He wondered if she'd forgotten what else was in his kitbag. Better not to think about that or he would find himself in an embarrassing situation.

Southampton, being the home of the Spitfire, was full of RAF uniforms as well as several ATA pilots, all of whom wanted to stop for a chat. The women delivered most of the Spits, but the occasional guy greeted them as well.

They went to the flicks and saw the latest cartoon, *Jungle Book*, which wasn't his cup of tea but she seemed to enjoy it. The newsreel showing the Yanks marching through Britain was greeted with a cheer by the audience. He reckoned if Japan hadn't bombed Pearl Harbour they would have left Churchill to carry on by himself.

All the GIs were grinning at the cameras, waving and obviously happy to be here. The contrast between their well-fed appearance and that of the Brits was stark. The friendly invaders wouldn't have to endure rationing like everyone else. He doubted much of their luxurious rations would filter into the local population.

The local girls would be only too happy to mingle with the Americans if it meant they got access to nylons, chocolate and other items no longer available here. Perhaps he was being cynical and things wouldn't change. Life was grim, food was short and everyone who could work to help the war effort was doing so. Why wouldn't they want a little excitement and luxury in their lives?

They snagged a lift back to the ferry pool and, as promised, her suitcase and his bag were waiting for collection. The building was deserted, which was hardly surprising as the women would be busy delivering Spitfires and so on and rarely returned until dark.

'It's a good thing I didn't bring much,' Ellie said. 'I wouldn't fancy carrying anything heavier for the two miles to the cottage.'

'Pull the other one, honey, your parachute weighs a lot more than that and you lug that about without complaint.'

He slung his kitbag over his shoulder and was ready to walk when someone called her name.

'That's Alison – I'll not be long.'

He had a horrible feeling she was about to be asked to ferry something urgent. Then she poked her head through the door and beckoned him. He dropped his bag next to hers and hurried inside.

'Jack, I've just been asked if I can deliver two Priority One Spitfires to be taken to Debden,' Alison told him. 'Sorry to ruin your leave, but would you be prepared to help out?'

'I don't have my gear with me. If you can find me something that fits, I'll be happy to.'

'Come with me, I think I can find you a Sidcot suit and possibly boots that will do.' Ellie pointed in the direction of the locker room. 'I seem to remember seeing some men's stuff in a cupboard left over from when they used to be here as well.'

The boots were a bit tight but the flying suit was perfect. After a deal of rummaging they found a helmet, goggles and a glove that would do as well.

'Ellie, whilst waiting for the paperwork there's something I want to show you. The kites we're taking are fully operational and you need to be able to use the instruments if the weather closes in.'

'We've got twenty minutes before the car comes – is that long enough?'

'More than enough. What I need is some paper and a table – I've got something to write with in my pocket.'

When he'd finished explaining and had drawn the necessary diagrams, he was certain she would be able to implement his instructions if the situation called for it.

'I think it's bloody stupid not training you girls to instrument fly. For God's sake, if you can fly a twin-engined bomber safely then you should be allowed to use them. It might well save your life one day.'

She carefully folded the paper and tucked it into her pocket. 'It's against all the rules, but thank you so much for teaching me.' She glanced outside. 'It's only a couple of hours' flying time and the Met office report is excellent. We'll be there long before dark and might even be able to catch a taxi back.'

They had already stowed their bags but not before both of them had removed the necessary items for an overnight stay. His clean shirt, collar and shorts, plus his shaving gear, were in an old shopping bag and hers in something just as disreputable.

They had done the obligatory visit to the Maps and Signals Office, collected the paperwork and then ran out to the waiting car. His borrowed parachute was slung over his shoulder. He had to assume that this had been abandoned because the owner had left the service and that it wasn't faulty.

'Don't look so worried, Jack, you won't have to use that. This delivery is a piece of cake. In fact, I'd rather be flying a Spitfire than anything else in the world.'

'Even spending the night with me?' He whispered into her ear as they settled on the back seat of the car.

'Ask me again in a day or two. However, I doubt anything can beat a Spit.'

He pulled her tight against him and gently nibbled her earlobe. 'I'm looking forward to proving you wrong, darling.'

The car braked sharply as it turned onto the road throwing them both sideways and breaking his hold. Probably for the best. He wanted her calm and relaxed when she scrambled into the cockpit, not thinking about him.

A Priority Wait One chit meant that whoever was collecting the kite had to hang about until it was ready even if that meant waiting for hours. This time they were lucky and the handover took barely half an hour.

'We've done this before, Ellie, follow me…'

'I outrank you, Jack, so if anyone's going to be following, it's you.'

He watched her walk to the Spitfire, confident she was as able as he to deliver the kite.

Ellie ran through her preflight checks and waited for the signal to taxi onto the runway. The green light flashed and she took off smoothly. Flying this aircraft was a delight; however many types she flew, this would always be her favourite.

She quite liked the idea that Jack was somewhere close by but she didn't see him on the two-hour flight. After landing she taxied to the perimeter, following the ground engineer with his waving paddles. As she scrambled out, the second Spitfire arrived.

'The Anson's waiting, miss, you both arrived in the nick of time,' she was told by the young officer. He pointed to the far side of the airfield and her heart sank to her boots. He saw her expression and grinned. 'Don't worry, you just have to get the other side of the strip. They'll taxi to you.'

Jack joined her. 'I'm glad we didn't have to fly over any muck. I want to make sure you know how to use your instruments before you do that.'

'Shush – you know it strictly forbidden for any of us to go above the bad weather.'

He laughed and slung his arm around her shoulder. 'Come on, our carriage awaits. We'll be back in time for supper in your excellent canteen.'

They were greeted with a chorus of boos when they took the last two seats on the taxi. 'Sorry we kept you waiting, guys and gals, but we're here now. Everything's tickety-boo.'

She recognised the pilot, Jim Mollison, as she had flown with him several times before. She nodded her thanks and he gave a nonchalant wave and turned the aircraft onto the strip.

It was impossible to hold anything but a shouted conversation once they were airborne. The rattle of the fuselage and the thunder of the engine drowned out normal speech. She had the seat next to a small window and was enjoying being a passenger for once when she saw two aircraft in the distance.

She tugged at Jack's sleeve and pointed to the window. He leaned across and looked out. 'Christ almighty! They're ME-109s – bloody Germans.' Even in the racket she heard what he said and so did the two sitting behind them. Jack surged to his feet and grabbed the pilot's arm. She couldn't hear what he said but when he pointed the pilot nodded.

The enemy aircraft flew towards the Anson. The unmistakable rat-tat-tat of machine-gun fire made her hair stand on end. The enemy were so close she could see the whites of the pilots' eyes.

Then Jim took evasive action. He pulled the nose up, opened the throttle and the plane screamed into the clouds. The German fighters didn't follow. They were safe. She turned to speak to Jack but he wasn't beside her. He'd still been on his feet when the plane had climbed so steeply and he'd been flung backwards.

He was crumpled, unmoving, in a heap at the tail end of the Anson. She was about to rush to his aid but a man was there before her. 'It's okay, I'm a doctor,' he yelled. 'I'll see to him – you stay in your seat.'

Reluctantly she did as he suggested. Her heart was pounding – her hands clammy. Why didn't Jack wake up? Had he broken his neck in the fall? If she lost him, she'd never recover from the pain.

Then someone touched on the arm and shouted directly into her ear. 'He's all right, Ellie, just knocked out for a few minutes. The doc's checked him over and he's conscious.'

The interior of an Anson was too cramped for her to see for herself. There was only room for the nine passengers and their parachutes if they remained seated. Moments later Jack was back beside her looking none the worse for his experience. He put his mouth next to her ear.

'Ellie, I'm fine. Banged my head when I fell but nothing else is damaged apart from my dignity.'

She couldn't stop the tears of relief. He put his arm around her and held her close whilst she sobbed into his shoulder. The Anson landed at White Waltham to allow the men to get off and then took off again to take them to Hamble.

By the time they landed a second time she was fully recovered. It was now dark and Jim would have to overnight here.

'Thank you for an eventful flight, Jim, it's one I won't forget in a hurry,' she said.

'Sorry about your head, Jack, but I had to...'

'Forget it, mate, you did the right thing.'

'Do you have anywhere to stay tonight, Jim?' Ellie asked quite prepared to invite him to come back with them.

The pilot smiled and nodded. 'I've arranged for a billet in the local pub. Your CO wanted me here for taxiing duties tomorrow anyway. You heading for the canteen?'

'We are – why don't you join us?' Jack said.

They enjoyed a tasty supper of stew and jacket potatoes followed by spotted dick and custard. All washed down with two mugs of strong tea.

They were the last to leave the canteen and offered to help stack the chairs but were waved away with a smile.

'We've still got to collect our things and walk back to the cottage. Are you quite sure you feel well enough to do that, Jack?'

A pinprick of light flashed in their eyes. 'Jack, Ellie, I'll run you back. It's the least I can do after all the excitement and the fact that you gave up your leave to help me out.'

'Alison, have you been waiting for us? That's so kind. You should have fetched us from the canteen as we were just sitting there chatting.'

'I finished my paperwork whilst you were eating. The car's over there and your bags are already inside.'

They arrived at the cottage a few minutes later to find that Amanda and Nigel were there before them. This meant Jack had no alternative but to sleep in her bedroom and she'd decided she really didn't want to pre-empt their marriage.

'Jack, shall we get married immediately? I do want to sleep with you but I want to be your wife first.'

Seventeen

Jack dropped his kitbag and with one arm snatched Ellie up and swung her around. His triumphant shout brought Amanda to the front door. He could see her silhouette in the darkness. He ignored her.

'If I was still in the RAF the padre could marry us. I can't believe you've changed your mind. I love you so much and I promise I'll not let you down.'

'I'm sure you won't, darling, but put me down please. Let's go in and decide how and when our wedding's going to take place.'

The torch was somewhere on the ground, the tiny beam pointing towards the cottage. For some reason it seemed to be moving about. Spinning around hadn't been the best idea after banging his head. He was dizzy and didn't want to collapse out here and leave the girls to drag him inside. He dropped Ellie and gritted his teeth. For some reason his feet didn't want to go in the right direction. His legs were baggy. A wave of nausea overtook him and he just managed to turn away from the front door before he threw up.

From a distance he could hear voices then he was thrown over someone's shoulder and his world went black.

He opened his eyes to find Ellie hovering by his bedside. 'Thank God. Doctor Pearson said if you didn't come round he was going to send for the ambulance.'

A man moved into his line of vision. 'Right ho, young man, you have a nasty concussion. Nothing life-threatening. Bed rest for the next few days. I'll call again tomorrow morning. If he becomes comatose again call an ambulance.'

The two of them moved away. He drifted back to sleep and when he woke a second time, she was asleep in the chair beside him. The curtains were drawn, the blackout still up, and the bedside lamp had been put on the floor so it didn't shine in his eyes.

His mouth was dry and his head thumped unpleasantly but apart from that he was okay. Fortunately, she was on his right side and he reached out and touched her arm. She was awake instantly.

'Oh, Jack, thank goodness. I've been so worried about you. How do you feel?'

'I'm okay. I could do with a drink of water if there's any up here.'

'Small sips, the doctor said you mustn't have too much to drink and nothing to eat today.' She held the glass to his mouth and he swallowed a few mouthfuls.

'What's the time?'

'Three o'clock – you've been asleep for hours.'

'I don't want you sitting on that chair. Get in beside me. I promise your virtue's in no danger at the moment.' Only then did he see that he was undressed. In fact, in his birthday suit. No wonder she hesitated.

'Don't come between the sheets. Just lie on the top and pull the bedspread over you.' Talking was becoming more difficult. The light hurt his eyes He was drifting off again but wasn't going to pass out until she was safe beside him.

'If you're sure, I'll do that. I won't bother to undress.' The bed dipped, blessed darkness filled the room and from somewhere he found the energy to speak to her again. 'I'm sorry.'

She smoothed his hair and dropped a light kiss on his forehead. 'Don't be silly. I'm just glad Nigel was here to carry you in.'

It took a further two days before he was well enough to get up. The cottage was silent – Ellie, Amanda and Nigel were back at work. He was on sick leave until the quack signed him off. He swung his legs to the floor and stood up. His head remained clear. So far so good.

He hated the fact that he'd had to piss in a pot and Ellie had had to empty it. He rubbed his fingers over his chin. He needed a bath and a shave and then he'd find something to eat.

He heard movement in the kitchen and froze. Then the cheerful face of Ellie's neighbour appeared in the doorway.

'Good heavens, Jack, you weren't supposed to get up today. I was just about to bring you up some breakfast.'

'I feel great, thanks, and whatever you're making I'm ready to eat it. I need to get back to White Waltham today.'

'You'll do no such thing, young man. Ellie left you a letter – you sit down and I'll give it to you.'

Obediently he took a seat at the kitchen table and she handed him the folded paper.

Jack,

The doctor said you can't return to work for a week. Flying with a concussion would be dangerous for you and the aircraft.

I'll be back this evening and we can start making wedding plans. I've written to Dad and Mabel and Mum and George. We can't marry from Glebe Farm but I thought we could get married in St Albans. That's far enough away from London.

I love you.
Ellie

How typically Ellie – practical and unsentimental, but that was one of the reasons he loved her. No slushy romantic nonsense from her. She got to the point as always. Her suggestion that they marry in St Albans suited him just fine. His lips curved. He hoped she wasn't thinking of the cathedral as that would be a bit too grand for him.

A plate of scrambled eggs and toast was placed in front of him and he devoured it enthusiastically. He'd not eaten anything solid for three days. Ada plied him with hot toast and mugs of tea until he was full.

'That was great. Did Ellie tell you to keep an eye on me?'

'She did, but you're a sensible young man and I'm sure you're not going to do anything silly like return to work.'

'I've no intention of leaving here for another day at least. Thank you for the splendid breakfast.'

'I'll be getting along then after I've tidied up.'

'No, I'll do that. You've done more than enough.'

'If you're sure you can manage…'

'Having one arm doesn't stop me washing up, Ada. It just takes me longer.'

Ellie's neighbour bustled off, leaving him to put the kitchen back the way it should be. He pottered about the cottage for a while and then decided he would have a kip so he was on top form when Ellie got back.

He could hardly believe his luck. The most beautiful girl in the world finally loved him and would soon be his wife. He'd opened the bedroom window when he'd got up to air the room and he heard something bang upstairs. The wind had got up. He frowned at the thought of his beloved being buffeted by an unexpected storm.

No point in getting het up. She was a better flyer than him now and would cope with anything the elements threw at her. Whatever kite she was delivering she would get it to its destination safely. The window had become unlatched and was swinging back and forth making the clatter he'd heard downstairs.

After pulling it closed, he decided to draw the blackouts and the curtains just in case he slept longer than he thought and it was dark when he woke up. He'd been told that his lounge suit and shirts were hanging in her wardrobe. He'd better check that his uniform was fit to wear as he would need it tomorrow.

All his clothes were pristine. Someone had sponged his jacket clean and his two uniform shirts had been laundered and pressed. His eye was caught by the box pushed to the back shelf above the clothes. Curious he turned it round and saw it had come from Dunlop's solicitors. He had no intention of opening it but would certainly ask her what was in it when she returned.

Ellie's final delivery of the day was to take a Hurricane to Kenley. She hadn't flown one for a while but she was very familiar with this fighter's idiosyncrasies. The fact that this had been the aircraft Jack had flown made the flight more enjoyable.

She took off smoothly but the undercarriage refused to retract correctly. The starboard leg had done so, but the port leg remained out. This was one of the problems the Hurricane was infamous for but she'd never encountered it until now.

There was no point in continuing her journey to Kenley unless the undercarriage could be successfully retracted. She tried the emergency routines she'd been taught but to no avail. One leg remained down the other up whatever she tried. She waggled the wings and heaved on the lever. Still no joy. After half an hour trying to get the undercarriage up safely she had only one option left to her.

Her circling of the aerodrome had attracted attention. If she couldn't sort the problem out, she would have to attempt an emergency landing and they had already cleared the runway in readiness for this. She would try a highly irregular and dangerous procedure. She took her hands and feet off everything and grabbed the selector lever.

The fighter zigzagged through the sky as she heaved with both hands. The port wheel came up. That was better than nothing. Despite the danger she was calm. She made a final circuit and performed a smooth crash landing.

The hurricane slithered to a stop on its belly. She released the straps but for some reason she couldn't move. Her heart was pounding, her hands slippery inside their gloves. Then the cockpit was thrown back and she was being lifted out.

'Out you come, miss, don't want to sit in there all day.' Two hefty airmen removed her from the Hurricane and dropped her onto the ground. Her breathing steadied and she was in control again.

'Thank you, but I was quite capable of getting out myself. Whilst you're up there, please could you chuck my overnight bag down?'

The first concern was how much damage had been done to the precious fighter. She stepped back to look and apart from a few scratches she could see nothing untoward.

'Them wheels are a bugger, miss, you did well to land in one piece,' one of the chaps who'd pulled her out said. 'We can sort this out, but it won't be ready to go until tomorrow.'

'Then I suppose I'll have to stay here and wait for it.'

She settled her parachute more firmly on her shoulder and picked up her bag. She'd better report to the office and try and find herself a bed for the night. Three laughing RAF pilots greeted her with a familiar ditty.

'I am in the ATA
I break up whatever I may
I am what I am
And I prang what I can
Whatever they give me today, poop poop!'

This was sung to the tune of 'Popeye the Sailor Man' and she joined in when they sang it a second time. She bowed and they clapped.

'Well done, couldn't have done better myself,' one of them said.

'Thank you. I know the undercarriage is notorious but it's never happened to me before.' She smiled and hurried into the adjutant's office. She had to make a report to Hamble and hopefully someone would take a message to Jack so he wouldn't worry when she failed to return.

She reported the incident and it was noted without comment. A message would be given to Amanda to take to the cottage. She got a decent meal at the Officers' Mess and found a bed in the WAAF's accommodation.

Life was usually fairly uneventful, but now she'd experienced two potentially fatal incidents in quick succession. This just confirmed her determination to marry the man she loved at the earliest opportunity. This horrible war could go on for years even with the arrival of the Americans. Jack had already lost his arm fighting for his country; he deserved to have some happiness in his life.

When she'd left that morning he'd been sleeping peacefully beside her. She was certain he wouldn't hang about to wait for her return but would leave and report for duty at White Waltham tomorrow. This meant their wedding plans would have to be arranged by letter unless she was given a delivery to his pool. This was quite possible, as now aircraft that were needed further north had to be delivered to White Waltham and ferried on from there.

*

As expected, when she eventually returned home, Jack had gone but he'd left her a letter.

Darling,

I'm not a malingerer so have returned to duty. Don't worry, I'm fighting fit but will get checked out by the doc and get a clean bill of health before I resume flying. I think it a great idea to marry at St Albans as long as it's not in the cathedral!

Another suggestion for you to consider – we could go to the nearest registry office next time you're here. You don't need to give notice anymore. I'll understand if you want to wait until we can have a proper do but you know how I feel.

What's in the box from Dunlop's solicitors? I didn't look but am curious.

I love you and knowing that you return my feelings makes the world a brighter place.

Jack

Good grief! Thank goodness he didn't look inside or he might have got the wrong idea. She would always have fond memories of her first love but it bore no comparison to how she felt about Jack.

The sound of a car pulling up outside made her go to the front door. It was Amanda who'd persuaded the local farmer to give her a lift. Her friend waved and with her overnight bag in one hand ran down the path and flung her arms around her.

'I can't tell you how glad I am to see you in one piece. You could have gone for a Burton the other day.'

'Are you talking about almost being shot down by German fighters or the incident with the Hurricane's undercarriage?'

There was so much news to exchange that Ellie didn't get to bed until midnight. Amanda had also decided to legalise her relationship with Nigel and they were going to avoid any unnecessary fuss and pop into the nearest registry office.

'Why don't we have a double do? Not St Albans but somewhere midway between the four of us – like Oxford.'

'Amanda, that's a splendid idea. Do you think the men will agree?'

'If it means no parents, speeches or fuss, they will be thrilled.'

Being married anywhere but in a church would have been unthinkable before the war but things had changed. She would be married in her uniform and there would be no reception. It was a relief not to have to worry about finding a pretty frock. In fact, there wouldn't even be guests. Amanda and Nigel would witness her marriage and she and Jack would witness theirs. She was sure her parents would understand and just be happy for her. She doubted that Amanda's family would feel the same but that wasn't her problem.

Before she turned out the light, she wrote a quick note to Jack telling him what she wanted him to do. Nigel was based at Hatfield; she and her friend were at Hamble and Jack was in the middle at White Waltham. Therefore, it made sense for him to arrange things at the nearest registry office to his base – which would be in Oxford probably.

She would inform her mother and Fred and Mabel after the event – not before. Amanda intended to do the same. It couldn't be simpler – she didn't even need to worry about who to invite or how to find enough food to feed a room full of guests.

When Jack presented himself to the medic he was told he couldn't fly for another two days, which was a damned nuisance. He should have remained at the cottage and spent the time with Ellie. Sod's law and nothing he could do about it. Frankie was overjoyed to have him back early even if he couldn't resume delivery duties.

'You can take over from me for a couple of days – we were the same rank in the RAF – you've been here long enough to know the ropes. I'm needed for an op and thought I wouldn't be able to do it.'

'Okay – I'd rather be busy, even on admin duties, than sitting about doing bugger all.'

He rather enjoyed being in charge but was eager to get back to flying as soon as possible. A letter arrived from Ellie that tilted his world. He couldn't believe his luck – he was perfectly positioned to make phone calls at the moment. He could also, in his temporary capacity as CO, speak to Hatfield and Hamble and coordinate leave for the four of them.

Saturday 13th June would be his wedding day. More than three weeks away but the first date that all of them could be here. The necessary paperwork had to be completed in advance and he didn't have the details for Amanda or Nigel. He'd left a message for both of them to contact the registry office in Oxford as soon as possible.

He put the receiver down and couldn't stop smiling. His obvious happiness was noted by one of the many admin blokes. When he explained he was thumped on the back and congratulated.

'You can't have a double wedding with our fellow ATA members without a knees-up afterwards. I know you don't want a fuss but, if we all chip in for the sandwiches and beer it won't cost you a penny,' Norman, a balding bloke in his fifties, said.

Before he could prevent it, word spread and it appeared that anyone and everyone had invited themselves to the wedding and the party afterwards. God knows what the others would think – but as long as he and Ellie were married on the 13th, he didn't care what happened afterwards.

Eighteen

Two days after writing to Jack she was called to the telephone in the admin office. The chits weren't ready as it was still early so nobody objected to her taking a call.

'It's your young man, I recognise his voice,' Jenny said with her hand over the mouthpiece.

'Jack, is something wrong? I thought we didn't ring except in an emergency.'

'Hi, sweetheart, nothing wrong and no emergency although it is something we have to talk about immediately. I've an awful feeling you and Amanda are not going to be very pleased with me.'

'What have you done? Have you booked the ceremony at some ungodly hour?'

He chuckled. 'No, two o'clock on the 13th, it's not that. I suppose I'd better come clean. The past two days I've been acting CO, which meant I was able to use the telephone to arrange things. The downside of this meant that everyone at the base knows about the weddings.'

She had a good idea what he was going to say next but left him to flounder. 'Go on, I'm listening.'

'It's like this, it seems that now we've got at least fifty guests to both the ceremony and the reception. I know you said you didn't want any fuss but the occasion is unique. Four ATA pilots getting married at the same time demands a celebration of some sort.'

'As long as I don't have to organise anything then I'm actually pleased. I'm sure Amanda will feel the same. Where on earth are we going to hold a party for so many?'

'One of the guys has booked a room at a pub close to the Town Hall. They will supply the alcohol, tea and soft drinks but we've got to find our own spread. I've got a list pinned up on the board and everyone who's coming is writing down what they can contribute.'

'That sounds absolutely splendid. You can spend as much as you need to. I'm sure, just this once, we can splash out on luxury items from under the counter.'

'You're not cross with me for blabbing our business all over the shop?'

'I'm delighted we're going to give the ATA an excuse to have a party. There have been sixteen fatalities so far this year – we all need cheering up. Don't worry, I'm sure that Amanda and Nigel will be equally pleased. What neither of us wanted was anything formal, elderly relatives, speeches and so on. It will be so much better with just people like us.'

'You'll never believe it but Dora, who runs the canteen here, is going to contribute a wedding cake. It won't be fruit, but it will be delicious if it's anything like her other bakes.'

'Less than two weeks and I'll be Mrs Reynolds. It's a good thing there's no objection to married women in the ATA. Do you know there are even a couple of grandmothers, let alone mothers, on the books?'

'It doesn't surprise me. I stopped thinking of women as the weaker sex a long time ago. I'd better go, I'm delivering Spits to Scotland again today. They arrived here yesterday. Do you know what you're doing?'

'Alison said it should be Wellingtons to Lincolnshire. That'll be fun – I've not flown many of them so far. The last time I delivered one the RAF officer receiving refused to believe I was the pilot then actually had the barefaced cheek to climb into the plane in order to check a man wasn't hiding in the cockpit.'

'God knows what that idiot would think if one of the other girls delivered a bomber. You're taller than most of them.'

'That's true, but I'm still one of the youngest. I'd better go, the chits are out and I want to tell Amanda your good news.'

'Let's hope she and Nigel think it *is* good news. I have a sinking feeling we'll get a lot more than fifty turning up. Probably guys we've never even spoken to.'

'The more the merrier. As long as they contribute to the buffet and the beer doesn't run out, it'll be a wonderful celebration.'

She hastily dropped the receiver and rushed out as she saw Amanda at the door. She'd neglected to say goodbye to Jack – but he'd understand.

Her friend took the news well. 'I'm absolutely fine about it – don't look so worried. Jack's right though, anyone within fifty miles of Oxford with a few hours free will turn up.' She laughed and slung her parachute over her shoulder. 'God knows what mysterious items will arrive on our buffet table.'

The Anson dropped Ellie at the MU where the repaired Vickers Wellington was waiting to be returned to a base in Lincolnshire. These medium bombers were being replaced by the larger and faster Lancaster and Halifax so she wasn't sure how many more times she would get the opportunity to deliver one.

She went through her preflight checks oblivious to the stunned expressions of the ground mechanics who'd reluctantly handed over the kite to a girl. This was the third time she'd flown a Wellington and she foresaw no problems ahead. The Met report was excellent and after Jack's excellent instruction on how to use the instruments she was confident she could fly through bad weather without coming to grief.

However, she'd be a good girl and land at the nearest airfield as instructed and not attempt to continue unless visibility deteriorated so fast she had no other option.

Take-off was perfect, she retracted the undercarriage and climbed the regulation 2,000 feet and headed for East Anglia. This lumbering bomber was relatively easy to fly and the cockpit gave her a clearer view of the surrounding countryside. Trying to peer over the nose of a fighter was almost impossible for her, so she had to look sideways in order to know where she was.

Finding the correct airfield when there were so many proved more difficult than she'd expected. Every third field was an airstrip and the way they'd been camouflaged was nothing short of miraculous. Runways were sometimes covered with green and brown wood chips in a random pattern to disguise the strip. One airfield even dyed them blue and put them down in a meandering pattern to represent a stream. Hedges might be painted on the grass with bands of oil or maybe tar. Excellent camouflage from a distance, but obvious when you got closer.

The landing was as good as her take-off had been. This time she was received without comment and handed the paperwork to return a damaged aircraft to the same MU she'd just left.

Eventually she returned to Hamble, having spent more than five hours in the air and an equal amount messing around on the ground getting the necessary paperwork in order. At least she'd got home whilst the canteen was still serving hot food.

'Ellie, what a spiffing idea to have a double wedding and invite everybody,' Pamela trilled as she walked in.

Amanda was waiting for her and beckoned. 'Sorry, old bean, I only mentioned it to one person and word spread like wildfire.'

'Golly, I'm not sure just how big this room is at the pub. Let's hope the weather stays fine and there's a garden for the overflow.'

'Sit down, I'll get you beans on toast – that's all they've got left.'

Whilst her friend went to fetch her something to eat Ellie was beginning to have serious reservations about this impromptu wedding.

During the two weeks leading up to the big day, Jack was forced to spend several nights away from his digs and had no opportunity to contact Ellie. Three days before the event he returned to White Waltham oil-stained and knackered.

He'd lost count of the number of severely damaged fighters he'd ferried from MUs and their counterparts that he'd returned to their respective bases.

He hadn't eaten since the night before and the canteen was closed, which didn't improve his mood. Flying in the summer months continued long past the hours worked by the civilian staff. He'd been the last to land – the Hurry would be delivered to Kenley tomorrow. That would be his last delivery before the ceremony and two days' leave. If his bicycle had been missing, he'd have lost his rag, but it was propped against the wall where he'd left it.

Thank God it wouldn't be too dark to see for another hour at least. He didn't fancy pedalling two miles when the sun had set, as there'd be no moon tonight. His landlady took one look at him and shooed him upstairs.

'Off you go, Jack love, you look done in. Noisy crowd in the bar tonight, mostly locals – you don't want to go in there. I'll bring you up a nice bit of supper and a pot of tea. There should be enough hot water for you to have wash.'

'Thanks, you spoil me. Have there been any messages?'

'A few, but none from your young lady so don't worry about it now.'

Jack stripped off in the bathroom, dropping his filthy clothes on the lino. The water was tepid but he was too bloody tired to care. A proper bath would have been great, but sitting in the allotted five inches didn't appeal to him.

He almost fell on his face when he bent down to scoop up his discarded garments. The sound of snoring echoed from the neighbouring door – one of his fellow ATA pilots had retired early. No doubt he too had been working non-stop.

He preferred to sleep naked, but communal living meant wearing pyjama pants was essential. He hadn't had the time or energy to wash his hair and he could feel the grit and grease embedded in it when he ran his hand through.

'Here you are, love, get this down you and then get some kip. They work you boys too hard.' Vera put a laden tray down on top of the chest of drawers. 'Nice bit of Woolton pie, bubble and squeak followed by jam roly-poly. Plenty of tea to wash it down.'

'Just what the doctor ordered. Thanks, I'll bring the tray down tomorrow.'

She shook her head as she gathered up his laundry. 'You'll do no such thing. Leave it where it is and my girl will bring it down when you've gone.'

He wolfed everything and drained every last drop of tea. He fell on top of the bed and was asleep before his head hit the pillow.

He had an inbuilt alarm that woke him at six o'clock regardless of what time he'd gone to bed. The freshly pressed uniform he would be wearing tomorrow was hanging in the wardrobe. In some ways he was sad Ellie wouldn't have the opportunity to wear a pretty frock – but she would look stunning in a flour sack.

There'd been no opportunity to visit the venue but he'd been assured by several guys that he wouldn't be disappointed and neither would she. God knows what would arrive on the buffet table, but as long as it was plentiful nobody would mind.

As he was pedalling furiously towards the airfield he remembered Vera had said there were several messages. They would have to wait until he got back this afternoon.

Frankie was allowing him an extra half a day in honour of the occasion.

He didn't need to go into the office to collect any paperwork as the Hurry was a continuation of yesterday. The short flip to Kenley was a pleasure. He did the required circuit and waited for the green light giving him permission to land.

It seemed like another life when he had been stationed here and he no longer felt an affinity to the place. He looked at his watch and saw he had plenty of time to grab a cuppa and a wad before the Anson arrived to take him back.

The place was different nowadays – more relaxed – the blokes had fewer sorties to fly as the Jerries no longer came every day. Once the Yanks were up and running there'd be more to do but it would take them a few months to establish themselves, build their airstrips and the necessary accommodation for the GIs. They couldn't land their massive bomber, the Boeing B-17G, known as the Flying Fortress, until proper concrete runways were built. A lot of the RAF strips were still grass. Fighters could land on anything but heavy kites needed real strips.

Jack didn't think twice when the taxi pilot said he had a pickup to do before he could drop him off at White Waltham. They'd scarcely been airborne for fifteen minutes when they were circling to land at Hornchurch.

The pilot turned with a friendly smile. 'Half a dozen Spits coming here and I've to wait for everyone. Can't see anybody waiting so it might be some time. You might as well stretch your legs – I won't leave without you.'

'Okay. I'll take a stroll around the apron. Don't get enough fresh air.'

He smiled wryly. The smell of burning rubber, aviation fuel and cordite predominated. In the relative calm he could hear birds singing and he enjoyed the sun on his face. He knew better than to get in the way of the erks who kept the fighters airborne. Ground mechanics were best left to get on with their work unhindered and he didn't want to fraternise with the brown jobs manning the anti-aircraft guns around the perimeter. Soldiers were a tough lot and had no time for the 'soft boys' of the RAF or ATA.

He found himself a comfortable spot out of everybody's way but from where he could keep an eye on the Anson. He took off his jacket and decided against sitting on it. He would fold it instead and lean his head on it.

As he watched four of the expected six Spitfires landed. All the flyers were female but he couldn't identify any of them from this distance. The unmistakable sound of the last two fighters arriving meant it was time to tidy his appearance and wander across to join the waiting group.

There was a slight scuffle behind him. A searing pain on the back of his head and the lights went out.

Saturday, 13th June arrived like any other. Ellie rather thought she should have woken bathed in a beam of morning sunlight. Tonight she would be a new person; Ellie Simpson wouldn't exist. She wasn't sure about being referred to in future as 'Mrs Jack Reynolds' – maybe she could remain 2nd Officer Simpson for the duration?

She stretched and her skin tingled with anticipation at the thought of making love with Jack. She leaped out of bed and ran to the door. 'Amanda, do you want first bath or shall I go?'

A sleepy voice replied from next door. 'You go. Leave me some hot water.'

Ellie had washed her hair last evening and put it in pin curls. She patted her head. It was still damp. They had to be at the pool in an hour and a half so she couldn't leave it to dry. It would have to be up as usual.

Neither she nor her friend wanted breakfast. In their best uniforms they pedalled sedately to catch the Anson laid on especially for them and the four other girls who had the day off. Their overnight bags had been packed and left in the locker room yesterday.

'Are you nervous? I am.'

'Terrified, Ellie. The thought of committing myself to one man for the rest of my life is what scares me.'

She giggled and wobbled dangerously. 'Maybe that only applies if one's married in church. Do you know what we have to say? None of that *honour and obey* and *death do us part* stuff surely?'

'Not the foggiest. I expect they'll have to do the *does anyone here know of any impediment* bit. I expect there'll be something about exchange of rings and we'll have to say *I do*, but apart from that it's anybody's guess.'

'Did you know the legal limit of guests allowed at a reception is forty? I've a horrible feeling we might have double that if everyone who's spoken to me actually turns up.'

'That's not our problem, Ellie. All the bride has to do is look pretty and smile. By the way have you thought about photographs?'

'I'm sure Jack will have arranged something. Photographic materials are in short supply but one of the guests is bound to be someone with a pocket Brownie who can take a few snaps for posterity.'

Ellie had something important to ask and this was the last opportunity she'd have for such a personal question. She braked and got off her bike and leaned it against a five-barred gate.

'Amanda, I really don't want to have a baby before the end of the war. You and Nigel have been together for ages – how do you avoid unwanted pregnancies?'

'If you avoid the middle of your cycle…'

She couldn't help looking at the bike and her friend snorted with laughter. 'Your menstrual cycle, not that one. We only make love either side of my monthlies – I'm as regular as clockwork – and so far that's been jolly effective.' Amanda pulled a face. 'There are things a man can put on but I don't recommend them.'

Ellie didn't like to ask why not. 'I'm due the day after tomorrow and like you I'm always on time. I'll keep my fingers crossed it works as well for me as it has done for you.'

'It's all a bit of a lark, don't you think? I don't suppose Jack has managed to organise any champers for the toast. If there are as many people turning up as you think I expect the pub will run out of beer.'

'As long as there's plenty of tea I can't see the uninvited guests complaining. I still feel a bit bad not telling my family – what about you?'

'Pa will be happy he hasn't had to foot the bill but Ma will take umbrage. I'm twenty-five. Perfectly capable of making my own decisions. After all, in the ATA we're treated equally with the men and do the same job thanks to Pauline Gower. I shouldn't think there are any other women in a similar position.'

'Amazing to think we only got the vote just over ten years ago. Look at us now.'

Nineteen

The Anson taxied to a standstill at White Waltham and Ellie, Amanda and the others who'd accompanied them headed for the admin building.

'Jack said he'd arranged transport for us. I suppose he and Nigel will already be there as it's supposed to be bad luck for brides and grooms to meet before the ceremony,' Amanda said.

'It's only an hour to Oxford so we've got plenty of time to catch a bus if necessary.'

Her friend grabbed her arm. 'There's a chap in a dreadful suit heading this way. Do you know who it is?'

Ellie's stomach churned. She knew exactly who it was and if Mainwaring was here it couldn't be good news. She pinned on a smile. 'You and the girls go ahead, I'll speak to him. I think that's your transport waiting and there isn't room for all of us in it anyway.'

Amanda didn't argue. 'I expect that chap will drive you. See you in an hour.'

Jack's nemesis waited until they were alone before he spoke. 'I tried to contact you but you'd already taken off. I've got bad news. Jack didn't return yesterday. He was supposed to come in the taxi. They waited for half an hour for him but then had to leave.'

She swallowed the lump in her throat. Her brain refused to function and she couldn't think of anything sensible to say.

'We can't talk out here. There's an office we can use.'

He put his arm around her shoulders but she shrugged him off. She didn't want his sympathy. If something had happened to Jack it was this man's fault. He ushered her into an empty room and a few moments later a girl in uniform brought in a tray of tea and biscuits.

Ellie removed her jacket and took one of the chairs. Her heart was thudding uncomfortably; her hands were clammy. She sent up a fervent prayer to a God she didn't really believe in that Jack was safe. Whilst she waited for Mainwaring to pour her a cup of tea, she attempted to steady her breathing. He placed it on the edge of the desk where she could reach it, before taking a seat at the other end.

'We thought you were both protected. Jack had an hour's wait at Hornchurch and somehow the bastards must have got to him.' He cleared his throat and ran his finger around his collar. 'We found traces of blood where he was sitting but no sign of him anywhere on the base. I've got every man available searching for him.'

'When did this happen?' Her voice was commendably firm.

'Yesterday afternoon.'

For a second she was unable to take this in. Jack had been missing since yesterday and nobody had thought to tell her? She surged to her feet, and was tempted to throw the cup, saucer and contents in his face. Instead she just dropped it on the floor. Scalding tea and broken crockery landed on his immaculate trouser cuffs.

Immediately she regretted her actions. 'I'm so sorry.' Ellie grabbed the handkerchief that was poking out of his jacket pocket and dropped to her knees to remove the shards of china.

To her astonishment he half-smiled. 'I deserved that. No, don't bother, no serious damage done. Please sit down so we can finish talking.'

She added an extra spoonful of sugar to the remaining cup and held it out. He drank it without comment. 'I forgot to ask – did the tea burn you?'

'No, all tickety-boo in that department. Now, if you've quite finished there are things I didn't get a chance to tell you.'

She flushed at his mild reprimand and hastily resumed her seat. 'I'm not a violent person as a rule but...'

'Enough. The matter is closed. We received a demand from the kidnappers this morning, which is why I'm here. If the charges are dropped then they will hand over Squadron Leader Reynolds.'

She leaned forward. 'I don't see how telling me that makes things any better. Those villains aren't going to be released from custody.' She was unable to continue. She blinked back tears. 'Jack will only remain alive as long as they think you're going to do as they ask. I'm right, aren't I?'

'Exactly so. However, I'm confident the combined efforts of Scotland Yard and my department will be able to locate and return him safely to you.' He nodded as if that would convince her. 'Squadron Leader Reynolds is a resourceful young man. He might very well find a way to get free without our help.'

She was angered by his stupidity. 'If he had both hands, maybe, but he doesn't. We were supposed to be getting married today...'

She gulped and turned her back on him, not wishing him to see her face. She straightened her shoulders and put her head back. She was an officer in the ATA, not a silly schoolgirl.

'There are things I need to do. Please excuse me.' She marched from the room, determined to speak to Amanda if she could. She hurtled through the building in the hope that the car might still be there. It was and Amanda was standing beside it obviously waiting for her.

Ellie quickly explained the circumstances. 'You must go ahead with your wedding. I'm not sure what you can tell the guests. They will probably think that one of us got cold feet.'

'I'll tell them the truth. Jack's been abducted by some London criminals. It's not an official secret, is it?'

'I don't think so. Mainwaring won't be happy but... but do it anyway. Have a wonderful wedding day.'

Her friend hugged her. 'Chin up, old thing. You and Jack have been through so much together. We'll be dancing at your own wedding in a week or two.'

Watching the car drive away was almost too much. She stood in the sunshine trying to make sense of what had happened. Jack wasn't dead. He couldn't be. He was her life, her happiness, and she refused to believe he was gone.

Jack woke up. What the hell had happened? Where was he? Who could he hear talking on the other side of the room?

Some instinct made him remain slack, his eyes closed as if still unconscious. Slowly his brain started to function despite the filthy headache.

He tensed and relaxed his muscles and to his surprise discovered he wasn't tied or gagged. His momentary elation vanished. There could only be one reason why they hadn't bothered to restrain him – he was somewhere he couldn't escape from and where no one would come if he yelled for help.

He listened carefully. There were at least three men and from their accents they were Londoners. No point in dwelling on how they'd managed to get onto the base or how they'd got him off without detection. The fact that he wasn't already dead meant they needed him alive.

There was only one reason for this – they were holding him to ransom. His life and freedom in exchange for those that had been arrested because of Joe. The authorities would never agree to such an exchange. If he was going to get out of this alive he'd have to do it himself.

He focused on the voices. What he heard confirmed what he'd deduced. He'd been out of it for a few hours – it was now evening. Had anyone missed him yet? What would Mainwaring do? Ellie would be happily preparing for their wedding tomorrow, blissfully unaware that it couldn't now take place.

These men were the guards and thought a one-armed man no threat to them. No doubt they had guns and wouldn't hesitate to shoot him. One of the men was told to get fish and chips and he heard the door open and close.

Footsteps approached. He was kicked in the ribs.

'We know you're awake, you bastard. Sit up, I want to talk to you.' The speaker kicked him again to make his point.

No use pretending. He groaned as if in more pain than he actually was, and then very slowly used his elbows to prise his shoulders from the boards. Once he was leaning against the wall, he opened his eyes and groaned again.

He hadn't heard this man speak before. His diction was posh. Strange, his clothes were scruffy and he was unshaven.

'You know why you're here. You'll stay alive as long as I think you're useful.'

Jack knew better than to answer – whatever he said would only inflame the situation. Instead he nodded and then dropped his head, hoping this gesture would convince the man he was no danger to them.

'You move, you die. Got it?' This question was reinforced by a vicious kick in the ribs.

'Got it,' Jack managed to answer despite the agony that ripped through him. At least one rib had fractured that time. This was going to make it bloody difficult to escape but if he didn't, he would be dead anyway.

Mercifully, he was left alone to gather his thoughts. The guy masquerading as an East Ender was obviously the leader. There was no point in even contemplating a move if he was in the room.

He slowed his breathing and this eased the pain in his side. He must've been out for hours so most likely had a concussion as well. His mouth was dry. He could do with a drink but wasn't going to get one.

It had to be dark outside as the blackouts were drawn but it couldn't be that late if the fish and chip shop was still serving. His stomach growled. Fat chance of him being fed.

He dozed for a bit and was then jerked awake when someone came in. The appetising smell of hot chips and vinegar drifted his way. His mouth watered – at least it wasn't so dry now.

Knowing he was possibly listening to their conversation the three men spoke in muted voices so he couldn't hear what was being said. He guessed that at least one of the men would remain in the room, but he hoped the posh guy wouldn't stay overnight.

He just had to stay alive until either he got the opportunity to escape, or the spooks or Scotland Yard rescued him. Had the ransom note already gone out? How long would these criminals wait before they realised their demands weren't going to be met?

Maybe he'd got twenty-four hours, but realistically he doubted he had that long. Lying down wasn't an option with fractured ribs so if he wanted any kip, he'd have to do it propped against the wall the way he was at the moment. During the Battle of Britain he'd learned to catch sleep when he could – they all did. They couldn't have continued to fly constant sorties otherwise.

When he next opened his eyes the room was quiet, not even the murmur of voices coming from the table on the far side of the room. The main light, if a single light bulb hanging from a flex could be called this, had been turned out. The only illumination was from a table lamp.

Despite his desperate situation his mouth twitched. Table lamps were for front rooms in suburban semis – not for a den of hardened criminals. As his eyes adjusted to the gloom, he saw there was only one guard left and he was slumped across the table.

Was he asleep? Drunk? There was certainly the smell of alcohol in the room. Surely, the bloke would be snoring if this was the case? He narrowed his eyes and focused on the table. Yes – as he'd expected there was a gun within easy reach of the man's hand.

He needed a pee and he was damned if he was going to do it in his pants. At least he had a genuine reason for standing up. If he got up stealthily and the man was awake his movement would be considered a threat. If he just stood up, he might have time to explain he needed the WC before a bullet lodged in his chest. He used the wall to help him upright. The skin between his shoulder blades crawled as he expected a bullet to thump into his back at any moment.

Carefully he swivelled, rolled onto his knees. The man hadn't moved. He would brazen it out. He'd never get another opportunity like this. Perhaps if he didn't walk in the direction of the table the likelihood of being shot lessened?

He turned. His breathing steadied. His head no longer thumped but the slightest movement made him catch his breath. If he didn't move now, he would have to piss on the floor and be forced to sit in the puddle.

The door was directly behind the table. He would have to pass it if he wanted to get out. Every instinct made him want to creep on tiptoes but he walked normally, expecting at any moment to be discovered.

So far so good. Every step was agony – not just from his ribs but also because his bladder was bursting. He reached the table and without thinking snatched up the gun.

Should he crack the man on the head or make good his escape? He decided on the latter and reached the door. The key was on the inside. He snatched it out, stepped through, and rammed it back in the keyhole. He didn't breathe until the lock clicked.

He moved a few steps from the door and then unbuttoned his fly and with a sigh of relief peed on the floor. If all hell had broken loose, he couldn't have stopped. The sound was loud in the darkness but, thank God, nobody came to investigate.

They'd emptied his pockets so he no longer had his identity papers or his trusty torch. He slowly rotated hoping to see a glimmer of light coming from somewhere so he could orientate himself. For some reason he thought he was on an upper floor – in a tenement somewhere in the East End of London.

He shoved the gun into his waistband and, with his arm outstretched, inched his way along the narrow, stinking passage. Suddenly his hand was in empty space. Stairs. He was halfway down when a door opened below. Someone was coming up.

Amanda immediately told the others in the car why Ellie and Jack wouldn't be getting married today.

'Don't look so glum, ladies, I'm certain the powers that be will find him. Now we've got a second wedding to look forward to instead of just one.'

Despite her cheerful comment the atmosphere in the car was more funeral party than wedding.

There were at least two dozen assorted ATA pilots and admin waiting to witness the wedding. The service, if that's what it was called, went past in a blur. All she could think about was Ellie and Jack and how they should have been there too.

Nigel kissed her and, hand in hand, they led the guests down the road to the pub where the wedding breakfast was to be held.

'Good heavens! I've never seen so much food – where did it all come from?'

Nige laughed, delighted at her expression. 'I told everyone to get here early and go round all the cake shops and bakeries in the town and buy anything they could.'

'No one will go hungry, that's for sure. I see you have arranged for beer to be waiting. There must be thirty glasses on the table. Is that orange squash in the jugs? Where did you get that?'

'I'm told it's the welfare orange juice for children. I expect it's better than nothing.'

Jack had thought of everything – there was even a windup record player and a pile of records plus a spotty youth to play them. After several glasses of gin mixed with the orange drink in the jugs, she began to enjoy herself.

It got so crowded people spilled into the pub garden. There must have been well over the regulation forty as the event got into full swing.

There were no toasts, no speeches, no gifts – apart from contributions to the buffet table – just congratulations and smiling faces. Absolutely spiffing!

'Nige, where are we staying tonight? Do you mind if we slip away? I don't think anyone will notice as they're all having such a good time.'

'Absolutely, darling.' He pulled her close and kissed the top of her head. 'I miss them too, but not as much as you do. They should have been here and then today would have been perfect.'

Together they left made their way through the streets to The Royal Oxford Hotel. There would be an empty room there tonight. What must her dearest friend be going through right now? Life could not be so cruel as to take away Ellie's happiness a second time.

Twenty

When Ellie returned to the office it was empty. The tray and broken crockery had also vanished and someone had mopped up the spilt tea as well.

If she kept repeating to herself that Jack was alive, that he would come home to her in one piece, maybe she could get through this without falling apart. If she had her flying gear with her she could volunteer to help out here, but everything was in her locker at Hamble.

As she dithered about in the passageway, she got several sympathetic looks, but no one approached her. Did they know the truth or did they think she'd been jilted?

There was no point in her staying here – wherever Jack was, he wasn't anywhere near Oxford. He had been abducted in Hornchurch so she would try and catch a flip to the Hatfield ferry pool, which was close to the RAF base. That way she would be nearby when he was found. The villains who had taken him were based in the East End of London and it was only a few miles from her first ferry pool to the city.

He wouldn't come out of this unscathed – but hopefully his injuries would be superficial and, in a week or two, he would be fully fit and they could rearrange their wedding. Next time she would get married in her own church, the one the family had attended for generations, and make sure that her mother, brother and Fiona were invited.

For this wedding she would find a traditional, white wedding dress and Jack could wear his smart lounge suit. Thinking positively helped. She would find herself a lift immediately and not hang about waiting for Mainwaring to come back. He wouldn't want her anywhere near London and it would probably be sensible to disappear before he gave her a direct order.

A Tiger Moth was waiting to take off and a helpful RAF chap told her it was going to Hornchurch. She raced across the apron, waving frantically, and the pilot was only too happy to take her.

'Climb in, it's not often I get to fly with a pretty popsy like you,' the young man said with a leer.

'Thank you. Much appreciated.' She scrambled in and settled into the front seat, the one reserved for the passenger or trainee pilot. It was going to be cold without her Sidcot suit and flying jacket, but the weather was mild and she'd flown in far worse in the early days before they had been issued with protection from the elements.

As soon as they took off, she relaxed. The pilot might be an idiot but he was obviously a good flyer. This little kite would always be a favourite as it was the one she'd learned to fly on seven years ago when she was still a schoolgirl.

The landing was as smooth as the take-off and this time her thanks were genuine. Not waiting for him to make another pass at her, she dashed to the admin building, determined to discover how the kidnappers had managed to evade security. First, they'd got onto the base without being seen and, even more extraordinary, they'd then been able to take Jack out.

Someone saw her approaching through the window and came out to meet her.

'Miss Simpson, I cannot tell you how sorry I am about what happened to Squadron Leader Reynolds. Come in, you look frozen. I'll rustle up something hot to drink. Would you like a sandwich or something to go with it?'

She had been about to refuse both but realised she hadn't eaten since the night before and was ravenous.

Over a plate of spam sandwiches and a pot of tea, the adjutant apologised profusely but was unable to explain how the abduction had taken place.

'We're still investigating, of course, and although we've yet to prove it we think it was one of the soldiers on the gun emplacements who was the inside man.'

'I'm guessing they took him out in a vehicle – I've watched the gate on this base and others often enough to know that vehicles are usually just waved through – not searched. They would have been relying on that.'

'Unfortunately, that was the case here. Not anymore. Although I fear that horse has already bolted.'

The conversation lapsed and she munched her indifferent sandwiches and drank the tea – which was somewhat better.

'I need somewhere to stay until this is resolved. Can you find me a billet on the base?'

'I'll do that now.'

He left her alone while he made the arrangements. The telephone rang noisily, making her jump. She picked up the receiver. 'The adjutant's office, Hornchurch.'

'Is that you, Miss Simpson? Mainwaring, here. You shouldn't be there. It isn't safe so close to London.'

'I hardly think they will attempt the same thing a second time. I'm as safe here as anywhere else and I want to be able to get to Jack quickly when they find him.'

'We've heard nothing on the grapevine so far that would indicate Reynolds is still alive.' His words were hardly reassuring but what else could he say in the circumstances?

'You can contact me at this base as I intend to remain where I am. I'm not foolish enough to go to London and attempt to look for him myself.'

'Very well. Stay alert, Miss Simpson, your life might depend upon it.' With that less than encouraging comment the line went dead.

Amanda and Nigel would be married by now and the reception in full swing. She refused to believe that she and Jack wouldn't be together soon.

The adjutant returned with a WAAF. 'If you would like to come with me, ma'am, I'll take you to your billet.'

The female accommodation had only been built recently and was much better than some of the places she'd been obliged to sleep in when a member herself. As expected, she wasn't taken to a communal dormitory but offered a single room. An officer's billet – she might not be in the services but she was a second officer in the ATA with the gold braid to prove it.

'Here you are. The Officers' Mess is in the main block. There's an orderly assigned to this accommodation so you only have to ask if you need anything.' The girl saluted smartly and left Ellie to unpack.

The only nightwear she had with her was the filmy negligée set Amanda had insisted she bought for her wedding night. She put this back in her bag – it wouldn't be worn until she and Jack were married. She would have to sleep in her knickers and bra – not something she was accustomed to doing. Did Jack sleep in pyjamas like the men in her family did? One of the American girls who joined the ATA recently said men over there preferred to sleep with nothing on at all. Jack had adopted some Yankee mannerisms and his conversation was liberally sprinkled with American words. Had he also taken on this risqué habit?

She hung up her spare uniform, put her toilet things out on the shelf above the sink, and she was done. Sitting about twiddling her thumbs wasn't in her nature – there must be something useful she could do whilst she was here.

Nobody wanted her assistance – she wasn't one of them – it wasn't like overnighting at a different ferry pool where she could have worked in the office, answered the phone without a second thought. Fortunately, she discovered a shelf of tatty books in the Mess and took three of them back to her room.

She wasn't hungry so didn't go in search of supper. She retired early and hoped she could sleep away the hours. Waiting was torture. A frantic knocking on the door roused her some hours later.

Jack couldn't go back and certainly not down. Whoever was approaching would have to be silenced. His hand was shaking as he withdrew the gun. He didn't think he could shoot a man in cold blood so would have to knock him out.

His legs were threatening to give way. He had to brazen it out as he had before. He'd passed at least half a dozen closed doors in the passageway so there must be other people living in this tenement.

Somehow, he forced himself continue. It was bad luck to pass someone on the stairs. Would it be his, or the shadowy figure he could see just below?

He turned sideways, grunted a greeting and pushed past. The man responded in the same way and continued, apparently unbothered by finding him on the staircase.

Jack returned the gun to his belt. He probably had only moments to get out of the house before the guy realised who he was. His fingers closed over the key from the door, which he'd dropped into his pocket without thinking.

The man would have to kick the door in to release the other bloke – this should give him a few minutes more. He took the final few steps two at a time and burst out into the street.

His knees buckled and he only prevented himself from crashing to the ground by clutching at a nearby lamp post. Movement of any kind was hideous and jumping those stairs had been stupid.

He couldn't hang about here if he wanted to see his beloved Ellie again. His night vision was excellent, thank God, and despite the lack of light he could make out shapes of buildings on either side of the road.

What was that? He was near the Thames – he could hear the sound of ships moving on the water. If he made his way towards the river he might be lucky and come across a dockyard where he'd probably be safe.

He didn't make the mistake of hurrying. His steps were measured, and became slower and more laboured the further he went. The metallic taste of blood in his mouth told him he was in trouble.

He couldn't go any further. There was a large gate ahead of him. If he could just get that far he could lean against it until the morning and just pray he wasn't found by his captors before then.

Ellie heard the knock and, forgetting she was in her underwear, rushed across the room and flung open the door. The young airman's eyes widened and he turned smartly so he was facing the other way.

'Urgent telephone message for you, ma'am – you must come to the adjutant's office immediately.'

'Give me five minutes.' She slammed the door and was dressed in less than the suggested time. This was achieved by omitting to put on her socks but she doubted anyone noticed.

She'd not stopped to put on her watch either so had no idea of the exact time – she thought she'd been asleep for several hours so it was probably almost dawn. There was one other person in the office, a WAAF who was talking to whoever was on the other end of the line. The receiver was handed to her without comment.

'Miss Simpson, Ellie, Jack's alive. He's at the London Hospital in Whitechapel. I've no idea what shape he's in. I'm sending a car to collect you and it should be with you in the next fifteen minutes.'

She hadn't realised she'd been holding her breath. The world and the roaring in her ears receded for a second. Then she recovered her composure and was able to speak.

'Thank you, Mr Mainwaring. I'll be ready.' She put down the telephone and ran through the deserted building, across the concrete and into her digs.

The car was there when she returned and she tossed her bag in the rear and jumped in behind it. There was a faint red haze on the horizon indicating the sun was on the way up.

Her cheeks were wet, her hands trembling. She had to calm down before they arrived. Jack needed her to be strong, not weep all over him.

The drive was short as the roads were empty at that time of the day. The only delay had been when the driver was obliged to drive around the potholes and debris still not cleared from the last air raid.

She'd expected to get out at the front of the hospital, but the car turned into the ambulance bay at the rear. There was a uniformed policeman waiting at the door.

The hospital was eerily quiet. None of the usual sounds she associated with such a place. It smelt the same – disinfectant and boiled cabbage. The last time she'd set foot in one had been to see Greg just before he died.

Their footsteps echoed down the empty passageway. The policeman made no attempt to talk to her – in fact he was taciturn to the point of rudeness. Like many of the constabulary he was middle-aged. No doubt the younger men had been called up or volunteered for active service.

Small wonder the criminals had taken hold of parts of London and were able to abduct and murder people without being apprehended. The fact that there was a uniformed presence of any sort filled her with foreboding. This could only mean that the authorities still considered Jack to be in danger.

She refused to even contemplate the idea that he was seriously injured. If he had managed to escape from captivity he couldn't be that badly hurt. After walking through endless draughty passageways, up several flights of stairs, she followed her escort through a door. She bit her lip. Ahead of her were two soldiers. They were armed.

There was no sign of Mainwaring so she must have arrived ahead of him. One of the guards nodded and held open the door.

She hadn't been sure what to expect, but certainly not this. Jack was not only alive but sitting up in bed. Apart from a transfusion attached to his arm and a bandage around his head he looked reasonably well. He'd been watching the door and his smile was blinding when he saw her.

'Ellie, darling, I've been praying you'd come.'

She flew across the room, too overcome to speak. She put her arms around him and he flinched. Immediately she sat back.

'I've been so worried. Mainwaring didn't know if you were badly hurt or not. Why are you being guarded? Do they expect you to be attacked in here?'

'I doubt it.'

'Then they must think you're the danger. That doesn't make sense.'

'I don't bloody well care, sweetheart. All that matters is that I'm alive, and you're here.'

She kicked of her shoes, removed her hat and jacket and stretched out beside him, resting her head on his shoulder. 'Tell me what happened and how you managed to get away.'

When he'd finished, she was impressed and horrified in equal measure. 'Thank God the dockers found you so quickly. You might have bled to death or, even worse, been recaptured.'

He chuckled and grimaced. 'Don't make me laugh, honey. It hurts too much.'

For a second, she was puzzled by his laugh then realised what she'd said. 'You know what I mean. Anyway, to have come out with a mild concussion, a few stitches in your head and a couple of broken ribs, is amazing.'

'Don't forget my perforated lung. They're leaving it to heal itself so I'm *hors de combat* for several weeks.'

'That's good news.' He shook his head and smiled. 'You're impossible, Jack Reynolds. Stop making fun of me.' She smoothed a tumble of red hair from his forehead. 'I suppose we'll have to wait for Mainwaring to arrive to discover why there are armed men outside this room.'

She pressed her lips to his. He responded with more passion than she'd expected for an injured man. After several enjoyable minutes she relaxed into his embrace. His left hand was missing but he still had his upper arm.

'Amanda and Nigel enjoyed their day but said it wasn't the same without us.'

'Sorry to have missed it.'

'Idiot. We missed our own wedding – that's far more important.' She settled more comfortably and then continued. 'I want to marry at home, in the church where Neil was buried and Dad and Mabel got married.'

'Good idea. Not sure when I'm out of here but as soon as I am, we can do it. I'll wear my RAF uniform; you wear a pretty frock.'

His breathing slowed and he fell asleep. He'd just managed to stay awake until she got there. With a sigh of happiness and relief she closed her eyes.

Twenty-One

Jack woke, with Ellie still sleeping beside him, to find Mainwaring slumped on a hard wooden chair at the foot of the bed.

'Good, I didn't want to wake either of you. We've found the place you were held. It was, of course, deserted. Can you give me a description of the three men?'

'Only the one who spoke to me – I didn't see the second man at all and only the back of the head of the third.' He told what he knew but was certain it wouldn't be enough to find the perpetrators.

'Ellie told me there's an armed guard outside – is that for my benefit or yours?'

Mainwaring pushed himself upright. 'Good God, you don't think we have you under arrest, do you? It's for your protection. Until you're well enough to go somewhere safe I fear you might be a target. London Hospital is in the centre of Whitechapel.'

'It's going to be several weeks before I'm fit to fly. We want to get married from Glebe Farm…'

'Absolutely not. That's the first place they'll be looking. I've arranged for a couple of my men to masquerade as farm labourers and keep an eye on things down there. Mr and Mrs Simpson flatly refused to leave.'

'Sounds like Fred and Mabel.'

Ellie swung her legs to the boards, fully awake. She had obviously followed the conversation. 'Why would these men still be interested in us? They must realise whatever they do, the men in jail won't be let out.'

'They are vindictive and will be looking for revenge. None of you are safe until this is sorted.'

Jack's happiness deflated. Mainwaring was right – they were nasty buggers and would be looking to murder him or his loved ones now. He would give his life to protect Ellie. Maybe he would have to.

'What about St Albans? My mother, brother and his wife live there.' She ignored the implications and spoke as if everything was fine.

'If you keep the event small, no reason why not. If you can persuade your father and his wife to come that will be one less thing for me to worry about.'

Jack glanced at the door. The nurse was coming in to attend to him.

'Sweetheart, you go with Mainwaring and find yourself some breakfast. Come back in a bit – I'm not going anywhere.'

She smoothed back his hair and kissed his forehead. Her smile was radiant. He was the luckiest guy in the world to be alive and have this wonderful girl in love with him. As they disappeared two white-coated doctors came in. His smile faded at their grim expressions.

'Squadron Leader Reynolds, your last blood test shows that you are bleeding internally. You are going to be prepped for surgery now.'

'I feel okay, I can breathe, so how can I be in trouble?'

'Do you have any pain elsewhere?'

'I hurt everywhere I was kicked, but nothing I wasn't expecting.'

The nurse folded back the crisp sheet and bedspread. Even he could see his stomach was distended. He'd expected it to be purple and blue after the kicking he'd got, but this was different. The medics prodded and poked. He gritted his teeth.

'It's not your broken rib that's causing the problem. I fear it could be your spleen. It will have to come out, young man.'

Things moved fast after that. Before he had time to explain what was happening to Ellie, he was being whisked down the empty corridors to the operating theatre.

A foul-smelling rubber mask was put over his face, he was ordered to count to ten and then the world faded. His last conscious thought was he hoped he woke up again.

Ellie returned to Jack's room to find it empty. She caught the doorjamb to steady herself. God – not again. Her eyes filled and she stumbled into the room to collapse on the bed. Running footsteps echoed in the passageway and a flustered nurse burst in. Nurses didn't run. She feared the worst.

'Miss Simpson, I'm so sorry, I was told to wait here and explain where your fiancé has gone. He's been taken to theatre.'

Tears of relief streamed down Ellie's face. 'What for? Is he going to be all right?' Her voice was punctuated with gulps and snuffles.

'He's a strong man. Mr Benton is the best surgeon we've got. He's in good hands.'

'How long will he be there? What went wrong?' She dried her eyes and blew her nose.

'Internal bleeding. If you would care to accompany me I'll take you to the waiting room set aside for relatives.'

Her pulse had just about returned to normal when she was ushered into the less than welcoming relatives' waiting area. There was sufficient room for a dozen hard wooden chairs to be positioned around the edges of the wall, a small rectangular window too high to look out of, and a light bulb hanging in the centre of the room with no lampshade.

'I don't know how long he will be in theatre, but I think it will be an hour at least. Someone will come and speak to you as soon as he is out.'

Ellie was left alone to her thoughts. Mainwaring hadn't stopped to talk to her but hurried off to do something important. She looked around the bare room and decided not to remain there, but find somewhere more convivial to sit.

There was a small café opposite the hospital where she'd been told she could get some breakfast. It hadn't been open when she'd first looked but should be by now.

She made her way to the front entrance and was about to step out when a man spoke from behind her. She almost went headfirst down the steps.

'Miss Simpson, you must remain inside the hospital at all times. It isn't safe for you on the street.'

She spun to see a military policeman staring down at her. It wasn't one of the soldiers who'd been outside Jack's door earlier.

'It's not me they're interested in. They've never seen me anyway so I'm sure I'm perfectly safe, thank you. I'm going to get some breakfast. You're quite welcome to join me if you wish.'

His expression lightened and he grinned, making him look much younger and less formidable. 'That's a kind offer, ma'am, but I'm afraid I can't allow you to go. Your uniform is too distinctive – it wouldn't take a genius to realise you must be a pal of Squadron Leader Reynolds.'

'How silly of me, I should have worked it out for myself. If I can't go, could you go and get us both a mug of tea and a bun of some sort? I promise I'll remain out of sight whilst you do so.'

He nodded. 'Fair enough. Don't see that breaks any rules.'

She handed him a few shillings and then moved back inside the foyer to watch the nurses hurrying in to take up their duties. In their navy-blue cloaks, stiffly starched white aprons and caps, they looked very businesslike and smart.

Her stomach growled so loudly it was overheard by three of them as they walked past. They looked round and laughed. One of them spoke to her.

'You'll get a good breakfast over the road.'

'Thanks, I'll go across and buy something.'

The policeman returned carrying two steaming mugs in one large hand and two paper bags containing not only buns but also sausage rolls.

'I'll take the food if you'll bring the tea. I did wonder if they'd allow you to bring the tea over here.'

'All tickety-boo, miss, I gave the girl a tanner and she was only too happy to oblige. I'll return them when we're done.'

'There's a nasty little waiting room upstairs – we can take it there. If you've got to stay with me then no one can object to you being in there.'

He dropped the change into her hand with a happy smile. She supposed he didn't often get fed whilst on duty.

She wolfed down the food, which was freshly baked and quite delicious. The sausage meat was probably more breadcrumbs than pork, but nevertheless tasted wonderful. When the last drip of tea was drained, she handed the mug to the waiting soldier.

Whilst he was gone, she went in search of a WC and eventually found one on the ground floor. On her return the soldier was in the passageway. His look of relief was comical.

An interminable time later an elderly, white-coated gentleman appeared accompanied by a bevy of fluttering nurses and junior doctors.

'Ah, Miss Simpson, I presume. I'm delighted to tell you that your young man came through surgery with flying colours. We didn't have to remove his spleen, we repaired the damage and he should be good as new in a few weeks. He will be back from recovery shortly.'

'Thank you so much. Can you tell me when he will be well enough to leave hospital? We were supposed to get married yesterday and I want to rearrange the ceremony whilst he's on sick leave.'

'Good heavens, young lady, he will need at least two weeks in here before he's fit to be discharged. I think your wedding plans will have to be put on hold for a while.'

Jack was still asleep two hours after his return but the nurse assured her this was normal.

'We see it all the time. When a firefighter, ambulance driver, or anyone else who is deprived of sleep, comes in here with an injury they're exhausted and their body takes the opportunity to recuperate by keeping them asleep.'

'Then I shall stretch out beside him and catch up too.' She didn't ask permission and knew she was breaking every rule, but they were in a side room so nobody would be able to see them apart from the nurse.

'You do that, Miss Simpson, you deserve your sleep as much as he does. I'll bring you a blanket and close the door so no one should disturb you. I have to come in and check the patient every half an hour but I won't wake either of you unless I have to.'

Apart from a nagging pain in his belly, Jack decided he was fine. Ellie was sleeping soundly beside him and all was well in his world. Time enough to worry about the bastards who had put him here when he was on his feet again.

Two weeks later he was pronounced ready to leave. His stitches had come out days ago and, as far as he was concerned, he'd been well enough to be discharged last week. Ellie had returned to duty and apart from her daily letters he'd had no contact with her until she arrived this morning.

'Jack, darling, stop prowling around the room. The paperwork will arrive soon,' Ellie said.

'It's not *that* we're waiting for, honey, it's that damned spook. He wants to talk to both of us before we go.'

'I don't care. As soon as your discharge papers arrive, we're leaving. The car's outside and will be moved on if we don't get down there soon.'

'Okay. Mainwaring knows we're going to St Albans so can find us there.'

'By the way, Fiona's wedding dress is now a perfect fit – you'll love it. Dad and Mabel have got your RAF uniform with them. Are you sure you can get married in that, as you aren't officially in the service now? Impersonating a policeman is an offence, you know.'

'I've spoken to Frankie and he cleared it with the bigwigs. It seems exceptions can be made. After all, I'm still referred to by my rank, aren't I?' He grabbed her and kissed her hard. 'I'm more interested in removing my uniform than putting it on, sweetheart.' He couldn't resist teasing her and loved the way her cheeks turned pink at the mention of their wedding night.

They were still entangled when the nurse walked in to give him the necessary papers. She hastily dropped them on the chair and retreated.

'We've had more than enough excitement in our lives, darling, I just hope from now on it's going to be plain sailing – or plain flying I should say.' He released her long enough to pick up the envelope.

'I don't know what the hell happened to my kitbag – it was left at Hornchurch when I was kidnapped.'

'I've got it in the car. Someone brought it to White Waltham first and then I picked it up from there last time I delivered a kite for onward transport up north.'

He was still a bit stiff and sore but didn't think that would be a problem tonight. He still had a further two weeks' sick leave but Ellie only had her regular two days' break before she was back on duty.

As they settled into the back seat of the car she looked at him and, instead of looking happy, she was the reverse.

'I wish we could have invited some of our friends. Amanda and Nigel are going to be really hurt we got married without them – in fact loads of people will be.'

'It can't be helped; until they round up the last of those involved it's just not safe. For all we know they're being watched too.'

She twisted round so she could peer out of the rear window. 'How do we know we're not been followed right now?'

'I'm certain that we are. We're not driving to Oxford as you thought, Mainwaring has arranged for us to transfer to another car and that will take us to the Luton pool. From there we're getting a flip to White Waltham and another car will take us to St Albans.'

'You arranged all that from your hospital bed? Sounds really complicated and it's going to take us far too long. We'll be late for the service.' She paused and then continued. 'What did that man want to say to us? He's obviously fully involved with all this already.'

'Not a clue. The ceremony isn't until four o'clock this afternoon so that gives us plenty of time, as long as you don't spend too long getting ready.'

Her mouth tightened but then she laughed. 'It's a bride's prerogative to be late.'

Eventually, the last car delivered them at the house in St Albans that Ellie had found for her mom in ample time for them both to get changed.

'You've got to make sure you've left for the church before I come down. We really don't want any more bad luck.'

Mrs Simpson embraced Ellie, not something that would have happened years ago. Then Mabel and Fred did the same. There was no sign of Fiona or George.

A voice called from upstairs and he recognised it and his future sister-in-law. 'Hurry up, Ellie, you'll never be ready in time. George is waiting to help Jack in the dining room.'

Jack shook hands with Fred and kissed both ladies on the cheek before heading for the rear of the house. George greeted him warmly.

'Good show. You don't look as bad as I feared, old chap. Let me help you get that lot off.' Jack was about to protest. He was quite capable of undressing himself. 'No time to spare, old boy, if we want to snatch a quick half before the fun starts.'

'Fair enough. I'm going to need something stronger than beer.'

With George's help he was redressed in his old RAF uniform in record time. 'Why aren't you in yours? My best man should be in uniform too.'

'Good idea. Give me a minute and I'll dash up and put it on. Will confuse the others but will be good to feel a part of the old crew again.'

Jack glanced at his watch. Still three-quarters of an hour before the service. The dining room was already set out for the reception. He was astonished at the two-tier wedding cake. Surely icing was banned since sugar rationing? Then he examined it more closely and saw it was made of cardboard. He hoped there was some sort of cake underneath.

As there would only be seven of them at the wedding there'd been no need to book a hall. There were plates of dainty sandwiches, sausage rolls and the pretending cake. More than enough for them to enjoy the occasion. No sign of any alcohol but as Mrs Simpson was teetotal maybe it was going to be a dry reception.

George returned looking smart and they made their escape to the local hostelry where he downed a whisky to steady his nerves.

'Here, Jack, have a half as well.'

A while later he was feeling more relaxed. He glanced out of the window and his beer slopped onto the table. Walking past was his bride. Ellie looked like a princess from a fairy tale. Then he understood the gravity of the situation. 'Bloody hell, George. We should be waiting at the altar not swilling beer in here. Some sort of best man you are.'

He was about to dash after the wedding party when George grabbed his arm. 'No, there's a shortcut through here. We can hardly run past her. She'll never forgive you, or me, for that matter.'

They startled several old biddies as they dodged around them but they arrived before Ellie and the others appeared at the corner. The distance from the house to the church was a five-minute walk, so little point in using a car.

He just made it to the front of the little Norman church as the organist struck up the wedding march. Only then did he see there were already two other guests. One, Mainwaring, he'd half expected. But, Ellie's grandfather, the fascist, Sir Reginald? How the hell had he found out about the wedding? Had he come to make trouble?

Twenty-Two

Walking through the streets of St Albans in a wedding dress was a novel experience, Ellie decided. With her arm through her dad's she tried to think of it as just walking down a very long aisle.

'Good thing it's not raining, Fred,' Mabel said from just behind her.

'We would have had to use umbrellas and run,' he said.

By the time they reached the entrance to the church they'd gathered quite a following.

'Ellie,' her mother whispered, 'do you think all these people intend to come in?'

'I don't mind if they do. With only seven of us the church will be very empty so a few more in the congregation won't bother me.'

Her mother, Mabel and Fiona stepped around her. 'As long as they don't want to come back for the wedding breakfast – there's not nearly enough food.' They hurried in, leaving her alone for a few precious moments with her dad.

'You look beautiful, Ellie love, I can't tell you how proud I am of you. You and your Jack have been through a lot – let's hope this is the start of something better.'

She shook out the skirt of the lovely borrowed gown, adjusted the veil, and was ready to begin the procession to the altar.

The organ struck up the wedding march, she smiled at her dad, and they set off. It was so long since she'd seen Jack or her brother in RAF blue, she scarcely recognised them. They looked quite different.

Jack's smile was blinding. Her heart skipped a beat and she wanted to abandon the slow progress and run to stand beside him. She handed her small bouquet of garden flowers to Fiona. The bride was supposed to stand on the groom's left, but tradition had been abandoned today to accommodate Jack's disability.

As there was another wedding immediately afterwards there would be no sermon or readings or hymns. She repeated the words and the ring was put on her finger. They were pronounced man and wife at last.

Jack put his arm around her and spoke quietly in her ear. 'Your grandfather's here. Thought I'd better warn you.'

She was about to turn but his grip tightened. 'No, ignore him, he's not going to ruin our wedding day.'

They signed the register – Dad and Mum were the witnesses – and were then ready to leave. George was taking snaps so there would be a permanent record of the day.

'We can do the rest of the photographs in the garden, Ellie. I don't think it would be appropriate to do them in the churchyard when there's another wedding party arriving almost immediately,' Mum said.

'Do you think Sir Reginald is going to tag along? How did he know we were getting married today, Mum?'

'I certainly didn't tell him and neither did George or Fiona. I expect Jack and George can prevent him from coming in if you want them to.' The two men nodded.

'No, it's my wedding day. I don't want it spoiled by unpleasantness.'

She'd expected to make an equally solemn progress back down the aisle but the organist had vanished and the guests for the next ceremony were already taking their places in the pews.

The vicar smiled apologetically. 'If you would like to exit through the vestry, you might find that easier in the circumstances. I'm afraid that as you gave me so little notice I was obliged to squeeze your service in between two others.'

'And we appreciate it, Vicar. We're married and that's all that matters,' Jack told him.

'What about Fiona, George and Mabel? They'll wonder where we've gone.'

Mum peeped around the vestry door. 'It's all right, I just saw them leave. You will be pleased to know that your grandfather is no longer there either.'

Jack led them down a narrow path between the back gardens of two rows of ancient cottages and they emerged beside the pub they'd passed on their way to the church.

The others were waiting for them there. There was no time to enquire how her new husband had known about this shortcut, but she had every intention of investigating the matter later.

Hand in hand they dashed the short distance back to the house and George was there before them unlocking the door.

'I think we've given him the slip. I'll lock the door behind us just in case.'

Whilst Fiona and her mother removed the damp tea towels from the sandwiches George went to get them all a celebratory drink.

'I've an admission to make, Mrs Reynolds.'

She stood on tiptoes and kissed him. 'If it's to tell me you had a few drinks in the pub before you came, I know that. You taste of beer and whisky.'

'Dutch courage, darling. Blame your brother – that's also how I knew about that path. I... bloody hell! We've forgotten Mainwaring.'

'Does he know this address?'

'Absolutely – spooks know everything about everyone.'

'Then presumably he'll knock on the door. I hardly think he'll expect us to go in search of him as he wasn't actually an invited guest.'

No sooner had she finished speaking than there was a loud bang on the front door. George was nearest and raised a hand to indicate he was going to answer it.

Ellie turned back to continue her conversation with Jack. She loved the fact that she was no longer a Simpson but a Reynolds. Loud voices in the entrance hall interrupted them.

'Good grief! Sir Reginald has barged his way in. What do we do now?'

'Leave this to me, darling, you go into the dining room with the ladies and George and I will sort this out.'

Her father overheard this remark. 'Count me in, son, I don't want that fascist ruining your wedding party.'

Mabel and Mum were already in the dining room, fussing over the food. She grabbed Fiona's arm and hurried her in to join them. After closing the door firmly, she explained the reason.

'Oh dear! I feared he might try and follow us when I saw him in the church. He can only have come to make trouble,' her mother said, wringing her hands.

'Don't worry, Mum, Jack and George can eject him forcibly if necessary. We can remain here and enjoy this delicious spread. Is there actually any cake at all under that splendid edifice?'

Her comment distracted them as she'd hoped it would. Fiona seemed unbothered by the unwanted guest's appearance.

Mabel carefully lifted the cardboard cake to show there was a Victoria sandwich underneath. 'Fresh cream and strawberry jam, Ellie love. Better than fruit cake if you ask me.'

Whilst her stepmother and mother discussed this thorny question Fiona took her to one side.

Jack charged across the sitting room and into the entrance hall to find Mainwaring standing in the path of Sir Reginald.

'Congratulations, Reynolds. I hear you've had some trouble recently.'

'None of your business. You're not wanted here.' Jack said.

'I want to speak to my daughter and grandchildren.'

'Not today. Send a letter and something might be arranged.'

'I intend to speak to them now. I have something important to tell them.'

'You're not coming in. Whatever you have to say can wait. I'll not allow you to ruin a perfectly good wedding.'

This seemed to be enough provocation for the burly chauffeur to step in. This unpleasant individual shoved past his master and swung a punch at Mainwaring.

To Jack's astonishment the spook swayed aside and the blow whistled past harmlessly. Before the chauffeur could lash out again, he was floored by an uppercut to the jaw. Mainwaring was bespectacled, slimly built and several inches shorter than his opponent, but he'd still triumphed.

Ellie's grandfather roared his disapproval and pushed George violently, sending him crashing backwards into the delicate, spindly-legged table by the door. This collapsed with a hideous splintering sound. It had probably cost a fortune too.

Jack grabbed Sir Reginald by the back of his collar and ran for the open front door. It gave him a great deal of satisfaction to pitch him onto the pavement.

The semiconscious chauffeur was heaved out of the house by Mainwaring and George. Jack dashed back inside and someone slammed the door and bolted it.

'My word, that was fun. Before you ask, Reynolds, I boxed for my college at Oxford.'

Jack had acted without thinking, had quite forgotten about his recent injury and the fact that he was supposed to be taking it easy for the next few weeks. He would probably feel tickety-boo again if he sat down for a bit.

'You don't look too clever, Jack lad. I reckon you've done yourself a mischief throwing that man out of the door.'

He was about to protest that he was fine when Ellie dropped to her knees beside him. 'Here, let me have a look. We don't want to take any chances.'

She gently unbuttoned his jacket and then his shirt. 'Does this hurt when I press? Here, or here?'

'No, not particularly. I can breathe easily – I don't think I've re-fractured my ribs.' What he thought he could have done was reopen his surgical wound. He daren't look down in case he saw red seeping through his vest.

'Your incision is fine too. You just overdid it. The surgeon said it would be several weeks before you're fully fit again. I'm sure he didn't intend for you to be throwing large gentlemen out of doors so soon.'

He grinned. 'Absolutely right, darling girl, I expect he wanted me to wait another month before I got into any fights.'

Before she could move away, he pulled her onto his lap. There was an ominous ripping sound. She had removed her veil, which was fortunate, but the silky material of her wedding dress became entangled on the chair arm.

'Sod it, and the dress doesn't even belong to you.' His expletive had been heard by everyone in the sitting room.

Fiona waved gaily. 'Absolutely no problem at all, I didn't intend to wear it again anyway. It's now done two family weddings so it doesn't matter a jot if it's torn.'

Ellie was struggling to get up in order to examine the damage.

'Stay where you are, I'm an injured man, a hero of the RAF, and I need the comfort of my wife.'

'What you need, Jack Reynolds, is to apologise to Fiona and me for being so clumsy.' The words were stern but her eyes were dancing.

'I most humbly apologise, Mrs Simpson.' He stopped as he realised there were not one, but three Mrs Simpsons in the room. 'I am referring of course to my sister-in-law, not my mother-in-law or my stepmother-in-law.'

'Here, have a glass of champagne and shut up, so we can do the toast,' George said as he handed them each a brimming glass. This was the only alcohol on the premises.

An hour later George made a suggestion. 'If you change into your uniform, Ellie, we could go to the pub and have a few drinks, make this a proper celebration.'

'What about Mum, Dad and Mabel?'

'They are happy for us to go. What about it?'

'Sounds like an excellent plan.'

Ellie scrambled from his lap and dashed off. Ten minutes later they were on their way, all with torches to see them home.

'This is absolutely perfect; after all, the reception we missed was in a pub. I wonder if anyone will play the piano so we can have a bit of a singsong?'

'I don't remember if there was a piano, do you, George?'

His brother-in-law nodded. 'It's my regular. There's definitely a piano and usually an old chap who can play it. If we tell them we're celebrating your nuptials, and buy a round of drinks, it will soon seem like your own personal party. You deserve to have a real knees-up.'

There were only about a dozen in the saloon bar but, when word of free drinks spread, those in the public bar came in to celebrate with them. The beer was flowing for the men, and some of the women too. She and Fiona were happy to drink lemonade with a dash of gin.

The chairs and tables were pushed back and the dancing started. Initially it was too lively for Jack to risk joining in but they enjoyed watching the others having a good time.

'This is more like it. Are you enjoying yourself, honey?'

She kissed him instead of answering. Those watching cheered and she pulled away, embarrassed by her display.

'I wonder if we can find somewhere else to stay tomorrow night, Jack. Being under the same roof as all my parents as a bit inhibiting, don't you think?'

'I've waited this long to make love to you, darling, so one more night won't matter. Do you mind if I get plastered? I'll sleep downstairs.'

George overheard and slapped him on the back. 'We'll get legless together, brother-in-law, and the girls can have one room and we'll have the other.'

Fiona was sitting close by. 'Shall we leave our husbands to it and go home? George will take care of Jack; you don't have to worry about him. He needs to let his hair down this once after all he's been through.'

'I know. He wouldn't do it if this was going to be our wedding night but we've decided to postpone it until we can be really alone. If we leave now it won't be dark and I can find somewhere decent for tomorrow night.'

There was no need to say goodbye as Jack waved. She wasn't sure consuming vast quantities of beer would be good for him so soon after his operation, but her brother would make sure Jack came to no harm.

The remainder of the evening passed in a haze of alcohol. He vaguely remembered being half-carried to bed by George but nothing after that until he woke up the next morning. He had a thumping hangover and his mouth felt like the bottom of a parrot's cage – not that he had any personal experience of this. He sat up slowly, knowing what to expect. With extreme caution he swung his legs to the floor. So far so good. Surprisingly, apart from the headache and filthy taste in his mouth, he didn't feel too bad.

He found the bathroom, had a strip wash, shave and cleaned his teeth. He was ready to go in search of his wife and find out where they were sleeping tonight. He hardened at the thought of finally making love to Ellie. No other woman would have been so relaxed about him drinking himself senseless on their wedding night. They only had one more night together before she was back on duty and he was damn sure he was going to make it a night to remember.

He was an idiot. He had another two weeks' sick leave and was going to spend it at the cottage. They had all the time in the world to get to know each other's preferences in bed. There was no need to rush things.

'This wasn't how I expected to spend my wedding night, but I just didn't want it to be here,' Ellie said to Fiona from where she was curled up in a comfortable armchair with a much-needed cup of tea the next morning.

'I don't blame you. Thin walls and all that. He'll be happy with the hotel you've booked and the champagne supper.'

'I really enjoyed the impromptu party last night. It didn't matter that only George knew any of the guests.'

Mabel came in to join them. 'Well, you're safely married, love, that's the main thing. That nice Mr Mainwaring explained why he didn't want us to return to Glebe Farm.'

Ellie sat up, curious to know what had been said.

'Those varmints who took our Jack are still looking to hurt him and anyone one else he knows. Even my Fred agreed we're better off away from home for a while.'

Mainwaring seemed to be now a firm favourite with everyone after he'd knocked out the chauffeur so efficiently.

Her mother came in from the kitchen. 'They are staying here with us until it's safe to go back. I love my son and his wife, but they are not of my generation, and don't remember the last war and they find me very old-fashioned.'

'It was ever so nice of you, Mrs Simpson – it's going be a bit of a holiday for both of us. There's plenty to look at in St Albans.'

Mum laughed. 'Jack was quite right to say that having three Mrs Simpsons in the house is very confusing. Please, won't you call me Charlotte?'

Mabel beamed. 'That would be lovely, and you call me Mabel. Who would have thought that we would all end up as best of friends – a funny old world we live in. Do you think that horrible man will come back?'

'As long as he doesn't press charges, I don't care what he does. He said he came to tell us something. Perhaps you should contact him, Mum, and see what it was?' Ellie said as she drained her tea and stood up. 'I was thinking about your wedding dress, Fiona. Would you let us cut it up and make it into christening gowns? You and George will have another baby. Jack and I don't want to start a family until the end of the war, but we definitely will have children at some point.'

'That's a good idea. Make some use of it,' Fiona replied.

'Mabel, do you think we could get started on that whilst you're here? I have a serviceable treadle machine for the main seams but the rest will have to be done by hand.'

The sound of someone coming down interrupted the conversation. Jack appeared looking remarkably well and not at all hung over.

'Good morning, Mrs Reynolds, I hope you slept well – I certainly did.' He held out his hand and she took it. Their kiss was everything it should be. She drew him to one side and quickly told him what she'd arranged.

'Sounds perfect, darling. I want to say goodbye to George before we go. He wasn't there when I woke up. Has he gone out?'

'Yes, to get the Sunday paper. Mum's getting breakfast ready for when he gets back. Can you face it?'

'Ravenous and not at all hung over.'

'Another thing I'm so happy about is the fact that you'll be living with me at the cottage for the next two weeks. We won't see much of each other once we're both back on duty.'

'I suppose we have to stay for breakfast.'

'No, not if we don't want to. Let's just go. No long goodbyes. George will understand.' His smile made her toes curl.

The hotel was still serving breakfast and they ate in the grand dining room whilst their room was being prepared. A waiter ceremoniously put their room key down beside him.

He was tucking in but she couldn't swallow a mouthful, not sure if she was excited or nervous. He glanced up at her and dropped his cutlery on the half-cleared plate.

'Shall we go up?'

He kept his arm around her waist as they climbed the stairs. She felt as if everyone in the foyer was staring at them, knowing why they were going up when everyone else was coming down.

'I love you, Ellie, and you love me. We can take things as slow as you want.'

'We've waited so long and I'm afraid I'll be no good in bed and that you'll be disappointed.'

'Jesus H Christ!'

His blasphemy was overheard by two elderly matrons in mink coats who were passing them on the wide staircase. Their shocked exclamations and tutting made her laugh.

'Jack, really. And on a Sunday too.'

'Sorry, love, but I couldn't help it. You disappoint me? How could you think that? Making love is exactly that – and you know what they say? Practice makes perfect.'

Her fears and doubts vanished and they were almost running by the time they reached the door to their room. He unlocked it and they were inside; his arms were around her and they were kissing. They removed their clothes in double quick time and tumbled, naked into the waiting bed.

Sharing her body with him was everything she'd hoped and she finally understood what all the fuss was about.

'I love you so much and don't know why I waited so long.'

He smoothed back her hair, which was falling in a tangle over her bare shoulders. 'If a bomb dropped on us now, I'd die a happy man.'

'Jack, don't tempt fate. I want us to grow old together so we must both promise not to take any unnecessary risks in future. If the weather is bad, we don't fly. Agreed?'

'There's a war on, sweetheart, we'll do what we must. It's not a promise either of us can make.'

She was going to insist but he lowered his head and kissed her and heat flashed through her and nothing else mattered but this.

Twenty-Three

The months passed and summer turned to autumn. Apart from the occasional snatched night with Jack she might as well not have been married. The powers that be had decided it would be simpler for her to remain as Second Officer Simpson and not become Second Officer Reynolds.

She'd decided not to replace Amanda with a new housemate, which meant when Jack did get a couple of days' leave, they were able to enjoy being alone. Her heart skipped a beat at the thought that he would be with her tonight. The first time in ages they had had leave together.

The cottage was their first home and she would always remember it fondly. Of course, she went to White Waltham on her days off and they booked into a bed and breakfast near the ferry pool. She had no intention of being leered at by the other ATA men who shared Jack's billet at the pub.

Despite the fact that the Americans were now fully engaged in the war, things didn't improve on the home front. They had no rationing on *their* bases but as far as she knew they weren't sharing with the local populace. Their bombers flew in the daytime escorted by their own fighter planes and the RAF continued with night bombing.

The nights were drawing in, there was a nip in the air and the trees were shedding their leaves. It would soon be November and she prayed that she and Jack would be able to spend their first Christmas together at either St Albans or Glebe Farm.

She arrived, as always, before the chits were out. The only good thing about the winter months was that flying time was shorter but it also meant they were often marooned away from base.

'Amanda, I've not seen you for ages. You look well. Married life is obviously suiting you. How do you like flying bombers now?'

'Still prefer the fighters, but the extra few shillings each week is useful. Isn't it about time you were sent to do the next level?'

'I'm perfectly happy doing what I'm doing. Look, the slips are being put out on the table. I wonder where I'm going today.'

Amanda waved a piece of paper at her. 'A Wellington to Lincolnshire, Ellie, I don't envy you that. The Met office has given an absolutely beastly forecast for East Anglia.'

'What about you? Where are you going and with what?'

'I'm the taxi driver today. You'll be with me to collect the Wellington and it looks as though I might be picking you up later.'

Ellie gathered up her other chits. 'You're right, I'm ferrying Wellingtons back and forth all day to the same base.'

After checking with the Met girl, she wasn't encouraged. 'Heavy rain and poor visibility are expected to drift in from the North right across East Anglia by teatime, Ellie. I shouldn't think you'll get all your deliveries done today.'

'Only to be expected at this time of year. I've got my overnight bag. I'll find a bed somewhere and carry on tomorrow.'

Fortunately, it was a short flight to the MUs, the place where she was collecting the repaired aircraft, and she was expected. She had called in here several times over the past few months so they no longer looked shocked to see her.

'Morning, miss, all tickety-boo. See you later. Hope the one you're bringing us isn't as knackered as this was when it came in last week,' the ground mechanic said cheerfully.

With the necessary paperwork signed and collected she climbed into the bomber and took her place in one of the seats in the cockpit. It always seemed a bit eerie flying with an empty space beside her, but she'd got used to it.

The flight was uneventful, her landing perfect, and the skies were still relatively free of cloud. She was invited to delay her departure to eat lunch but she refused.

'Thank you, but I've got two more new kites to bring here and I won't get them both to you if I delay.'

'Guessed you'd say that, Miss Simpson, so I've got a flask of tea and a couple of sandwiches ready for you to take with you.' The young RAF officer handed these over with a smile.

'That's so kind and much appreciated. You'll get the flask back later.' This journey wasn't so comfortable as there were several large holes in the fuselage and one of the engines wasn't functioning properly. She grinned. Hardly surprising as this was a damaged Wellington. She'd flown worse and as long as the weather didn't deteriorate she'd get it safely to be repaired.

Whilst waiting to collect the next lot of paperwork she finally got time to drink the tea and eat the sandwiches. The weather forecast for this second delivery was ominous.

'I doubt you'll get the kite to the base today. Hope you have somewhere in mind to land if you have to,' she was told by the chap who was doing the handover.

'I'll be fine – I've flown this route many times. But if it's too bad I might well not be back to collect the third one today.'

'More important that you don't take any risks, Miss Simpson.' As she waited for the green light she was pleased that at least if she was flying into bad weather it was in a fully functioning aircraft and not a damaged one.

The last time she and Jack had been together he'd gone through her instrument training again. She'd only had to use this new skill once but was confident she could fly in any weather if necessary.

Halfway to her destination visibility suddenly deteriorated. The Wellington was being buffeted by savage gusts of wind; the rain lashed the cockpit. She would have to find somewhere to land.

Jack put the phone down and nodded his thanks to the admin girl who'd fetched him to speak to Mainwaring. It had taken months, but finally he was done with the mess Uncle Joe had left him.

'Well, old chap, you look happy. Seeing your beautiful bride tomorrow?' It was Nigel – he wasn't stationed at

White Waltham but quite often delivered or collected from there.

'I sincerely hope so – the first time in weeks that we've got consecutive days off. How's Amanda? I know Ellie misses her company at the cottage.'

'She's a bit peaky at the moment, since you ask. Told her to go and see the medic but you know what these women are like – take no notice of us chaps, do they?'

'I'm glad our wives are independent, capable young women. They couldn't do the job if they weren't.'

'Probably right, old bean, but I'll be glad when this bloody war is over and my wife is where she should be – at home, and not risking her life every day.'

Nigel had been promoted to Class V and was ferrying the largest aircraft back and forth. Jack was just happy to stick to fighters. He loved every second he was in the cockpit of a Hurry or a Spit, even when sometimes they were barely airworthy.

He got his deliveries and collections completed in record time and was able to get a flip to Hamble just before the weather closed in. He hurried to the admin office as he and Ellie had agreed to meet there and cycle home together.

'Hi there, is Ellie back?'

'No, she's not.' Alison looked grave. His stomach lurched. 'She should have caught the last Anson but she hadn't arrived at the base. We've had no communication from her for several hours.'

He was too shocked to speak. Then his head cleared. 'What's the weather like in Lincolnshire? If it's as bad there as it is here, she will have landed somewhere and she'll be waiting it out.'

'Then why hasn't she reported in? That's procedure and Ellie's always a stickler for following the rules.'

'How the hell should I know? If there'd been a crash it would have been reported. She's fine. She's found somewhere to stay until the weather improves.'

Alison didn't look convinced. 'If she's gone down somewhere in a field in the middle of nowhere it might be hours before anyone notices.'

'For God's sake, you'll put a jinx on her talking like that. Ellie can instrument fly – I taught her – so she can go through anything without being at risk.'

Her expression lightened. 'I was hoping you'd say that, Jack. I'm feeling more hopeful now. I know we're not supposed to fly above the clouds but Ellie's an excellent pilot, the best I've got – if anyone's going to keep safe in difficult circumstances it's her.'

He wasn't surprised that this breach of protocol was applauded. He'd always thought it daft not to allow ATA flyers to use instruments in bad weather.

'If you don't mind, I'll hang about here. She's bound to ring soon and I want to be able to talk to her when she does.'

Ellie was enjoying the challenge of flying blind, of using her new skills efficiently. Above the clouds it was clear, bright and sunny. If she stayed where she was and continued on this path, she would arrive at her destination safely.

When she was fairly sure she was directly above the RAF base she flew down through the clouds, hoping once she got below 2,000 feet, she'd be able to see the ground.

She caught her breath. The kite was pitching and shuddering in the gale-force winds. Visibility was almost zero through the rain. The ground might as well have been non-existent.

No need to panic. She checked the instruments. The Wellington was flying more or less straight and the airstrip should be directly below. She circled slowly. Her heart was hammering. Nothing but solid rain – no view of even a field to land in.

On her third circuit, this time much lower, she saw what she was looking for. The base was half a mile ahead – not quite where she'd expected it to be – but nothing had ever looked so wonderful as that strip of concrete.

On her second tight circuit of the base the landing lights came on. They knew she was coming. Her hands were wet inside her gloves. She didn't want to make a mess of this. The angle of descent was different from her previous visits. No time to worry about that.

The wheels touched, bounced a little, and then settled. Not a perfect landing but better than it could have been. Nothing to be ashamed of. Two caped figures appeared waving their paddles in order to guide her off the main runway.

She applied the brakes, checked everything was as it should be, and grabbed her overnight bag and parachute.

When she dropped to the ground she was delighted to find transport waiting. Her Sidcot suit was pretty weatherproof but even that wouldn't keep her dry in this torrential rain. A clap of thunder drowned out the rain and was immediately followed by sheets of lightning.

The passenger door swung open as she approached and she hopped in. Her eyes widened. She didn't know who was more surprised, herself or the driver of the vehicle.

'Holy cow! A broad. I can't believe you brought that bomber in safely when our guys are grounded today.'

The young man was in the uniform of the American air force. She must have landed in error at one of their bases.

'I can't tell you how pleased I am that I found your base. I was beginning to worry I wouldn't be able to land before I ran out of fuel.'

'Well, ma'am, you'll sure be the talk of the base. I'll take you to the Officers' Mess. They'll take care of you. You sure won't be going anywhere else today. It's just swell to have you here.'

They sped off through the rain and in a few minutes arrived in a screeching halt outside an unprepossessing Nissen hut. It was a very large hut, but nevertheless she'd expected better from the Yanks.

The young airman saw her expression and laughed. 'I bet you can't figure out what's inside, ma'am. It sure isn't what you think. It cost more dough to set that up than it would to buy your Wellington. I guess you'll be impressed when you see inside.'

Ellie thought this probably an exaggeration but was too polite to say so. The driver was out of the jeep and around to open the door before she could move.

'Here, ma'am, let me take your chute. You make a run for the door.'

She wasn't going to argue although she wasn't sure she should just barge in uninvited. There were two windows but these were blacked out so she couldn't see if he was speaking the truth. A second roll of thunder right overheard made her jump and then the lightning lit up the sky. The rain intensified.

She ran to the door but hesitated under the porch, unwilling to go in without her escort. She wasn't even sure if female officers were allowed in the men's Mess.

'Just push the door, ma'am, it's never locked.'

She did as instructed, and for a second time was astonished. The inside of the building was like a hotel foyer. Gleaming chrome and luxurious furniture – just as the airman had said it would be. The only drawback was the noise of the rain as it hammered onto the metal roof.

Within moments she was surrounded by officers and offered coffee, chocolate, nylons and a whole variety of other things that weren't available on the other side of the Nissen hut door.

Eventually she escaped – she wasn't comfortable being treated like royalty and praised as if she was another Amy Johnson. She'd just been doing her job. The same one that every ATA pilot did several times a day.

She was given excellent accommodation and hastily vanished inside the room and locked the door behind her. Only as she was removing her flight suit did she realise she hadn't telephoned to say she was safe.

After tidying her appearance and washing the inevitable oil and dirt from her hands and face she was ready to brave the onslaught of flirting and enthusiasm from the exuberant Americans.

No sooner was she out of her door than a lurking officer pounced on her. He introduced himself as Dean Reigate – she didn't catch his rank. He insisted on giving her a conducted tour despite her protests.

'Excuse me, but I must ring Hamble. They'll think I've crashed if I don't let them know I'm safe.'

'Gee whiz, I sure am sorry. I'll take you to the adjutant – you'll be able to make your call from there.' He led her down a maze of corridors and halted outside a door.

'Here you are, ma'am. I'll wait for you...'

'No, thank you, I'll return to my room when I'm finished.'

She explained her requirements to the curious Americans who were gracious and friendly. She was about to make the necessary calls when the lights went out.

The language from those in the office made her ears burn. She had the sense to remain where she was and not blunder about getting in the way.

Loss of power was not uncommon in storms and at home one just lit candles and turned up the paraffin lamps until electricity was restored. Sometimes this could take a few hours, sometimes days.

However, this was an American Air Force Base and they couldn't afford to be blacked out for long. They must have backup power – generators that would kick in within a few minutes.

Sure enough the lights flickered and came back on although somewhat dimmer than they had been before.

'Sorry, ma'am, but the wires are down and you won't be able to make your call right now. Why don't you give me the numbers and I'll do it for you as soon as we get things put straight.'

She got the message. He didn't want her to hang about and clutter up the place. 'Thank you, that would be kind. I'll write them down.'

She found pencil and paper and printed the names and numbers of the RAF base the Wellington was to be delivered to and Hamble. Jack would be waiting for her and tearing his hair out with worry. No, he wouldn't – he'd know she was safe somewhere.

On reaching the sanctuary of her room she found that someone had delivered a delicious tray of freshly made sandwiches, a flask of coffee and a large slice of cake.

She devoured the lot and wished she could have shared it with Jack. They had both been so looking forward to spending two days together and now it was unlikely she would get back in time to spend more than a few hours with him.

After a mostly sleepless night she was dressed and ready to leave at dawn. The silence told her the weather had cleared. She refused breakfast as she was eager to complete her deliveries and get back to Hamble. Her bag was weighted down with gifts from her temporary hosts. When she landed at the airbase, instead of being pleased to see her, the Squadron Leader who was waiting for the kite was furious.

'Where the hell have you been? Didn't it occur to you to let us know you were safe? We've wasted hours searching for wreckage...' He held out his hand for her paperwork, his expression glacial. 'I always knew having bloody girls flying our kites was a bad idea.'

Arguing with him was probably not a good idea but she wasn't going to stand there and be publicly berated when she'd done everything she should have. 'I apologise—'

'I should bloody well hope so—'

'That's quite enough, Squadron Leader. If you would allow me to complete a sentence I'll explain. I landed at an American base and they were stuck by lightning. The phone lines went down. I was turfed out of the office and told the calls would be made as soon as the lines were functioning again.' He was now looking slightly less belligerent. 'Obviously the calls weren't made. Please could I ring Hamble. My husband will be waiting by the phone.'

'Already done it. You were spotted on your way in. My dear girl, I should not have shouted at you. As it's so early I take it you didn't stop for breakfast?'

'Actually, I would still like to use your telephone. My husband will be frantic even though he knows I'm perfectly fine.'

He escorted her into the office. Although it was early she was certain Jack would be there to answer the phone. He wouldn't have left until he'd spoken to her.

'Hamble base.'

'Alison, I'm so sorry about the misunderstanding.' Ellie quickly explained what had happened and then asked to speak to Jack.

'He's gone to the cottage to get some sleep. We were both here all night.'

'Never mind. I should be back just after lunch. If it's any consolation to you I didn't sleep much either.'

She hung up and accepted the mug of tea and two slices of toast with enthusiasm.

'I'm afraid the Wellington you're returning for repair is in poor shape. After your experience yesterday, do you still want to take it?'

She swallowed the last mouthful and nodded. 'Of course I do. I don't see any other ATA pilot here to do it.'

This flight back was tricky and she was relieved she'd had training in landing with one engine as one cut out on her final circuit. She touched down safely. The admin was completed in record time and she was fortunate to find an Anson waiting to take her home.

Hamble was quiet as all the girls were still out. She reported to the office, dumped her chute and suit in the locker, and went in search of her bicycle. Amanda's bicycle had been handed on to Jack, as her friend no longer needed it.

It was where she'd left it but the other one was there too. She stared at the cycle Jack was supposed to have taken to pedal to the cottage and her heart sank.

When he'd heard she was perfectly fine but had just not reported in he must've been so angry he'd decided to go back to White Waltham and not spend the remainder of their leave together. She didn't blame him – she would have been angry too in the circumstances.

Sadly, she picked up her bicycle and, blinking back tears, pedalled the two miles to the cottage. She removed the key from its hiding place and let herself in. Too dispirited to make herself anything to eat she trudged upstairs.

Twenty-Four

Jack flung his arms around Alison on hearing that his beloved Ellie was safe. 'Thank God for that! I wish we'd known last night but I'm sure there's an explanation. I feel ten years younger.'

She returned his embrace. 'She'll be contacting us as soon as she lands.'

'I don't need to talk to her, I'm going home to get some kip.' In the early morning sunlight, the world looked wonderful. He wasn't given to conversing with the man upstairs but his prayers had certainly been answered.

He was about to collect his bike when he heard the unmistakable rattle of the first bus to Southampton heading for the bus stop directly outside the base. He sprinted towards the gates and the soldier on duty stepped out of his box and waved to the bus driver. Jack signalled his thanks, raced through and jumped on.

'Thank you, much appreciated,' he said as he went past the driver. He took the nearest seat, one next to a middle-aged matron in a smart red felt hat and matching jacket.

'Good heavens, young man, you cut that a bit fine.'

He hadn't expected someone from the upper classes to be travelling on the local bus. 'I didn't know I was going to catch this until I heard it coming. I want to buy my wife a gift.'

'Splendid, splendid. Frightfully good idea. Do you have children?'

He was a bit taken aback by the personal question but answered anyway. 'No, we only got married in May. She's an ATA pilot too.'

'My gal is doing something hush-hush. Not seen her for months. I was in the land army last time – never been happier.'

'My father-in-law's a farmer and has a team of land girls working for him. He couldn't produce his quota without them.'

The bus was packed by the time it arrived in Southampton and it was a relief to get off and be able to breathe fresh air again.

He headed for the nearest bakery and managed to buy two sausage rolls and two sticky buns. That was supper taken care of.

Nowhere else was open so he found a café, bought a copy of the *News Chronicle*, and waited for the city to get going. He had no idea what to get Ellie until he passed a pawnshop. In the window was a tray of jewellery that caught his eye.

He pushed open the door and the bell rang noisily. He'd expected an elderly man to appear but instead a girl of no more than fourteen or fifteen bounced in.

'Good morning, sir, what can I do you for?'

'I'd like to see the tray of items in the window. I'm looking for a gift for my wife.'

The window display was behind a locked grille. He waited patiently whilst the girl removed the padlocks, then the tray, and refastened the locks. Did she think he was going to run off with something?

He wasn't sure what he was looking for but his eye was caught by a pretty gold locket. It was intricately carved, and the chain had similar engravings. It was perfect. Ellie could wear it underneath her uniform.

'How much is that?'

'It's twenty-two carat, sir, very old and all. At least a hundred years, I should think.'

'I can see that, but how much is it?'

'I can let you have it for £5. It's a bargain as it was £7.50.'

This was an eye-watering sum but he wasn't in the mood to haggle. 'I'll take it if you can find something nice to put it in.'

'I'll just put the tray back, if you don't mind waiting. You can't be too careful nowadays.'

He wasn't sure if she was referring to him or to the fact that Southampton was full of jewel thieves just waiting to barge in and steal things.

She produced a blue leather box, with a pristine, cream satin lining, and it was perfect. He handed over the required amount, received the locket and a signed receipt. He intended to catch the next bus but bumped into a couple of mates and they went for a quick half at the nearest pub. Ellie wouldn't be back until after lunch so he had plenty of time.

Unfortunately, the midday bus was cancelled. Either he had to hitch a lift, walk, or wait for the next one. There was already a large queue of disgruntled ladies and he didn't fancy his chances of getting a seat against these odds.

He had been walking for an hour when an army lorry rattled to a stop next to him. He scrambled in the back and they dropped him off at the gates. Ellie's cycle had gone. He swore under his breath and snatched up the remaining bike.

He could see the curtains were drawn in their bedroom, so she was asleep. He was knackered – he would have a quick to kip in the spare room – not wake her up. They still had two nights to be together so there was no rush. The door was unlocked, which was fortunate as the only key was kept under the flowerpot at the side of the house. She would obviously have removed this in order to get in herself.

He drew the blackouts just in case it was dark when they got up again. He put the buns and sausage rolls in the kitchen but kept the gift in his pocket.

As always, he'd removed his boots and left them by the front door beside hers. There was sufficient light even with the blackouts drawn for him to make his way upstairs without using his torch. He paused at their door and carefully lifted the latch and looked in.

Ellie was sound asleep, but still dressed and lying on top of the candlewick bedspread. He so wanted to wake her and make love. But that wouldn't be fair.

After removing his jacket, he flung himself on the spare bed, the one that had been Amanda's, grateful that the landlady had provided two double beds rather than twins. He was instantly asleep.

*

It was dark when Ellie woke and she couldn't remember if she'd drawn the blackouts. She would have to blunder about and hope she didn't stub her toe on anything before she put on the light. Her stomach gurgled loudly, reminding her she hadn't eaten since the previous day. In her overnight bag she had two large bars of chocolate, a tin of butter, two pairs of nylons and, best of all, a tin of real coffee. The Americans had been more than generous when she'd left the base.

She really should have had a wash before she slept – but she would do it now. There was always water in the china jug on the nightstand in her bedroom and that would have to do tonight. She would have a bath tomorrow morning. She stripped to her knickers and bra and got on with it. She shrugged into her dressing gown and was ready to find something to eat.

She'd left her torch downstairs in her bag so this would mean she'd have to negotiate the stairs in darkness. Halfway down she paused. Why was it so dark? Surely there should be a glimmer of moonlight from the windows? She felt her way to the front door in order to draw the blackout and to her surprise found this had already been done. She was certain she hadn't done this when she got in.

She switched on the light and the first thing she saw were Jack's boots placed neatly beside hers. With a squeal of excitement she raced upstairs and flung open the spare room door.

He jack-knifed and was across the room in three strides. 'Darling, I can't tell you what a bloody awful night it was. I couldn't imagine my life without you. Don't frighten me like that again.'

'I'm sorry. I love you so much and I thought you'd gone back to White Waltham because you were cross with me.'

'I went to Southampton to buy you a gift. I'll give it to you later. Something more important to do now.'

Before she could protest, she was tumbled onto the bed. Removing his clothes added to her excitement. Her knickers and bra joined his things on the floor. Skin to skin was how it should be.

By the time they emerged from the bedroom it was almost midnight. Hand in hand they made their way to the kitchen. 'We have eggs and half a loaf of fresh bread, butter and milk. Even better, we've got real coffee.'

'I've brought sticky buns and sausage rolls to add to the feast.'

They didn't need alcohol to celebrate – real coffee and chocolate was more than enough. They carried this through to the sitting room and curled up together on the sofa.

'Jack, what are we going to do tomorrow? No, that should be today as it's after midnight.'

'We've got enough to eat so there's no need to go looking for any more. Let's stay here and do nothing.' He nibbled her ear and her pulse skipped. 'Well, nothing apart from this…'

They were both sad when they had to lock the cottage, hide the key, and pedal to the base.

'I thought we could visit St Albans on the next leave we both have together,' he said.

'I'd like that. I'm really pleased that Mum and Mabel are now firm friends. Alison has promised I can have Christmas

Day and Boxing Day this year as I was on duty last time. Everyone will be at Glebe Farm and I'm really looking forward to it. When will you know if you're getting the time off?'

His smile made her wobble and her front wheel dropped into a rut. With a despairing cry she flew over the handlebars and landed in the ditch.

His laughter didn't help. He reached down and removed the bike, allowing her to scramble up. 'That was most enjoyable. Haven't laughed so much in years.'

'Horrible man. It was your fault I tipped up. Don't smile at me like that.' She brushed herself down and was ready to continue. 'By the way, I'm not hurt, thanks for asking.'

'I know, honey, do you think I'd have been laughing otherwise?'

'At least it wasn't too wet. Is my bike damaged?'

'All tickety-boo, darling. It's November today, did you know?'

'Trying not to think about it. At least there are fewer flying hours in the winter, so not all bad news.'

The canteen at the ferry pool would be open for breakfast, as it didn't get light until much later – although the clocks going forward would help.

Jack was collecting a Spitfire from the nearby factory and taking it to Hornchurch. She was once again on the Wellington run.

There was no place for tearful goodbyes. There was a war on and they both had work to do.

*

The weeks passed and Christmas was only a few days away. Both she and Jack had volunteered to work over New Year so she didn't feel at all guilty having three days off for the festive season. There was a feeling of optimism after Montgomery and his desert rats had been victorious at the battle of El Alamein. The constant day and night raids against Germany were lowering the morale of the German civilians.

Jack had arrived the day before and came to meet her from the train.

'Merry Christmas, honey, our first as a married couple.'

'I'm going to try and forget about the war and imagine it's all over and we're just a normal family celebrating together. Even the weather is on our side this year.'

'It's grey and overcast but no frost or snow. I remember the first Christmas I spent with you – I've never seen so much food. No mince pies or Christmas cake this year but Mabel and your mom told me we won't go short.'

'I expect we'll have something with apples – I don't really care as long as there's plenty of it.'

There was no petrol available for private use anymore so she was unsurprised to find Jack had borrowed a pony and trap. 'This vehicle now belongs to Glebe Farm. No idea where Fred managed to find them, but it's all there is for transport nowadays.'

'I didn't know you could handle the reins – where did you learn to do that?'

He grinned. 'Molly doesn't need any direction. All I have to do is hold the reins and click my tongue. Haven't tried to reverse so far but going forward's okay.'

'I learned to ride at school but have never driven a cart. Can I have a go?'

'Absolutely. It's bound to be easier with two hands than one. Good thing Fred has plenty of fodder for the cows and a row of empty stables. The dogs are enjoying the company.'

She took her position on the box, picked up the reins, released the brake and clicked her tongue encouragingly. To her delight the obliging animal moved off without hesitation.

'It was snowing the last time we all spent Christmas here, not sure how this contraption would deal with snow.'

'People managed perfectly well with horsepower in the olden days so I'm sure Molly won't let us down.' She flicked the reins on the horse's hindquarters and the animal tossed her head, flicked her ears, and lumbered into a trot.

As they turned into the lane that led to the farm the two dogs rushed up to greet them, barking and trying to get on the cart. The pony ignored them. With so much noise it was impossible to talk. She pulled on the reins and told Molly to halt and the pony did so.

Everyone had come out to greet them. Fiona was enormous; her baby was due any day.

'Leave Molly to me, Ellie love. I'll untack and put her away,' Dad said with a beaming smile. 'I can't tell you how glad we are to have you both home.'

She ran from one to the other, hugging and kissing each in turn. How much had changed in the past year – now she would say that Mum and she had a good relationship, something that would have been impossible before then.

Mabel held up her small bag. 'This is all you've got, love, no glad rags to put on tomorrow?'

'Remember, Mabel, my civvies are here. Don't worry, I'll wear a pretty frock for Christmas Day.'

The house had been decorated, the tree was up and everything looked perfect. She should have been overjoyed to be here with those she loved the most, with her first niece or nephew about to put in an appearance, but something was missing.

Being here with Jack was going to be more difficult than she'd anticipated. The ghost of her beloved brother Neil, who had died during the evacuation of Dunkirk, was accompanied by that of her first love, Greg.

She had done up an old bicycle for each of them – Jack was still using Greg's at White Waltham. Of course, George and Fiona had been with her parents and Mabel had still been the housekeeper last time.

Now she was married to Jack, Mabel was married to her dad, and Fiona and George were about to become parents. After losing their first child so tragically earlier this year this baby was even more special. She had thought Fiona had been pregnant at their wedding in June but she hadn't mentioned it.

She pushed her unhappy thoughts aside and turned to her sister-in-law.

'Fiona, when are you due?'

'On January 5th. George was a bit worried about me coming here so near the date especially after what happened before. The consultant who's looking after me told me as long as I'm back before the New Year he had no objection.'

*

Jack left Ellie nattering to Fiona and took her bag upstairs to the room that was now theirs. George and Fiona had, naturally, his old room and they had Ellie's. Mrs Simpson was in the unenviable position of sleeping in her dead son's bedroom. He had a nasty suspicion the two dead guys were going to cast a shadow over what should be a happy family celebration. Maybe it would have been better if they'd all gone to St Albans – there was certainly enough room in the house as they'd stayed there for the wedding.

If Neil and Greg's absence was affecting him, God knows what it would be doing to Ellie. Both guys had meant a lot to her. He didn't doubt that she loved him, but this Christmas was going to remind her of the last one they'd all spent together when he'd just been a friend of the family. Last year had been different as only he and Ellie had been at Glebe Farm.

He dumped her bag on one of the beds, wishing they had a double as they had at the cottage. The door opened and she came in and saw at once what the problem was. He frowned – surely there had only been one bedstead in the room before?

'These won't do. If we push them together, we can make it into a giant double bed.'

He leaned down and grabbed the headboard with his hand and shoved. The bed was on casters. It shot across the space and he fell flat on his face. Her laughter echoed around the room.

'Serves you right. Now we're even.' She was mopping her eyes as he staggered to his feet. Before she had time to react, he pounced on her and tumbled her onto the centre of the two beds.

They separated and for a second time he was on his arse on the floor, but this time with Ellie on top of him. What happened next was inevitable. They emerged hot and dusty from between the beds a considerable time later.

'We're going to have to remove the casters, honey, or keep them separate.'

'My old bed had a solid frame – I've no idea where Dad and Mabel got these. I didn't think new furniture was available even if you had enough points saved up.'

After a deal of heaving and shoving they had a double bed. What they didn't have were double-sized sheets and blankets. Ellie came up with an ingenious plan. By turning one set of covers sideways the problem was solved.

'I suppose we can't try this out?'

'You're incorrigible, Jack Reynolds. We've been far too long up here as it is and I want to change before we go down. I think we might be going to the midnight service and I want to be anonymous tonight.'

Twenty-Five

Despite the house being festooned with paper chains and tissue-paper decorations it didn't feel at all jolly. However, everyone was putting on a brave face and pretending they didn't notice two people were missing.

Ellie wandered into the kitchen to see if there was anything she could do but she was shooed out.

'Run along, love, your mum and I can manage perfectly well. We just had soup for lunch as we wanted to save our main meal for when we were all here.' Mabel was busy making pastry whilst Mum was kneading dough ready for tomorrow's bread.

'If you're quite sure, both of you, then I'll join the others in the sitting room.'

'All of you work ever so hard and deserve to put your feet up for a couple of days.'

'I've made a pot of tea, Ellie, if you'd like to take it through. There are even some biscuits to go with it,' Mum said.

The tea was received gratefully – no one offered to help pour. Fiona was like a beached whale, Jack had only one arm, but there was no reason why her brother couldn't have offered. Dad was asleep.

There was a modest selection of gifts under the tree but no stockings. They had all agreed to keep it simple this year. She had managed to find suitable books for everyone at WH Smith's but had been obliged to buy them way back in November. These were from both her and Jack.

She handed round tea in the best china only used on special occasions.

'Sit down, Ellie, we're going to put the wireless on. It'll be nice Christmas carols,' Dad said.

'That reminds me, are we going to the midnight service or tomorrow morning?'

'I'm not going to either, Ellie – too fat and too lazy to walk that far,' Fiona said from the sofa where she was stretched out with her feet on George's lap.

'I expect Mother will want to go. I suppose we'd better go with her,' her brother said with a resigned sigh.

'What about you, Dad? Mabel will want to go, won't she?'

'To tell you the truth, Ellie, we've not been going regularly. The vicar has become an army chaplain and the old chap who replaced him is deaf, and blind as a bat. He rambles on and last time we went we were there for over two hours. No heating in there and we were all frozen solid by the time we got out.'

Jack's delighted smile at the thought that he might not have to attend church parade made her laugh. 'In which case, we can all have a drink tonight and go to bed when we want.'

To her surprise Mum wasn't upset about missing church. 'There'll be a service on the wireless tomorrow. I'm content to listen to that. We go every week in St Albans so I don't feel at all guilty.'

After supper Fiona went to bed and George decided he would go with her. He was very protective and she didn't blame him. Losing a baby so late in the pregnancy would make anyone anxious.

Not long afterwards Mum stood up. 'If you don't mind, everyone, I'll go up too. All this fresh country air makes one tired, don't you think?'

Ellie scrambled from the chair and kissed her on the cheek – the gesture was returned. Jack stood up and embraced her. Dad and Mabel smiled.

He took her hand and squeezed it. She got his message.

'Good night, Dad, Mabel, see you in the morning.'

They had to wait for the bathroom to be free and this gave them an opportunity to talk.

'That was the first time ever that Mum and I kissed each other in this house.'

'Everything's different this year. But no one seems full of Christmas cheer.'

There was a lump in her throat and she blinked back tears. As he'd brought the subject up, was now the time to tell him how difficult it was for her?

Jack instantly regretted his remark. He didn't want to hear how much she was missing Greg or Neil, but understood it must be hard for her to be reminded of the last time they had all been together at Glebe Farm. He took the coward's way out and kissed her. Soon they were making love and fell asleep naked in each other's arms.

He woke and reached out for her. The other side of the bed was cold and empty. Ellie had been up for some time. His watch said it was only six o'clock. Why had she got up so early? It was their first Christmas Day together and she should have been here, in bed, with him.

Her dressing gown and slippers were on the chair. She was dressed. Even worse. He pulled on yesterday's discarded clothes, didn't stop to shave or wash, and went in search of his errant wife. The house was cold, no fires lit anywhere as yet. He was about to walk into the kitchen when he stopped. She was in there and talking to Fiona.

He didn't want to intrude if they were having a girl talk.

'I'm so excited about becoming an aunt. The way Jack and I are behaving I don't suppose it'll be long before we start a family of our own.'

'I should wait until the end of the war, Ellie. What you're doing is far more useful than producing a baby. I wish I could contribute more.'

He pushed open the door and the way Ellie's face lit up told him what he wanted to know.

'I'm parched – is there tea going? I'll just get a mug and then take it into the sitting room. Happy Christmas to you both.'

They stared at him as if he was speaking nonsense. Then they both laughed. 'You'd forgotten, hadn't you?'

'We had. Somehow it seems wrong to be enjoying ourselves when so many people are dying from the bombing going on both sides of the channel,' Fiona said.

'Don't you approve of dropping bombs on the Germans? They've killed thousands of our civilians and destroyed cities.'

'But it doesn't make it right for us to do the same to them, does it? I think war is beastly. It was much better when only soldiers and politicians were involved and the rest of the population got on with their lives as usual.'

Ellie hugged her sister-in-law. 'I agree – the Napoleonic wars seem romantic compared to the last world war and this one. Jack, now the Americans have joined in do you think it will be over this year – I mean next year?'

'We're certainly doing better in Africa and the Russians are pushing Hitler's troops back. But somehow, I doubt it will be over next year or even the one after. Let's not talk about that today – let's just enjoy being together.'

'Well said, son, just what I was thinking.' Fred came in wearing his dressing gown and slippers. Ellie almost fell off the chair on seeing him.

'Dad, you're not dressed.'

Fred chuckled. 'You always were quick off the mark, love. I wouldn't have known I was in my pyjamas if you hadn't pointed it out. I'm getting old and probably losing my marbles.'

Now Jack was astonished. He'd never heard Fred make a joke, let alone appear anything but fully clothed.

'I'm going to leave the ladies to their chatting, Fred. Why don't you bring your tea into the sitting room with me.'

'I said I'd take a cup of tea up to Mabel, her Christmas treat, like.'

Ellie handed him two mugs and he wandered off humming to himself. Married life was certainly agreeing with him.

The blackouts were still drawn and he had no idea if it was light yet. 'Doesn't your dad have to go out and do the pigs or cows anymore?'

'The land girls take care of everything – he just has to oversee and do the paperwork. They even do the chickens for Mabel.'

'After his stroke, it's better that he doesn't have to work so hard.'

'The only drawback,' Fiona added, 'is that there aren't as many eggs and so on coming into the house as everything has to be recorded and sent somewhere or other.'

'I'll help you with the fires, Jack; we need to get the house warm. It's Christmas Day after all.' Ellie carried the tea and then told him to sit down whilst she applied a match to the waiting newspaper and kindling. At times like this he resented having only one arm – she shouldn't have to do everything. He was supposed to be taking care of her. That was the way things should be.

He thought back to the conversation he'd overheard earlier. 'Sweetheart, do you think there's a chance you might be expecting?'

She didn't answer his question. 'There, this room will soon be lovely and warm. Shall I turn on the Christmas tree lights whilst the blackouts are still drawn.'

'Bugger the lights. Answer my question.' He hadn't intended to sound so abrupt but it certainly got her attention. The tongs dropped noisily into the scuttle.

'Don't talk to me like that, Jack Reynolds, I don't appreciate it.' She jumped to her feet and faced him, her expression fierce. 'I suppose you were eavesdropping outside the kitchen door earlier. I've no idea if I'm pregnant, but I could be – I won't know unless I miss my monthly.'

Getting to his feet was more difficult than it used to be for some reason and this only served to make him feel even more useless.

'If you are, you'll have to leave the ATA. I don't want you to stay in the cottage, so I suppose you'll have to move to White Waltham to be near me.'

Her mouth tightened. He should have kept his mouth shut – he'd just dug himself into a deeper hole.

'Then I sincerely hope that I'm not for I've no intention of leaving the ATA. As for moving to White Waltham, that isn't going to happen. If I move anywhere it will be here or to St Albans.'

'I don't think you understand how things work now. You're my wife, my responsibility, and you should live where I am, not with your parents.' Things might have been salvaged if he'd had the sense to keep his mouth shut and not blunder on. 'Amanda moved in with Nigel. We're married for God's sake and you don't even use my name.'

He was about to apologise but she stared at him as if she didn't know who he was.

'I think it would be better if you moved into the spare room down here. I'll make the bed up.'

Why on earth had she said that? Jack looked stunned for a moment but then furious.

'Don't bother. My place is in bed beside you. I'm your husband and don't you forget it.'

'I'm not likely to when you start issuing orders and behaving like an idiot. I might have said I was going to obey you in the marriage service, but we both know that's not going to happen. I'm your equal – no – I'm your superior at work, and I'm the one with the money. So don't try and tell me what I'm going to do or where I'm going to live.'

Mentioning the fact that she was rich wasn't tactful. This had always been a sore point as the money she had had come from Greg.

Tension crackled between them. His face was hard, uncompromising, and she regretted having been so outspoken.

'I see. Now the truth's coming out at last. You don't think I'm good enough for you – I've always been your second choice. I'll move downstairs to the servants' quarters where you think I belong.'

He didn't give her the opportunity to take back her hasty words. He walked past as if she didn't exist and she heard his heavy footsteps on the stairs as he went to collect his belongings.

From the moment they'd arrived things had been strained between them – now they'd had their first real row and on Christmas Day too.

She hurled the entire scuttle of coal onto the burning kindling and the fire went out. Was this a bad omen? Had the spark gone from her relationship so soon?

Her throat was tight. She wasn't going to cry. Tears wouldn't help. What she had to do was find Jack and put things right before the rift got bigger.

First, she must resurrect the fire, as newspaper was in short supply. She removed most of the coal and was relieved to find a small flame still burning. After blowing on it she carefully added bits of paper and wood until she was certain the coal would catch too.

Her hands were filthy; no doubt she had smudges on her face as well. She didn't want to speak to Jack looking like this so she used the downstairs cloakroom to repair the damage. People were now up, despite the early hour, and she wasn't sure if Jack was in the kitchen or upstairs. She hadn't heard him go past.

Her bedroom – their bedroom – was empty, the beds pushed apart and remade as singles. How had he had time to do all this? She didn't need to check the wardrobe or chest of drawers to see if his clothes were still there. He had taken them.

It was going to be difficult talking to him when the rest of the family were about but it had to be done. If she didn't put things right it would ruin Christmas for everyone and that would be unforgivable.

She slipped past the kitchen and dashed to the rear of the house to the rooms where Mabel had lived when she'd been the housekeeper. There was no sign of Jack, but more worrying his belongings weren't there either.

She swallowed the lump in her throat. If he wasn't here then he must have left. Where would he go on Christmas Day?

He could be a mile away by now and she could hardly run after him without telling everybody what had happened. The room was icy – the furniture under covers – it didn't look as if he'd come in here at all.

She crept into the passageway, found her wellington boots and coat, and slipped out of the back door. With any luck they would just think she and Jack had gone for an early morning stroll. The sky was grey, heavy with rain, barely light enough to see.

Could he have gone into the stables? If she yelled his name the others would hear so she would have to search in silence. The dogs were dancing around her feet, ecstatic to see her so early.

At first the significance of this didn't register. Good heavens! They would have followed him if he'd left the farm so perhaps he was still here somewhere after all.

Jack stormed into Ellie's bedroom, ripped the beds apart and remade them. He then stuffed his belongings into his kitbag and was about to leave when the door flew open.

'What's going on? For God's sake, Jack, don't do anything stupid. If you've had a row with my sister, put it right.'

For a second he wanted to punch George, but then sanity returned. 'I don't know what happened. One minute we were okay the next everything blew up.'

'Are you walking out on Christmas Day?'

'Leaving her? Of course I'm bloody not. I love her – but at the moment I'm too angry to see her without making things worse.'

'Right. Fiona's already downstairs. We can talk in our room whilst you calm down. That's if you want to tell me what this is all about.'

In George's room, Jack paced the floor while trying to put his thoughts in order. George was a good bloke and had just stretched out on the bed waiting for him to be ready to speak. When he explained what had happened it sounded pathetic. George slapped him on the back.

'Find Ellie and apologise. Doesn't matter whose fault it was. Easier if you do it. Works with Fiona when we have a row.'

A sudden gust of wind blew rain onto the window. 'I don't envy the land girls out in this today. It's torrential.'

'Then it's a good thing we can all stay inside. I can smell toast downstairs. Shall we go down? Ellie will be in the kitchen acting as if everything's fine.'

However, when Jack looked in, she wasn't there. She hadn't been upstairs and wasn't in the back rooms either. George joined him in the icy passageway.

'She's not been in there. Christ! Her coat and boots have gone. Why the hell would she go outside in this?'

'To find me. She thinks I've left her.' There was another blast of rain and wind and the back door flew open. Two small, bedraggled shapes rushed in. The dogs whined and barked, bringing the others out to investigate.

'Shut the door, George, the rain's coming in. What are these two doing in here anyway?' Mrs Simpson spoke as if this were still her house.

Ignoring her, Jack snatched up the largest coat he could see, rammed his feet into a pair of boots and, without explaining, ran into the storm. The dogs raced past and he followed them. If anything had happened to his darling girl he would never forgive himself.

Twenty-Six

The top half of the stable door slammed hard against the wall, making Ellie jump. Jack was either still inside the farmhouse or skulking in one of the outbuildings. Before she looked for him, she would check on Molly as she could hear the pony crashing about inside the loose box.

'It's only the wind, old girl, nothing to panic about.'

The pony's ears were flat against her head and her eyes were wild. Something more than the weather had frightened her. There was no option but to go in and calm her down. Jack could take care of himself – the pony couldn't.

Molly was technically a pony but was almost tall enough to be a horse. Talking softly all the time, she approached the terrified animal. As she did so she was scanning the stable to see what had caused the upset.

Something moved in the straw. Her heart leapt into her throat. The dogs were going frantic outside. It was too late to open the door and let them in to deal with whatever was hiding.

She placed herself between the moving straw and Molly and this seemed to do the trick. 'There, nothing to be frightened of. Here, let me take your halter; you've got the lead rein tangled around your neck.'

This rope should have been removed before the pony was put in to the box but obviously Dad had forgotten to do it. Whilst she was soothing the still-trembling pony, the heavens opened. The rain sounded like bullets on the roof and drowned out her voice.

The bottom half of the door crashed open and Molly bolted past sending her sprawling into the straw. By the time she'd regained her feet the wretched animal had vanished. The dogs were busy dispatching the rats that had been unwise enough take refuge in the stable. She left them to their grisly task and stepped out into the appalling weather. The dogs could get out if she left the top half of the stable unlocked but she would close the bottom door.

This took her a few moments as the wind kept snatching it from her hand. She was now soaked to her knickers even with a waterproof coat and wellington boots on to protect her.

She could hardly leave Molly wandering about in the rain so set off in search of her. In the distance she heard the sound of a lorry pulling up. For a moment she was puzzled, then realised it was the team of land girls being delivered at the end of the drive. There was a faint glimmer of light on the horizon indicating dawn was approaching. It must be later than she thought.

She trudged in the most likely direction the pony would have taken – the drive – and halfway up was met by a cheerful call.

'I say, we've got the pony. Don't worry. We'll put her away and give her a good rub-down.'

Ellie could vaguely see half a dozen girls approaching. 'Thanks very much. There were rats in the stable and it spooked her. A merry Christmas to you all. Please come to the house when you've finished. There'll be a hot drink and something to eat waiting in the kitchen.'

There was a chorus of 'thank you' from them and Ellie squelched her way back to the house. Jack appeared at a run and she was snatched from her feet.

'I was frantic when I couldn't find you, honey. I'm so sorry. I love you and I don't care where you live as long as I'm there with you.'

His lips were cold and wet but she returned his kiss with enthusiasm.

'I love you and I'm sorry too. Let's go in. I'm soaked through and we'll get pneumonia if we hang about here.'

He kept his arm firmly around her waist and together they ran to the back door. It opened as they arrived and they rushed in, grateful to be out of the wind and rain.

'What a palaver! Here, lovey, give me your wet things. You run along upstairs and jump in the bath. It's already drawn for you,' Mabel said as she helped her out of her sopping wet coat.

'Molly got out – but the land girls are bringing her back. Jack, you can have the hot water after me.'

Knowing him, he would probably expect to get in with her but with the family waiting downstairs, this wasn't going to happen.

The bathroom was deliciously warm and full of steam. She stripped off and stepped in the bath. Instead of the expected five inches it was half full. Such luxury – and whoever had run the bath for her had added bath salts. She wasn't sure Jack would appreciate smelling of lavender, but she loved it.

The door hadn't been locked and he appeared in his dressing gown. 'Don't take too long, darling, the rest of them are holding up breakfast for us.'

'I'm getting out now – I feel wonderful now I'm warm again.'

When she stood up he was holding a large towel open and wrapped her in it. She leaned against him for a second, but hastily stepped away when his arms tightened.

'Absolutely not, Jack Reynolds. Get in the bath and behave yourself.'

His laugh sent shivers down her spine. 'I've reassembled the bed, just needs making up again.'

'I'll do that whilst you're in here.'

This time she put on a frock and a pair of the nylons she'd been given at the American base. She was just applying a smudge of red lipstick when Jack came in.

'God, it's icy in here. Don't hang about waiting for me, Ellie. I'll not be long.'

'I've put out your clothes. Don't worry about the tie.'

'I'm not wearing a bloody cravat.'

'I'm relieved to hear it. Leave those for men like Nigel. With that pullover on no one will see your collar anyway.'

The rain stopped and the watery winter sun sent feeble light into the bedroom. They had both apologised, things appeared to be smoothed over, but there was a distance between them that hadn't been there before and she didn't know how to bridge it.

*

This was supposed to be a happy time. The war was going better, Ellie's family were reconciled but Jack was finding it difficult to relax. There were too many ghosts in this house for him to be comfortable.

Neither of them had mentioned Greg but his shadow lurked between them. It was impossible to compete with a dead man – he wasn't sure he wanted to carry on trying. When he'd said to her that he was second best, that had been nothing but the truth. If things didn't improve, if she didn't commit completely to him, then maybe this marriage wasn't going to be what he'd hoped for.

He would never leave her but he would now lower his expectations and settle for what she was prepared to give him. What he needed was a stiff drink, but alcohol of any sort appeared to be in short supply this year.

The mood in the kitchen was subdued, even Fiona was quiet and she was usually the most talkative. Mabel insisted she and Mrs Simpson had everything under control and they were instructed to remain in the sitting room and entertain themselves with party games and conversation. The gifts under the tree wouldn't be opened until the afternoon, which was a shame as this would have given them all something to do.

'Shall we listen to *Music While You Work*?'

'Yes, put the wireless on, Jack lad, a bit of music will be just the ticket,' Fred replied. 'I'm looking forward to the King's speech after lunch. Wonder what he'll have to say about the Yanks.'

'It's not his words, Dad, Churchill tells him what to say,' Ellie said.

'Doesn't matter, love, as long as he's got good news for us. This blooming war has gone on long enough.'

She was siting next to Fiona on the sofa and the only empty chair was on the opposite side of the room. He switched on the wireless set, tuned it, and then flopped into the chair. George dragged a wooden rocker over so they could talk quietly without interrupting the music. Wilfred Pickles usually made him smile but today Jack didn't feel in the mood.

'Bit of an atmosphere, isn't there? Have you and my sister not sorted things out?'

'We apologised and on the surface everything's okay – but she's different here.' He hesitated to say what he was thinking but George was a good friend and would listen without judging him. 'It's Greg.' He explained and his friend nodded.

'We should have had Christmas at St Albans away from the sad memories. I can't help thinking about my brother. Mum and Dad must feel it too.'

'What are we going to do to make things more cheerful?'

'Nothing we can do. We'll just have to get on with it.'

Ellie suddenly jumped to her feet. 'Golly! I'd forgotten I'd invited the entire gang of land girls in for a hot drink and something to eat when they'd finished.'

He exchanged a glance with George. This was exactly what the house needed – a bit of party. 'We'll make a hot punch. There's bound to be some leftover dregs in the bottles in the cupboard in the study.'

'Good idea. I'll see if I can make a few sandwiches or something. They'll be here in half an hour so we'd better get a move on.'

'Is that all right with you, Dad?' George asked.

'Just what the doctor ordered. I'll give you a hand. I'm pretty sure there's half a bottle of sherry hiding in the pantry.'

Ellie shook her head. 'Don't touch that, Dad – it's for the trifle for Boxing Day tea. Mum and Mabel would skin you alive if you used it for punch.'

'Glad you told me, love. There might be a bottle of wine, maybe some beer, but doubt you'll find anything else. You go ahead and search.'

He and George managed to find two bottles of wine left over from Fred and Mabel's wedding, but even better, they unearthed half a bottle of brandy.

'This will be more than enough to make the punch worth drinking,' he said gleefully.

'What we need are cloves, cinnamon and sugar – orange juice would be wonderful but I've not seen an orange for years,' George replied.

They took their bounty into the kitchen. 'I've put out my preserving pan, that's the biggest one I've got. There's also some sugar – not much – and half a bottle of orange cordial. I thought it might be good to add a jar of fruit. I've got plums and raspberries as well as some apples.' She pointed to the array of goodies and then vanished into the pantry.

The kitchen smelt of roasting chicken, Christmas pudding and roast potatoes. His mouth watered at the thought of sitting down to dinner later.

Mabel was getting into the spirit of this. Jack wondered how his mother-in-law was coping with things that used to be hers claimed by a new wife. The atmosphere seemed jolly enough so presumably both women were happy with the situation.

He'd never made punch before but George seemed to know what he was doing. He tipped everything into the pan, put the spices in a bit of muslin and tossed these in as well.

Ellie was busy making ham sandwiches and smiled at him. Perhaps he'd been imagining there was a distance between them. George had wandered off to take Fiona a cup of tea, leaving him in charge.

'What do I do with the fruit? Do I just chuck it in with everything else?'

'You need an equal amount of water to alcohol – have you added that yet?'

He hadn't and was glad she reminded him or the punch would have been too strong. 'I remember being in charge of a non-alcoholic brew…' He regretted mentioning the Christmas when Neil and Greg had been present as immediately her smile slipped. He turned away from her and grabbed everything they'd found and dropped it into the mixture.

He stirred and sniffed appreciatively. The aroma of spices, fruit and hot alcohol filled the kitchen. George returned and slapped him on the back.

'Have you tasted it? Can't serve it without tasting first.' He picked up the china ladle and dipped it in. Jack handed him two mugs and these were half-filled. 'Hey, you two, I want to try it as well.' Ellie poked him in the back and reached round and took one of the mugs from his hand.

'This is delicious, but I think you could do with more water as it's really strong.' She handed him back the mug and he drained it.

'You're right – we'll be plastered if we drink too much of this.'

He was about to fill a jug at the sink when there was the sound of voices outside. The land girls were coming. The water was forgotten and the heady brew served as it was. Mabel had put out more than enough glasses and even Fiona had some.

By the time the impromptu party was over the atmosphere had changed. They eventually sat down to a somewhat delayed Christmas dinner at three o'clock. If the chicken was overcooked and the potatoes a bit burnt, he didn't notice. It all smelled delicious. He would be happy to do the washing up along with George and Fred whilst the ladies put their feet up after the meal.

'It's almost three o'clock, Mabel love, if we get the plates out quick, we can listen to the King whilst we eat.'

'We'll do no such thing, Fred Simpson. Show a bit of respect. We've waited this long for lunch so we'll listen as usual in the sitting room before we eat.'

Jack suggested a compromise. 'Why don't we bring the wireless in here?'

Mabel wasn't too happy but reluctantly agreed to this arrangement. There was just time to dish up and sit down before the national anthem was played. Mabel wanted to stand but was persuaded it wasn't necessary.

"This year it adds to our happiness that we are sharing it with so many of our comrades-in-arms from the United States of America. The recent victories won by the United Nations enable me this Christmas to speak with firm confidence about the future. Tremendous blows have been struck by the armies of the Soviet Union, but

the lessons learned during the forty tremendous months behind us have taught us how to work together for victory, and we must see to it that we keep together after the war to build a worthier future."

'That was ever so good, wasn't it? It was a bit of a shock when his brother abdicated but I prefer him now. To think that he has a dreadful stammer and can still make a speech. He's an inspiration to us all.'

Everyone around the table agreed. Somehow, they all found room to squeeze in a helping of Christmas pudding and cream.

'Where did you find the fruit to do this, Mabel?' Ellie asked between mouthfuls.

'I saved up points for months. There's no mince pies or chocolate but it wouldn't be the same without a proper pudding.'

This was perfect time for Ellie to produce her contribution to the feast. 'Look what I've got for us all. Real coffee and two bars of chocolate. They were given to me when I landed on that American base and Jack and I decided to keep them for today.'

It didn't take long to wash up despite the amount of crockery used as all the saucepans, roasting tins and so on had already been done.

'George, take Fred into the sitting room. I'll do the coffee...' Ellie called.

'I've come to do it, darling. I've done nothing at all today apart from cause chaos, you made the sandwiches for the land girls.'

'That doesn't count. You've just helped with the washing up – it will be quicker if I do it on my own.'

He bit back the angry response at this tactless remark. Why did she always have to point out his deficiencies? Of course, it would be quicker if she made the coffee and carried it all through on a tray but she should realise he didn't need his nose rubbing in the fact every five minutes.

Ellie saw Jack stiffen at her offer. He really should have got over this sensitivity by now. It was just stupid pride that made him want to do everything one-handed just to prove that he could when it was so much easier to let someone else carry a tray of drinks or make the coffee.

Why was he so prickly suddenly? It must be because they were here and he was worrying unnecessarily about her feelings for Greg. It was silly really as they'd spent several weekends together here and they'd been perfectly fine. Perhaps it was because it was Christmas.

She ignored his black looks, picked up the tray and marched out, leaving him to simmer on his own. It was his hard luck if he missed out on the treat of real coffee and a few squares of delicious chocolate. Her arrival was greeted with delight.

'What a treat! Did this come from the PX?' George asked as he handed a mug to Fiona.

'I expect it did originally, but it was given to me. I know it seems extravagant to us, as we've lived without such luxuries for years. However, the Yanks have everything they could possibly want. No rationing for them.'

'Thank you, Ellie, for sharing your gifts with us,' Mum said.

'Talking of gifts, shall we open presents now? I've got a beastly back ache and am going to turn in soon,' Fiona said with a grimace.

'I've got a couple of Aspirins you can have,' Mabel said.

'That's kind, but no thanks. George is going to make me a nice hot water bottle and that will do very well.'

'If you go up now, you'll miss Tommy Handley in *ITMA*. It's on at eight o'clock,' George said as he took a seat next to her.

'That's a shame, but it can't be helped. I need to put my feet up in bed.'

The gifts were exchanged and exclaimed over. Mabel had knitted gloves for everyone. George and Fiona had got woollen scarves for the men and silk ones for the women. Ellie's books were also well received.

Fiona waddled off soon afterwards with her hot water bottle. George settled her in and then rejoined them. Jack was unusually silent and she was dreading having to share a bed with him when he was in such bad humour. She certainly had no intention of making love tonight, even if he wanted to.

Twenty-Seven

After *ITMA* was over Ellie made cocoa for everyone and took them in a generous slice of Madeira cake to go with it.

'I'm taking mine up. Good night everyone – it's been a lovely Christmas Day.' This wasn't really true but she could hardly involve her family in her marital problems.

Jack and George had decided to finish off the punch. They had reheated it and tipped it into a jug and then vanished to the study. From the raucous laughter and bawdy singing coming from behind the door they were obviously the worse for wear. She smiled as she recalled the night of her wedding – Jack and George had got drunk together then too. She hadn't bothered to take them a hot drink.

'Good night, Ellie love, make the most of your time off. You'll be back on duty soon enough,' Dad said.

She kissed him on the cheek and hugged Mabel. 'Sleep well, love, I reckon your Jack won't come up for a while from the sound of it.'

Her mother accompanied her to the door. 'It must be hard for you being here with Jack when the last time you spent Christmas here both Neil and Greg were alive.'

'Actually, Mum, we were here last year. But you're right, I think everyone's a bit subdued because of that. It took me far too long to get over Greg and realise that I love Jack. He thinks I'm still comparing him to Greg, which isn't true. I don't understand why he's jealous of a ghost.'

'He can't compete with a dead man. Greg was a fine young man but Jack is a better fit for you. You have so much in common. Don't worry – he'll get over it once you are away from here.'

'If we could spend more time together things would be easier. Unfortunately, we don't get our leave together very often. We haven't spent much more than two weeks under the same roof since we were married.'

'That's not good. Would you consider resigning from the ATA, starting a family like Fiona and George? It can't be easy for him having his wife his superior as well as only having one hand.'

'I can't put my personal feelings ahead of my duty to the country. I'm needed, and until this ghastly war's over I'll do what everyone else is doing – just getting on with it as best I can.'

'Actually, I think I'll go up too. I'll just collect my cocoa and follow you. I'm very proud of you – I don't know how you can work in a man's world the way you do.'

Ellie hurriedly changed into her night things and nipped to the bathroom whilst it was still vacant. Dad and Mabel would probably turn in as Mum was coming up now.

There was movement from Fiona's room. She tapped on the door and was called in.

'Thank goodness you've come. I've wet the bed and am too embarrassed to ask for clean sheets.'

'Don't worry about it. I know where everything is. I expect these things happen when you're heavily pregnant.'

Mum was about to go into her bedroom and overheard the remark. 'What things, Ellie?'

'Fiona's had a slight accident and I'm just getting her some clean linen.'

'Good heavens! It sounds as if her waters have broken. We need to call the midwife immediately.'

Ellie clutched the doorframe. 'She's had back ache since yesterday.'

'Oh dear – I wish she'd told me. This could well mean the baby's coming very shortly. There could well not be time for help to arrive.'

'What shall I do? I think George is drunk – I doubt if he's in a fit state to find a midwife for her.'

Fiona appeared at the door looking remarkably cheerful considering the circumstances. 'I'm about to drop this baby. I want to push. I hope you know how to deliver one, Ma.'

'Ellie, we need newspaper and old sheets. If George isn't capable then you will have to find a midwife. Before you do, I need hot water and clean towels.'

She paused long enough to tell Mabel and Fred and then grabbed the things Mum had asked for.

'I shouldn't think George is sober enough to ring anyone,' her father agreed. 'I'll get the car started but I've no idea where to go.

'Thank you, Dad. Can I leave you in charge of the hot water, Mabel? I've got to take these things up immediately.'

The bed had been stripped, Fiona was in a clean nightdress and all that was needed were the items she was bringing.

'Mum, what do you want me to do?'

'Get the bed ready so Fiona can lie down.' She sounded confident – probably having had three children of her own she knew what to expect.

'Were we all born here?'

'Of course you were. Now, Fiona, there's no time for you to have a bath or anything else. That will have to wait until afterwards.'

Once the expectant mother was safely on the bed Ellie went to the door to collect the obligatory hot water and clean towels. There was no sign of her brother.

'George?'

Mabel shook her head. 'They've both passed out. I've put a couple of pails beside them and Fred has covered them with blankets. They'll sleep it off in the study.'

'I'm not comfortable about being in here. Would you help Mum?'

'I might not have had any little ones of my own but I've attended a couple of deliveries. I'd be delighted to help. You run along, lovey – try and get some sleep as this might well take all night.'

'I'm going to fetch the midwife. Dad's just getting the car started. Is it still Nurse Smith who lives in the cottage next to the church?'

'It is. I don't have her telephone number or you could ring. Be careful driving in the dark, Ellie, we don't want any more excitement tonight.'

She was happy to leave them to it. Her reaction to Fiona's labour reinforced her decision not to have children of her own before the end of the war. She realised that she wasn't the maternal type and would much rather continue being able to earn her own living, especially if this involved flying.

Jack's little Austin Seven was still kept at the farm and it was this vehicle that was waiting for her.

'It's got a gallon of petrol in the tank and that should be more than enough to get you there and back. I'm off to my bed – babies are women's work. Give me a heifer and her calf any day of the week and I'm your man. I'll leave the back door open for you and the midwife.'

It was only two miles to the village and as there was a full moon she could see well enough even with the meagre light from the pinprick headlights. She pulled up outside the cottage and left the engine running while she ran to the door. She was raising her hand to knock when it opened.

'I heard the car coming. I've just got back from another delivery. I don't recognise you – which of my ladies have you come to fetch me for?'

'Nurse Smith, I'm Ellie Simpson – no – Ellie Reynolds now.' She quickly explained the reason she was there.

'That's no problem at all. Happy to help. Merry Christmas to you.'

'I'd forgotten it was still Christmas Day. I wonder if this baby will come before midnight.'

The midwife jumped into the front seat, her bag on her lap. 'From what you've told me this baby is eager to come into the world. This is a second baby so everything moves more quickly than it did first time. I just hope I'm there in time to catch it.'

The round trip had taken less than twenty minutes – surely not time enough for her niece or nephew to arrive in the world? No sound of a baby crying and worryingly no shouts and groans coming from inside the room.

'Nurse Smith, it's very quiet. Shouldn't my sister-in-law be yelling?'

'Not all women do, Mrs Reynolds. Why don't you make us all a nice cup of tea?'

The midwife stepped into the room. Ellie froze outside, fearing the worst. Her breath hissed through her teeth.

'That was quick, Nurse. Mrs Simpson is ready to push. You've arrived just in time.' Mum wasn't worried so everything must be tickety-boo.

Something jolted Jack to consciousness. For a moment he was disorientated. Where the hell was he? The noise that had woken him was George snoring. Someone must have come in and covered him with a blanket and turned the light out, which was why it was so dark.

The house was quiet so it must be the middle of the night. He was perfectly comfortable where he was but wanted to be in his own bed with his darling girl curled up beside him.

Carefully he pushed back the covers and swung his legs to the floor. He literally kicked the bucket and the clatter echoed around the room. He waited for his companion to stir but George continued to snore noisily.

He reached the door without further incident and pushed it open. To his surprise there were lights on everywhere – if he hadn't been so hung over he would have noticed the sliver of light coming under the door.

What he needed was coffee but he wasn't going to make himself any. Tea would have to do. His head was thumping, his stomach churning and there was a filthy taste in his mouth. Not the first time he'd felt so grim after drinking himself senseless.

He was a little unsteady on his feet and smiled. He wasn't exactly drunk, but neither was he completely sober. Maybe it would be better if he remained downstairs; he didn't think Ellie would appreciate him in this state.

His hand was raised to lift the latch when it flew open and she came out with a tray of tea and walked straight into him.

Instinctively he put out his missing hand to steady himself and his actual hand to try and prevent the tray from crashing to the flagstones. He failed miserably with both.

Ellie managed to keep her feet but he crashed into the wall and lost his balance, taking the tray and its contents with him. Being doused in scalding liquid cleared his head wonderfully.

'Stay where you are, Jack, don't try and get up.' She vanished for a second and then he was drenched in freezing water.

He spluttered and coughed and was about to protest when a second deluge landed on his chest. He was now completely sober and incandescent.

He was about to explode when she dropped to her feet beside him and began to run her hands over his face and chest. 'My God, are you burnt? That tea was red hot. I'm so sorry – I thought you were snoring in the study.'

Only then did he understand why she'd tipped water over him. 'I'm wet, cold, but not burnt thanks to you. You'll also be pleased to know I'm no longer plastered.' He held out his hand. 'Could you give me a hand up, please?'

Somehow, he staggered to his feet. He was standing in a pool of water and he shivered. 'Who were you taking the tray to? It's the middle of the night.'

'Fiona's about to have her baby. The midwife told me to make tea but, come to think of it, I think she just wanted to get rid of me.'

'George's still unconscious in the study. We need to wake him up and get him ready to greet his offspring. I'm going to change first and then get him on his feet. Would you make him a strong pot of coffee?' He squelched to the foot of the stairs and then turned. 'I'm really sorry about earlier…'

'It doesn't matter. We both said things we didn't mean. The kettle's already on again. I think we could both do with some coffee.'

He half expected the beds to be separate again and was relieved to find they weren't. He wouldn't blame her if she didn't want to sleep with him. He'd behaved like an idiot but he was going to make it up to her.

When he returned there was the wonderful smell of freshly brewed coffee in the kitchen but no sign of her. She must have made another tray of tea and taken it up.

He looked at his coffee longingly but decided getting George on his feet must come first. He added three spoonsful of precious sugar to the other mug and returned to the study.

He switched on the light. 'Come on, mate, you've got to wake up. You're going to be a father any minute.' He moved the bucket out of the way.

George groaned but didn't stir. Jack put the coffee down and went back to fetch a jug of cold water. It had been very effective on him so no doubt would do the same for his brother-in-law.

He carefully pulled back the cover so it wouldn't get wet and tipped half the cold water on George's head. The result was immediate.

He sat up instantly and surged to his feet with his fists clenched. Fortunately for Jack, George's eyes were still closed and he easily avoided the swinging fists. He hurled the remaining contents of the jug and hastily stepped aside.

'George, you idiot, I'm trying to do you a favour. Open your eyes, for God's sake, and get a grip, man.'

This time his brother-in-law opened his eyes. 'I'm all wet. What the blazes is going on?' He blinked and rubbed his eyes.

'Here, drink this, and then dry yourself with the towel. You're about to become a father. Fiona's upstairs with the midwife having your baby.'

George's legs folded under him and he sank back onto the chair. 'Bugger me! It's not due for another two weeks. If anything goes wrong this time she won't get over it.'

Jack put the mug of coffee in his hand and George drank it in a few gulps. He looked a lot better now. 'I'll fetch you a dry shirt – you can't go into your own room – obviously.'

As he rushed past his bedroom he heard the wail of a newborn baby. This made him an uncle by marriage and Ellie was now officially an aunt. He returned with the shirt – one from before his accident – and helped George put it on.

'The baby's here and it's fine – I told you that it would be. You can stop shaking and get upstairs to see your son or daughter.'

He walked behind him in case George fell backwards as he didn't seem very steady on his feet. The door opened as they arrived and Mrs Simpson stepped out.

'Good, you have a son; mother and baby are absolutely fine, which is more than I can say for you.'

'I'm going to be sick – excuse me, Mother.' He made it just in time.

'I'll look after him, Mrs Simpson. It might be better if he left it until tomorrow to make his apologies and see his baby.'

'Why you young men will insist on drinking yourself sick is beyond me. I don't know where Ellie is. I think she's probably gone to bed. Not quite a Christmas baby as it's now Boxing Day. Good night, Jack.'

Jack wasn't quite sure where he was supposed to put George as his bedroom was out of bounds, Ellie was in their room, and Mrs Simpson and Fred occupied the other two.

Eventually he escorted the new father back to the study and tucked him in with both the blankets. 'Congratulations, mate, now get some sleep. Tomorrow have a bath and shave. Don't go in and see Fiona until you have.'

There wasn't an answer as George was already snoring. He left him with the door slightly open so the room wasn't totally dark.

He crept into his own room, undressed as quietly as he could and then slipped under the covers, trying not to wake Ellie. He reached out for her but although he could hear her breathing there was a barrier between them. The beds were together but they'd been made up as singles.

She couldn't have made it plainer. She hadn't really forgiven him. He turned his back on her and closed his eyes but sleep eluded him. The third time he sighed she spoke from the other side of the bed.

'Has it come? What did Fiona have?'

'A boy. She's fine. George knows but passed out again downstairs.'

Her hand brushed his face. 'Sorry about the bed, darling, I didn't have the energy to make it again. We'll do it together in the morning.'

He kissed her hand. 'Okay. Good night, sweetheart, I love you.'

'I love you too. I can't believe we have a nephew to spoil. I'm so happy for George and Fiona.'

As he drifted off to sleep he imagined how he'd feel when he held his own child. In fact, the sooner Ellie was pregnant the happier he'd be. He'd be a father and have a blood relative again and she would be safe at home and not risking her life every day.

When they woke he would persuade her to make love and with any luck they would start a baby. He was wide awake and restless. He imagined their son or daughter being born in the autumn. Where would they live? He would rent a house near White Waltham so they could be together most nights. After the war was over he would go to university and study civil engineering, become a man who built things, someone who helped repair the damage the bombing had done. One thing he was certain of: he didn't want to be a farmer like Fred.

He smiled wryly. There wasn't a choice really as, with only one hand, working on the land would be almost impossible. Fred had left the farm to Ellie whilst he and George were estranged but now things were different. His brother-in-law would need employment so maybe he could take over instead of Ellie. After all, not only was George's son a Simpson, he'd been born at Glebe Farm. He couldn't wait to tell his darling girl what he'd planned for their future.

Twenty-Eight

The early arrival of Fiona's baby was more than enough to dispel the aura of sadness that had hung over the place up to that point. Ellie cooed and smiled when appropriate and was delighted for her brother and his wife. However, she didn't feel a rush of maternal love or an immediate desire to produce a baby of her own.

'He's such a little duck, isn't he, Ellie love? Imagine, another little Simpson born in this house. My Fred's over the moon at being a grandfather,' Mabel said.

'I wonder what they're going to call him – I hope it's not Noel as he was born on Boxing Day,' Ellie said.

'George told me they are going to call him Neil,' Jack replied as he munched his third slice of toast.

'Another Neil Simpson in the family – I think that's a perfect choice. All that alcohol last night doesn't seem to have affected your appetite. My brother looks decidedly the worse for wear.'

'That punch was lethal. We should have known better. Fiona and the baby will have to stay here, I suppose, until she's allowed to get up. He'll have to go back to work.'

Mother came in looking ten years younger. Being a grandmother obviously suited her. 'The midwife is very pleased with baby and mother. I overheard what you said, Jack, and you're quite right, they will have to stay here for a week, but can then travel by car – if one can be found with sufficient petrol – to St Albans after that.' She turned to Mabel who was busy making more toast at the range. 'I should like to stay as well, if that's possible, Mabel. Of course, if I'll be in the way I will go back with George.'

'You stop as long as you want, Charlotte. After all he's your grandson, not mine.'

'That's absolutely not true. He is in the fortunate position of having three grandmothers to spoil him. Fiona's parents have been informed but obviously they won't see the infant until we are all back home in St Albans.'

'That makes Sir Reginald baby Neil's great-grandfather. Are you going to tell him?'

'He can read it in *The Times* along with everybody else. I want nothing more to do with him. The obnoxious man has caused more than enough trouble for this family.'

Mum had conveniently forgotten she had run to her father when she'd decided she no longer wished to be married to Dad. At least they were all in agreement about keeping Sir Reginald away.

'Did anyone ever discover why he gate-crashed our wedding?' Jack asked.

'Perhaps he wanted to be reconciled with us, but he certainly didn't go about it the right way. To be honest, I was surprised he didn't press charges after you ejected him so splendidly, Jack.'

'Mum, is he very rich? I've never thought to ask that.'

'Actually, my dear, it's not something one discusses with one's parents. However, I do remember my mother saying there were several estates up north, as well as shipping and manufacturing interests.'

George came in and gratefully accepted the tea Mabel handed him. He shook his head and pulled a face when she offered him toast.

'I can't quite believe I'm a father. Fiona's in seventh heaven. She won't put Neil down and the midwife told her she'll spoil the baby if she doesn't do so.'

'Poor little mite, he just wants a cuddle. I don't like to hear babies cry.' Mabel sniffed her disapproval.

'She's ignoring that advice. He's a splendid little chap. And Fiona's forgiven me, as long as I don't make a habit of it.'

Ellie drifted out of the kitchen, intending to take the dogs for a walk. The sun was out and there was no frost. Jack joined her in the passageway.

'Good idea, I could do with a walk to clear my head.'

They hadn't gone far when there was the familiar roar of Spitfires approaching. They watched them fly overhead, almost low enough to see the pilots, and she prayed they all came back safely.

'Do you still wish you were with your squadron?'

'I wish I still had both hands but apart from that I'm happy with my lot. I doubt that any of the guys I flew with are still alive.'

They walked on, the dogs racing ahead, happy to be out with their favourite people. They didn't really need extra exercise as they lived outside.

Something belatedly occurred to her. 'They were flying really low. They should have been climbing to fighting height, shouldn't they?'

'Holy cow! There could be low-flying bombers heading this way. We'd better get back...'

His words were drowned out by the sound of the air raid siren. He grabbed her hand and they raced to the house. Dad had said they didn't bother to go down to the air raid shelter but today was different.

'I'll go and get Fiona and the baby, you tell everyone else.'

His lips tightened but there was no time to think about his sensitivities – lives were at stake. He couldn't carry a newborn baby with one arm.

'Down into the shelter immediately. Low-flying bombers coming any moment,' she yelled as she hurtled into the house.

She took the stairs two at a time and burst into Fiona's room. 'I'm almost ready. George will take the baby.'

'Do I need to bring anything for you?'

'Just grab some blankets, Ellie – it's going to be cold down there.'

Mabel had been in charge of pillows, blankets and flasks of tea from when the war started but she wasn't sure if this practice was still adhered to. She didn't have to worry.

'I've got everything we need, Ellie love. My Fred has taken pillows and blankets. I'm bringing tea and cake.'

'What about Mum?'

'Your Jack has taken her, along with the candles and such. I expect it will be nasty and damp in there.'

The Anderson shelter had been built to house half a dozen comfortably and it was going to be a bit of a squeeze with seven of them, plus the baby and the paraphernalia he needed.

She waited for Mabel to make her way down the slippery steps before closing the door.

'What about the land girls? Won't they want to come in?'

'No, they've finished for the morning and have gone on to the next farm. Only the livestock to see to at the moment,' Dad said from somewhere in the darkness at the back of the shelter.

'I'll stay where I am on the steps until you get the oil lamp and the candles lit. I don't want to fall over anyone.'

A match flared and there was light – not much of it – but enough for her to make her way carefully to sit on the end of the bench next to Mabel.

The baby was crying and the sound echoed against the tin walls, sounding louder than it would have done outside.

'He's hungry. I was about to feed him. I'll have to do so now so I suggest anyone who is likely to be offended looks the other way.'

Immediately Mum and Mabel stepped in. 'Here, we'll hold the blanket around you so you can have your privacy, Fiona love.'

There was the sound of shuffling and the wails of little Neil grew louder. Then blessed silence. The baby settled. Apart from the heavy breathing of those inside with her it was relatively quiet.

The unmistakable sound of a bomber approaching made her stomach flip. They'd arrived not a moment too soon.

She held her breath. The scream of Spitfires in pursuit drowned out the bigger aircraft. She pressed herself against the damp wall and wished she was sitting next to Jack.

The dogfight must be directly overhead as the noise was deafening.

The shelter shook violently and the candles went out. Jack was already on his feet and making his way to the end so he could be with Ellie.

He braced himself against the side with his hand and managed to keep upright. There was no point in calling her name as she wouldn't hear him.

He found her and pulled her against him. She was shaking and he held her close. She snuggled into his shoulder.

There was a second horrendous noise and then ominous silence. The baby was screaming, Mabel was crying, and he could hear George and Fred murmuring words of comfort and encouragement.

'Is everyone all right?' he called into the darkness. No one was hurt.

'Did a bomb drop on us or the house?' Fred asked.

'No, I think one of the planes crashed very close to us. George, will you come with me to investigate?'

'I'm coming. There could be people trapped and I don't care if they're German or British. I'm going to do what I can to help.' Ellie shrugged off his arm and was at the door before he could protest.

Someone managed to rekindle the candles, which made it easier for both him and George to follow her.

'The door won't open. I think there's debris blocking it.' Ellie spoke quietly so only he and George could hear.

'With three of us pushing we might manage it,' he said.

They put their shoulders against it and even with their combined weight it didn't budge even an inch. His heart sank. Something had fallen on top of the shelter and they weren't going to get out without help.

'I can't smell burning, Jack, so I don't think there's anything in flames on top of us.'

George moved down a step to give them more room. 'The shelter's too far away from the house for it to be debris from that. What the hell do you think it is?'

Fred spoke from behind them. 'I reckon it's the stables. They're close enough to block the shelter door if they got a direct hit.'

Ellie pressed her ear against the door. 'I can't hear anything at all. God, I hope Molly isn't crushed.'

'Better the pony than us, Ellie love.'

Jack thought carefully about what he said next as he didn't want to make matters worse by alarming everyone.

'It's possible no one knows we're down here. However, even if the rescue services don't turn up, when the land girls come back this afternoon to milk and so on, they'll raise the alarm. We've got food and drink and will be perfectly fine until then.'

There was a chorus of agreement from the others and the three of them took their places again. 'I'm going to get the oil lamp lit as it will give a bit of heat in here,' Mabel said cheerfully. 'Fred, as you're on your feet will you hand out the blankets and cushions?'

Jack was impressed by her resilience. Mrs Simpson was slumped against the wall. He prayed she had only fainted.

'Sweetheart, your mom doesn't look too well.'

'I'll see to her – she's not good with loud noises or small spaces.'

His mother-in-law rallied and took a tin mug of stewed tea from Mabel. The infant was quiet and both Fiona and George appeared resigned to their circumstances. They were wrapped in a couple of blankets with the baby between them.

Fred was sipping his tea whilst Mabel fussed over everyone. Only Ellie seemed tense and unsettled.

'What's wrong? Am I missing something?'

She grabbed his good arm and all but dragged him up the brick steps until they were standing next to the exit. 'It's all very well blithely saying it will be fine when the land girls come back. Put your ear to the door – can you hear anything?'

He did as she asked. 'No, but we wouldn't be able to if there's a pile of rubble on top of us.'

Her grip tightened. 'Think, Jack. It can't be the stables or the house, whatever Dad said to the contrary. Both are too far way from where this was dug out. There's only one thing that can have blocked the door. One of planes has crashed in the yard.'

He was about to disagree but then went over what had just happened. There had been the roar of an aircraft and then the shelter had shuddered. 'I think you could be right but I bloody well hope not. If it's the Jerry bomber he's possibly got unexploded bombs on board...' He couldn't continue.

'Are you saying that they won't be able to dig us out in case the bombs go off and kill the rescuers? That we could be left here to starve to death?'

She sounded remarkably calm about the possibility they were all going to meet a grisly end. 'I was going to say that, yes, but am now trying to work out what plan you've got in mind.'

'There are spades in here. I put them in myself for this eventuality. I'm sure we can dig ourselves out. Not this way, but from the other end.'

'Then we'd better get started. Are you going to tell the others, or shall I?'

Fred overheard this last remark. 'Tell us what, son?'

Ellie explained and not even Mrs Simpson panicked. 'I'm relieved no one has had to use the facilities behind the curtain.'

'I wish you hadn't mentioned that, Mother, now I need…'

'That is quite enough, George. I suggest you move the Elsan to the other end of the shelter, put it on the steps. Then Mabel and I will put the curtain back up whilst you men get on with the digging.'

'I'm perfectly capable of doing my share, Mum – I do the same work as a man every day.'

'Does anyone know what the back of the shelter looks like?' George asked as Ellie handed him a spade.

'I think I've seen a plan of one,' she said. 'It's made up of three pieces so with any luck we can dislodge one of them and dig between them.'

Jack obviously couldn't help – he must find this so frustrating. 'It's all very well saying we can dig our way out, Ellie, but now I think about it I'm not sure it's a good idea.'

She was standing with George and Fred. Jack spoke from behind them. 'What do you mean? I know there's a risk of soil coming into the shelter but with everybody at the other end I can't see that will be a problem.'

'If we remove one of the corrugated-iron supports I think there's a real danger the whole thing might collapse.'

Why was he being so difficult? 'So, you think we should sit here and wait, not do anything to help ourselves?'

'That's exactly what I think, Ellie. We might think we know what's blocking the door but we could be wrong. We've not given anyone a chance to help us. We've got the rest of the tea and cake as well as the emergency rations of water and tinned stuff. Let's wait a few hours before we do anything rash.'

Dad patted her on the shoulder. 'Your Jack's got the right of it, love. Better to sit tight and see what happens. It won't be pleasant in here but it might be a lot worse if we start pulling the shelter about.'

'Don't forget my son, Ellie. He's only a few hours old and needs clean air – what you're suggesting might well put him in real danger.'

'I'm sorry, I didn't think this through. You're all correct. I just hate sitting about if there's something that can be done.'

She pointed to the rudimentary WC. 'At least we don't have to move that.'

'I don't envy whoever gets that job as I need to use it urgently,' George said. He bundled them out from behind the curtain and she was smiling when she took her place on one of the narrow benches.

The time passed. She wasn't sure how long they should leave it before attempting to rescue themselves. Her brother's worry about polluting the atmosphere with dirt and its effect on the baby was a real concern.

At first they had played word games, chatted about this and that but after a couple of hours the shelter had fallen silent – well – no more speaking anyway.

More than one of them had cause to go behind the curtain and she was going to be next. She was dreading the indignity. Jack was asleep; in fact, she thought everyone was judging by the sound of the heavy breathing around her.

Carefully she extricated herself from the blankets she was sharing with him and crept up the steps and put her ear to the door. She stiffened. Was that a noise? She pressed herself closer and held her breath but the pounding of her heart was all she could hear.

Yes – only faint, but definitely a noise of some sort.

'Everyone, wake up. I got it wrong. There can't be an unexploded bomb or anything else dangerous on top of us. The rescue workers are digging us out right now.'

Jack was there in instant closely followed by George. She stepped aside so they could listen.

'I can hear something too. It might be another hour or so but we're going to be out of here.'

Mabel, ever practical, suggested they finish off the tea and cake as they no longer needed to conserve what they had.

'It might be a good idea to move to the far end whilst we wait,' Jack said.

They shuffled obediently along the benches, which meant that when she went behind the curtain it would be even more embarrassing.

She was being quite ridiculous. Why should she be bothered about being heard having a pee when they all could have perished in here?

When she emerged Jack and George were standing by the exit. The noise of digging was audible even from where she was. She coughed and cleared her throat.

Her head was pounding. The air in here was thin and breathing was becoming more difficult. Surely they couldn't be running out of oxygen so soon?

Twenty-Nine

Jack heard Ellie cough and looked round to see her anguished expression. He knew at once what she was thinking, that if the oxygen levels were low the baby might well be in grave danger. He was certainly quiet, hadn't made a sound for an hour or two.

'If you've got a handkerchief get it out and tip water on it then put it over your mouth and nose. It should help keep out the dust and muck that will come in when they knock through.'

He wasn't sure this would make any difference but it kept everyone busy. Once this was done, he couldn't think of anything else that might be helpful.

The banging was more audible now and he heard Mabel thanking God for their deliverance. His prayer was more practical – he prayed whoever was on the other side arrived quickly.

Then someone shouted. He was on his feet and at the door before anyone else moved. He put his mouth for the door and shouted. 'We're all safe in here. The air's not good and we have a newborn baby with us.'

The voice replied. 'The ambulance is here and so's the local doctor. We'll have you out in half an hour. Sit tight.'

The door opened sooner than that and they were all helped through the narrow opening. He stayed until everyone was out. In order to get out he had to climb over the rubble, which wasn't easy with one hand but he was damned if he was going to ask for assistance.

He gulped fresh air in gratefully and immediately looked round to see how his family was. The ambulance doors were open and Fiona and the baby were inside with George and, presumably, the man listening to the infant's heart was the doctor.

Ellie arrived at his side. Her hair had come down, her face was covered with dirt but she'd never looked more beautiful to him.

'Where are the others?'

'They've gone in to put the kettle on and clean up. It was the tail of the German kite that landed on us – fortunately for us they'd already dropped their bombs.

'What about the baby? Has he suffered any ill effects?'

'The doctor wants to take them both into hospital just to be on the safe side. Mum's gone to collect the things they're going to need. We have to say goodbye to them as we'll have to leave before they come back.'

'I'll wait until your mom comes back before I disturb them. Bloody hell! There's nothing left of the bomber. Did any of the crew bail out, do you know?'

'They did and some members of the Home Guard turned out and have captured them.' She came to stand beside him and he put his arm around her shoulders. 'After this I think

I might believe in God after all. It was nothing short of a miracle that everyone survived today.'

'I agree, honey. It won't take long for all this to be cleared away. A few tiles missing on the roof of the stable, broken windows on the house, but apart from that no damage at all.'

Fred and Mabel came out with Mrs Simpson and he and Ellie joined them to say their farewells to George, Fiona and the baby.

He watched the ambulance trundle up the lane, closely followed by the fire brigade and local bobby. The land girls had milked the cows, fed the pigs and gone home as if nothing untoward had taken place.

'It's certainly been an exciting Christmas, but not one I care to experience again,' she said with a smile. 'If we get the time off, I suggest next year we all go to St Albans.'

'A year is a long time, Ellie, I can't think that far ahead. I just wish this damned war was over – at least we know now that Hitler isn't going to take over the world.'

She stretched up and kissed him lightly on the lips. 'I love you and as long as we're together I can cope with whatever happens.'

Acknowledgements

I'd like to thank my editor, Hannah Smith, my copy editor and proofreaders for their excellent work. My book is so much better because of them.

About the Author

Fenella J Miller was born in the Isle of Man. Her father was a Yorkshire man and her mother the daughter of a Rajah. She has worked as a nanny, cleaner, field worker, hotelier, chef, secondary and primary teacher and is now a full time writer. She has over thirty eight Regency romantic adventures published plus four Jane Austen variations, three Victorian sagas and seven WW2 family sagas. She lives in a pretty, riverside village in Essex with her husband and British Shorthair cat. She has two adult children and three grandchildren.

Hello from Aria

We hope you enjoyed this book! If you did let us know, we'd love to hear from you.

We are Aria, a dynamic digital-first fiction imprint from award-winning independent publishers Head of Zeus. At heart, we're committed to publishing fantastic commercial fiction – from romance and sagas to crime, thrillers and historical fiction. Visit us online and discover a community of like-minded fiction fans!

We're also on the look out for tomorrow's superstar authors. So, if you're a budding writer looking for a publisher, we'd love to hear from you. You can submit your book online at ariafiction.com/we-want-read-your-book

You can find us at:
Email: aria@headofzeus.com
Website: www.ariafiction.com
Submissions: www.ariafiction.com/we-want-read-your-book

- @ariafiction
- @Aria_Fiction
- @ariafiction

Printed in Great Britain
by Amazon